Eleventh Hour

A Tale of Compassion, Service, Power, and Politics

Richard E. McDermott, Ph.D.
Kevin D. Stocks, Ph.D., CPA

D1231092

First Edition

Traemus Books

1447 South 235 West
Orem, Utah 84058
Phone: (801) 525-9643
Fax: (801) 426-4648
www.traemus-books.com

Email Authors:

Richard E. McDermott: richard@traemus-books.com

Kevin D. Stocks: kevin@traemus-books.com

Web page: http://www.traemus-books.com

ISBN 0-9675072-2-7

Acknowledgments

Special thanks to the following who reviewed the book and provided helpful input:

Denise Abbott, R.N., Instructor in Medical Anatomy and Physiology, Timpview High School, Orem, Utah

Christine Amos, R.N., Syracuse, Utah

Steven Bateman, Administrator, Ogden Regional Medical Center, Ogden, Utah

Kristen Davidson, R.N., Instructor in Medical Anatomy and Physiology, Northridge High School, Layton, Utah

Rich Fullmer, CEO, University of Utah Medical Center, Salt Lake City, Utah

Mark J. Howard, Administrator, Mountainview Hospital, Las Vegas, Nevada

Joseph McDermott, M.D., Pathologist, San Antonio, Texas

Richard McDermott Jr., D.D.S., Orthodontist, Glendale, California

Robert Parker, M.H.A., President, Emergency Physicians Inc., Salt Lake City, Utah

Candadai Seshachari, Ph.D., Emeritus Professor of English, Weber State University, Ogden, Utah

Ashley Smith Spencer, Editorial Assistant, Provo, Utah

Melissa White, R.N., San Antonio, Texas

Tara White, Editor, Traemus Books, Syracuse, Utah   .

Table of Contents

Acknowledgments   iii

Preface   vii

<u>Chapters</u>

1	Trip to McCall	1
2	The Board	7
3	A Change of Seasons	11
4	Resolve and Regret	25
5	High Noon	35
6	Never Give Up	43
7	Cultural Diversity	47
8	A Dynasty Falls	55
9	Why are Costs so High?	59
10	A Lesson in Medical Economics	63
11	Amy	73
12	Gaming the System	79
13	Adverse Incentives	83
14	Is There a Solution?	89
15	The Robbery	99
16	The Hospital Carnival	107
17	The Model	115
18	Rachel	121
19	The Plan Takes Shape	125
20	Inadequately Trained	129
21	Ramer	139
22	Direct Materials	145
23	The Revenue Equation	151
24	The FAA Report	155
25	An Audit of the Pharmacy	159

26	Facility Problems	163
27	Ramer's Reversal	167
28	Paradigm Solutions	169
29	First Management Reports	173
30	Improving Quality	181
31	Quality Assurance and Safety Practices	189
32	The Competition	195
33	Power of the Press	199
34	Anniversary Dinner	203
35	Last Official Act	209
36	Carnavali	211
37	The Boardroom	217
38	SWAT Team	223
39	The Dedication	225
	Epilogue	229

Preface

Eleventh Hour is an introduction to the healthcare industry. It is designed for those who either have limited background in healthcare, or have technical training in areas such as accounting, business, medicine, or nursing, but limited knowledge of how the system works in its entirety. Topics covered include:

- The history of the American healthcare delivery system
- The theory behind managed care and its impact on cost and quality
- A brief introduction to healthcare economics
- Healthcare ethics and legal issues
- The role of the professional
- Hospital organizational structure
- The impact of power, politics, and money on healthcare delivery

This text may be used as a supplementary textbook for college courses in business, accounting, healthcare administration, nursing, medicine, and allied health sciences. It may also be used by hospitals and other healthcare organizations to train trustees, managers, and employees on important issues pertaining to the 21st century healthcare environment in which they operate.

The format gives readers an opportunity to learn in context. Fiction is an effective tool for teaching technical material. For thousands of years, civilizations passed values to succeeding generations through oral histories, folk tales, poems, myths, and epics that taught the values of their societies.

A well-written textbook/novel can provide the following:

- **A smoother transition from academia to the world of work, or from theory to practice.** The authors—one a former hospital administrator and both current university professors—have observed the cultural shock that occurs when students leave school and enter the workforce. Traditional textbooks have difficulty portraying the shades of gray in the dilemmas healthcare professionals face. *Eleventh Hour* softens the adjustment by giving readers a simulated work experience in a realistic healthcare environment.

- **Learning in context**. Individuals learn better when they can observe how principles taught apply to real world settings, and education is more effective when it's fun.
- **Richer discussions**. A textbook/novel allows the instructor or facilitator to interact with learners in meaningful discussions. Discussions are more interesting than lectures, as they involve everyone in the learning process. Discussions can teach assertiveness, communication, and critical thinking.
- **Better integration of topics**. The real world setting in *Eleventh Hour* gives instructors the opportunity to illustrate how issues such as cost, quality, and medical ethics are interrelated.
- **Exploration of concepts from different viewpoints**. In the world of work, individuals can draw different conclusions from the same data. A textbook/novel allows the reader to explore varying viewpoints based on diverse values, agendas, and backgrounds. *Eleventh Hour* covers the dilemmas specific to healthcare when resolving issues such as cost and quality, while dealing with accessibility and human life.
- **Teaching critical thinking**. Most textbooks teach students to find the right answer by giving the question and furnishing the data needed for the solution. What they fail to do is teach students how to ask the right question. *Eleventh Hour* illustrates how asking the wrong question will give the wrong answer, and how, in many situations, there may not be one right answer.

Traemus Books specializes in textbook/novels for healthcare and business. A separate text, *Code Blue*, with supplementary materials is available as an introductory text for students of medicine, nursing and allied sciences. Additional information on *Eleventh Hour*, *Code Blue*, and *The Game* (an introduction to business textbook/novel currently in production) can be found on the publisher's website: http://www.traemus-books.com.

Richard E. McDermott, Ph.D.

Kevin D. Stocks, Ph.D., CPA

1

Trip to McCall

September 4, 2003—Salt Lake City International Airport

It was 7:30 a.m. and the shadows of the Wasatch Mountains blanketed runway three-four-left as a blue and white Cessna 340 pulled out of the hangar, rolled onto the taxiway, and stopped. The roar of the twin engines severed the crisp morning air, resonating off the metal buildings to the west. Inside the private aircraft, the pilot, Hap Castleton, pulled his flight plan from a dog-eared navigation book and studied it to find the vector that would take him to Twin Falls, Boise, and, finally, McCall, Idaho.

Hap had a broad, generous face, graying brown hair, and a large frame. Deep creases mapped a face that had weathered the storms of thirty years as administrator of a small hospital in Park City, Utah. Satisfied with the route, Hap gently nudged his traveling companion, Del Cluff, and traced the map with his index finger.

Del, a thin man with receding brown hair, looked up from an accounting journal. His rooster-like eyes pecked at the map momentarily. Nodding at Hap, he returned to his journal.

Hap was disappointed by Del's indifference, as he had invited Del on this trip to discuss changes in the hospital's finance department. The Board of Trustees was pushing for a major reorganization, and finance was a good place to start. Hap folded the aviation map and placed it next to his seat. Picking up the mike, he contacted ground control.

"Salt Lake ground—Cessna two-six Charlie requests taxi to runway three-four-left."

"Cessna two-six Charlie—cleared to taxi."

Hap increased his throttle, turning the plane onto the taxiway that would lead him to the assigned runway. The morning air was cool and the takeoff would be smooth. He tuned the radio to 118.3—the Salt Lake tower.

"Cessna two-six-Charlie requests clearance for takeoff."

"Cessna two-six-Charlie cleared for takeoff. Fly heading 320, climb to thirteen thousand feet, contact departure on 124.3," was the tower's reply.

Hap felt the freedom surge deep in him as he released the brakes, pushed forward on the throttle and started his takeoff roll. Flying and fishing were his favorite hobbies. Heavy responsibilities at Brannan Community Hospital made it difficult to find time for either. Today, things would be different.

The plane accelerated and Hap gently pulled back on the control yoke. With a soft thump, the wheels left the runway and the plane lunged skyward. The plane climbed to thirteen thousand feet, turning onto its assigned vector of 320 degrees. Hap studied the altimeter and compass, checked his airspeed and adjusted the trim. Satisfied the plane was on course, he turned his attention to Del.

Del Cluff had been with the hospital for nine months. A meticulous accountant, Del irritated Hap almost as much as he irritated the hospital supervisors. It wasn't just that he was a bean counter, although that didn't help. Hap couldn't understand why anyone would want to spend his day with his nose buried in accounting records. But that wasn't the main problem. It wasn't even the preference shown to Del by Edward Wycoff, chairman of the Board of Trustees, although anyone who could get along with Wycoff was suspect in Hap's eyes. No—there was something more to it, something he couldn't quite put his finger on.

Grabbing a sack from under his seat, Hap nudged Del's leg. "Do you want something to eat?"

Del managed a nauseous smile. Pointing to his stomach, he shook his head. Hap snatched a sandwich and took a generous bite, wiping his fingers on his flight suit. *Nervous stomach? Del takes life too seriously.*

The smell of eggs and mayonnaise filled the cockpit. Chewing ferociously, Hap tuned his navigation radio to the next VOR. The plane crossed the first radio beacon.

From the right seat, Del Cluff watched the pilot adjust the radio and wondered why he accepted the invitation to fly with Hap Castleton. *Hope this yo-yo knows more about flying than he does about hospital administration . . .*

Palms sweating, Del tightened his seat belt.

Hap's management style was an increasing source of frustration. He created more problems than Del and a small flock of hospital accountants could fix. Although his larger-than-life personality made him a hero to many of his employees, Hap was no hero to Del.

The situation at the hospital was desperate. A new payment system known as prospective reimbursement had cut revenues even as costs continued to rise. The hospital was facing insolvency and time was running out. It was the eleventh hour with no solution in sight.

Del frowned, thinking of the rumors that the Board of Trustees was planning a major change prompted by Edward Wycoff, chairman of the Board of Trustees. Wycoff was snooping around the finance department, reviewing records, and quietly interviewing select members of the staff. The operation needed a good review, but Wycoff scared the wits out of most of the employees. His efforts only made the situation worse.

Del folded his journal, slid it under his seat, and retrieved the navigation map. He studied it, then squinted nervously at the hostile terrain below. To the north lay Mount Ben Lomond, capped with snow from a storm that moved through the Rocky Mountains two days earlier. To the east were the cliffs of the rugged Wasatch Range, thrust high by catastrophic earthquakes thousands of years ago. To the west, the purple mountains of Antelope Island were reflected in the waters of the Great Salt Lake. Del shivered involuntarily. Folding the map, he returned it to the pocket by Hap's seat.

"Heard the rumors about Selman?" Hap asked, the irritation in his voice cutting through the cool air. "Board's pushing for a change—Wycoff plans on firing him Monday." Hap clenched his jaw—his habit when irritated. "As soon as Selman's gone, Wycoff wants to install you as controller."

Del's eyes, a good barometer to his emotions, jumped in surprise. Del would welcome Roger Selman's dismissal—the two had frequently been at loggerheads. He would even welcome the opportunity to run things his way, but he wasn't entirely sure the promotion would be up—*it might be out*. It was clear to Del that Selman's position was dangerously close to the edge. Del said nothing while Hap struggled with his anger.

"Accept the job and you'll get two new responsibilities." His words were clipped. "The first is budget director—Wycoff wants three million dollars cut from the budget—I want you to oppose him."

Fat chance! Del thought. *Half of our suppliers have us on a cash only basis; we aren't even sure we can meet payroll.* This wasn't the first time Hap had locked horns with Wycoff. He had no ally in Del Cluff.

"And the second . . .?" Del prompted.

"Project coordinator for a new accounting system." The yoke of the small aircraft started to pull. Hap adjusted the trim.

"Six months ago I asked a consultant to look at the operation, see if he could propose something. Insurance companies are killing us. The Board isn't going to allow me to take another HMO contract until we have a handle on the cost of our services."

Del's eyes showed approval. He smiled. "Our auditors have been after Selman for a year to get a system up and running. They think this should be our number one priority."

Hap nodded decisively. "It's now *your* number one priority. Wycoff's hired a CPA, a fellow by the name of Wes Douglas, to serve as a consultant on the project. Wycoff wrote a memo to him—read it."

Del smirked sarcastically. He'd seen the memo. Wes was an East Coast accountant who knew nothing about rural hospitals. He'd be more trouble than he was worth.

Earlier that morning, Hap had a briefing at the weather desk. An unstable air mass with high moisture content from Canada was moving into the state and was being lifted high by the steep terrain of the Rocky Mountains. Severe thunderstorms were probable.

Hap studied a dark bank of cumulus clouds at twelve o'clock. On the present vector he'd hit the storm head on. He fished in his shirt pocket for a note card, then pointed to a dusty manual on the floor.

"I need a radio frequency—Twin Falls localizer. Think the frequency is 122.4, but I'm not . . ."

Hap stopped mid-sentence. Mouth wide open, he glanced at his instrument panel, then gaped out the window. His expression changed from disbelief to terror.

A cold wave of anxiety engulfed Del. "What's wrong?"

As Hap replied, the color drained from his face. "The right engine—"

A thin ribbon of blue smoke was trailing from the engine. Hap reached for the throttle. Before he could cut power, however, a violent explosion rocked the plane, whipping Del's head so violently he could taste the pain.

Hap grabbed the yoke, trying to regain control of the aircraft.

"Fire!" Del screamed.

The plane banked dangerously while Hap reached for the radio.

"Mayday! Mayday! Mayday!" he shouted. "Cessna two-six Charlie. Lost an engine..." He glanced at the altimeter. "Descending out of one-two-niner. Request immediate vector—emergency landing!"

One engine dead, the Cessna pulled right, the centrifugal force created by the right engine pulling the plane into a spin. A flat spin would give the aircraft the flight characteristics of a pitching anvil—no lift; just spin, speed, and mass.

"I can't hold it!" Hap shouted, jamming his foot onto the left rudder. "Throttle back . . . cut the left engine," he muttered, trying to stay calm.

Hap lunged for the throttles, accidentally cutting power to both engines. The plane shuddered—then dropped like a roller coaster. Hap wrapped his arms around the control yoke. The veins in his neck protruded like steel cables as he pulled with all the strength of his two-hundred-fifty-pound frame.

At 280 knots, the burning engine disintegrated, its broken cowling ripping the horizontal stabilizer from the tail as it cleared the aircraft. A side window blew out.

Del grabbed for something to hold on to as the ride down got rougher.

Still struggling with the yoke, Hap turned the plane north in the direction of Highway 82. An alarm sounded—red and amber lights exploded on the instrument panel.

Heart pounding like a sledgehammer, Del gaped at the rapidly approaching terrain below. To the west were homes and apartment complexes. To the east, nothing but the foothills of the jagged Wasatch Mountains. Directly in front of the plane lay a freshly harvested hay field.

A farmer observing the plummeting aircraft jumped from his tractor and ran for cover. Hap's eyes desperately drank in every detail of the approaching terrain as he searched for a way out.

The hayfield was flat—but too short for a landing. At the far end was an elementary school. Children were already playing in the yard, waiting for the morning bell to ring. Del pointed. "Try for the field!"

"We'll hit the kids."

"They'll scatter."

"Can't chance it."

This idiot's gonna kill us!

Hap banked the plane east toward the foothills. Completing the turn, he dropped his flaps. An alarm sounded—the landing gear wasn't down!

Rough terrain—bring her in on her belly. Hap turned off the electrical system. The blue and white Cessna, engines silent, skimmed a row of cottonwood trees. The yoke was heavy and unresponsive. As Del screamed in terror, Hap tightened his harness and braced himself for the crash.

2

The Board

Edward Wycoff arrived at the hospital at 6:30 on Monday morning—a full half hour before an emergency meeting of the Board of Trustees. Rushing down the hallway, he ignored the greetings of the housekeepers. Without breaking stride, he threw open the large walnut doors of the boardroom and switched on the lights.

Throwing his briefcase on a small telephone desk, he inspected the room. A retired officer in the Army Reserves, he knew how to conduct an inspection. Pity the employee who failed to meet his expectations.

Consistent with his instructions, the housekeeper had vacuumed the carpets and polished the conference room table until it shone like the brass on his colonel's uniform. He picked up the phone and punched in the extension of the dietary department. The chief dietician answered.

"Wycoff here!" His commanding tone never failed to catch an employee's attention. "I ordered breakfast for the Board!"

Telephone in one hand, the chief dietitian motioned frantically at a transportation aide. The aide clumsily shoved the heavy cart toward a service elevator. "Cart's on the way, Mr. Wycoff. Would've been there earlier but—"

Wycoff hung up, unwilling to grant her the satisfaction of an explanation. For a moment, the room was silent as he admired his reflection on the marble surface of the boardroom table. His most distinguishing feature was the color of his eyes, the exact shade of chipped ice. As always, he was unstirred by currents of self-doubt. *Hesitate—even for a moment—and you'll lose. Compassion only dulls the victory.*

Dr. Ashton Amos stuck his head through the door. At six-foot-four, he looked more like a basketball player than the newly elected president of the medical staff. His boyish mannerisms—coordinated awkwardness and a grin—made him popular with employees and physicians, characteristics Wycoff could capitalize on.

Weariness from a twenty-eight-hour shift in the Coronary Care Unit lined Dr. Amos' voice. "Got your message," he said. "Just finished rounds . . . I can talk now if you'd like."

Wycoff nodded. "Come in," he said evenly.

Dr. Amos crossed the room, seating himself in a large leather chair across from Wycoff. Retrieving a clean handkerchief from his pocket, he wiped his face and then blew his nose.

"Spent the night at the hospital?" Wycoff asked.

The doctor's mouth drew into a grim line. He nodded. "Fifty-one-year-old patient." Removing his glasses, he slowly massaged his eyes. "Double bypass—complications." Wycoff was unmoved; he'd give no sympathy.

"Any word on the accident?" Dr. Amos asked, changing the subject.

Wycoff shook his head. "The plane hit fifty feet below the foothill summit. Sheriff thinks they were trying to reach Mountain Road. An FAA team arrived Saturday—I don't think they know anything yet. Have you heard anything about Hap's funeral?"

"It's scheduled for next Monday—noon. I've canceled surgery."

Wycoff nodded briskly. "What about Cluff? What's the report?" Dr. Amos was on emergency call the night they brought in Del Cluff.

"Life-flighted to University Hospital. Called his attending physician this morning. He's listed in critical condition, but they think he'll make it." The room was silent as Wycoff digested the information. The young doctor knew he hadn't been summoned to report on Del. Unless Wycoff needed Del's services again—a dubious probability considering the massive injuries he sustained from the crash—Wycoff would give no further thought to Del's welfare.

"What's the Board going to do about a new administrator?"

Wycoff pursed his lips as though it was the first time he'd considered the question. "It's been a difficult weekend for me," he started, saying the words he had rehearsed earlier. "Hap and I disagreed—disagreed often," he said, nodding in agreement with himself. "Still, I had respect for the man."

Wycoff was lying, of course. He didn't think Dr. Amos would know the difference. He was wrong.

Wycoff steepled his fingers, a gesture of authority he'd used with good effect on Wall Street. "I've spent the past two days agonizing over the best course of action for the hospital." He hesitated. "I have a proposal, but I'm not sure if the Board will buy it."

An ingratiating smile played on his lips as he leaned forward. He pointed an arthritic finger at Dr. Amos. "I need someone with your prestige to explain it to them," Wycoff said. "Someone they respect, someone they'll listen to!"

Everyone knew how patronizing Wycoff could be when he wanted something. The thin veneer of benevolence failed to veil the expression in his eyes of a cold rigor mortis—the reflection of a thousand enemies ruthlessly disposed of over the years. Dr. Amos felt mildly nauseous.

"It's been my experience that the Board rarely turns down one of your recommendations," Dr. Amos replied, his face masked and expressionless.

"It's essential the Board pick the right man to replace Hap," Wycoff continued. "It won't happen overnight. While we're interviewing candidates, we need an interim administrator."

Dr. Amos nodded, his face softening with relief. There had been rumors that Wycoff planned to bring one of his hired guns in from New York to be the administrator of the hospital. *An interim administrator would be okay,* thought Dr. Amos. *It would give the hospital an opportunity to recover from the death of Hap while providing the time to organize the medical staff, in the event Wycoff still plans a coup.*

"Someone strong enough," Wycoff continued, "to fully implement managed care at Brannan Community Hospital."

"Do you have any candidates?" Dr. Amos asked, his interest clearly written on his face.

"None of our department heads are qualified. We need a *financial* person," Wycoff said with emphasis. "Someone who can lead us out of our current budget crisis."

"Any suggestions?" Dr. Amos asked curiously.

"There's a new CPA in the community—a fellow by the name of Wes Douglas. The hospital hired him a few weeks ago for a consulting project. He has no preconceived notions and isn't involved with hospital politics."

"Does he have the time?" Dr. Amos wondered aloud.

Wycoff nodded. "I called him last night. He's still building his practice. He's not only got the time; he needs the money."

Dr. Amos smiled wryly. Wycoff could always identify a person's vulnerabilities—he had obviously found Wes'. Dr. Amos rose thoughtfully and walked to the French doors overlooking the west patio. It was 7:00 a.m. and the morning shift was arriving. Mary Sorenson was parking her car. A widow with four children, she worked as an aide at the hospital. Retrieving her lunch from the front seat of a battered 1992 Corolla, she hurried to the employee entrance.

As Dr. Amos watched her, he reflected on the hospital's financial problems and the effect closure would have on the employees who depended on it for their livelihood. He turned to Wycoff. "I don't have a better idea," he said with a shrug. "I'll support the recommendation. Of course, I can't speak for the other members of the Board."

3

A Change of Seasons

Thirty-one-year-old Wes Douglas stepped from his car to the sidewalk. He stretched the knots out of his back as he surveyed the wooded grounds of Brannan Community Hospital. The change of seasons had come suddenly this year. Colorful leaves blanketed the lawn like the patchwork quilts sold in the gift shop.

Wes enjoyed all the seasons, but fall—the season of change—was his favorite. Watching a gust of wind stir the leaves, he pondered the changes awaiting his career.

Wes Douglas had stood with Hap Castleton on this very spot on a hot day in mid-August. Hap explained the crisis that motivated the Board of Trustees to hire Wes as a consultant. The Board was concerned the hospital was losing money. They blamed it on managed care, a program designed by insurance companies to control cost. Hap asked Wes to design a new accounting system that would allow the hospital to track their cost. For the consulting engagement, Wes would be paid $50,000.

Wes spent less than a week working with Hap on the project but was impressed by his energy and enthusiasm. Hap was an extrovert with an expressive style that won consistent approval. Hap understood people and was a master at hospital politics. Unfortunately, he was weak in operations—at least according to Edward Wycoff.

Wes, on the other hand, understood finance and operations. At Lytle, Moorehouse, and Butler, his former CPA firm, he consulted with a host of manufacturing firms and assisted in the design of systems to control costs. Wes had a mind for detail and he was a workaholic. Long after the staff went home, Wes pored over production reports and product flow diagrams, identifying inefficiencies that slowed production and raised cost.

Wycoff noticed the difference between Wes and Hap during Wes' first interview for the consulting job. Wycoff and Wes had finished dinner and retired to a richly paneled lounge on the second floor of the Yarrow Inn.

"I want to tell you a story," Wycoff said, lighting a cigar as he settled into a large wing back chair. "One of my neighbors in New York was vice president of General Electric. When he retired, he had worked thirty years with the company. Four of the company's officers retired at the same time— three vice presidents and a director. Thanks to General Electric's retirement program, they retired wealthy, sure of their business ability."

Wycoff removed his glasses, placing them on a table by his chair. "Wes, sixty-five is too young to do nothing," he said. "After long vacations, they all started businesses of their own. They were full of confidence."

Wycoff paused for emphasis. "In three years, each lost his investment. One of them was even forced into personal bankruptcy. For a long time, I wondered why people who ran a billion dollar corporation couldn't succeed with their own company," he continued, puffing his cigar thoughtfully. "Want to guess why they failed?"

Wes shrugged. "Inexperience in a new industry?"

"That contributed, but I think the main reason was they no longer had the support and discipline of a team. At General Electric, the vice president of research had the vice president of marketing to remind him he had to develop products that would sell. The vice president of marketing had the vice president of engineering to make sure he wouldn't pre-sell a product they couldn't build. The engineering vice president had the vice president of finance looking over his shoulder, prodding him to cut costs so his products could be priced at a level the customer could afford."

Wycoff tapped his chin thoughtfully as he continued. "And the vice president of finance had the other three vice presidents to remind him that without marketing, engineering, and research, he wouldn't have a job!"

Wycoff smiled cynically. "My friends failed because they chose partners just like them—in experience and in aptitude."

"You're saying they failed to select people who could compensate for their blind spots," Wes affirmed.

Wycoff's eyes danced approvingly. "That's right. And that's why I'm interested in your experience." Wycoff pressed his lips together tightly as he studied the young consultant. "I think you could help us with more than the design of a new system for cost control. I'd like to see you serve as a permanent consultant to the Board in financial and operational controls."

Wycoff leaned forward as though he was going to share a secret. "I'll admit Hap is great with people," he whispered, "but he's poor with details, and he knows nothing about finance. He knows the politics of the hospital, but you understand management and cost control. *Alone*, neither of you could run a business as complex as Brannan Community Hospital. As a *team*, however, I think you'd be unbeatable!"

Standing on the front lawn of Brannan Community Hospital, less than a month after that first conversation, Wes realized Wycoff's proposal was no longer relevant. Hap was gone and, without him, there was no team. Without a team, there would be no consulting contract.

Losing the job would be terrible. Wes totaled his outstanding debts— *$1,000 for office rent, $600 for part-time secretarial services and a payment of $1,000 or so on a $24,000 hospital bill.* The last was the largest debt. The collections department at Community Hospital in Hartford was unsympathetic. A year earlier, Wes was involved in a serious automobile accident. His insurance only paid a small part of the hospital bill and he signed a note for the remainder. Since coming to Park City, he had been unable to make regular payments and the hospital's business office manager was threatening to turn it over to an attorney.

Wes bent forward to relieve the throbbing pain in his back. Muscle spasms caused by stress aggravated the damage from the accident—and today he was stressed. Gently stretching backwards, he noticed that there was less numbness in his left leg than there had been a month ago—a good sign. If only he could say the same thing for the numbness in his heart.

Flexing his knees so as not to bend or twist, Wes Douglas gently stooped to pick up his briefcase. Forcing a smile, he bravely crossed the lawn, entering through the large brass doors of the hospital's lobby.

A row of wooden chairs with upright backs stood sentry at the entrance to the lobby and the scent of ethyl alcohol and cresyl violet seeped into the hall from the small laboratory on the first floor. Wes' leather-soled shoes squeaked on the highly waxed linoleum floor as he crossed the lobby to the information desk. He spoke with the receptionist and then went directly to administration where Birdie Bankhead, secretary to the administrator, greeted him.

Birdie, a fifty-six-year-old divorcee with two grandchildren and a poodle, had worked at the hospital as long as Hap. With red eyes and splotched cheeks, she looked up from the newspaper. Hap Castleton's picture was prominently featured on the front page.

"I'm Mr. Douglas," he said, "I'm here to meet with the Board."

Birdie nodded in recognition. "They're running a few minutes behind. Would you like some coffee or juice while you wait?"

"No, thanks, I'm fine."

Birdie wiped the corners of her eyes with a handkerchief. She opened her purse and retrieved a small makeup compact. "Sorry," she said as she excused herself. "It's been a difficult morning. I'll be gone for a few minutes. If you need anything, Mary Anne in the next office can help."

Wes nodded understandingly as Birdie left. Hands in his pockets, he scanned the room. The office was twenty feet square and served as the reception area for the administrator's office and the boardroom. The door to the boardroom was slightly ajar and, from the conversation drifting through the door, he could tell the meeting was winding down. A woman was speaking.

"I'm not sure there's anything we can do but what you suggest," she said with a sigh of dissatisfaction. "While I don't like it, you've convinced me it's our best alternative."

"All in favor?" a male voice asked. There was a volley of "Ayes."

"Those opposed?" There was one vigorous voice of dissent.

The door to the boardroom opened wide, and Dr. Ashton Amos emerged, extending his hand in greeting. Wes shook it as the doctor apologized for the delay. "Hope you haven't been here long," he said. Wes shook his head as Dr. Amos gestured for him to enter the boardroom. Inside, four members huddled in quiet conversation around a large conference table. The tabletop was cut from a one-inch slab of white Tennessee marble in an octagon shape and rested solidly on a square platform of highly polished walnut. In the center stood an architect's model of the new hospital Hap Castleton had hoped to build—a project canceled three days before his death.

"I don't think you've met the entire Board," Dr. Amos said to Wes. "This is David Brannan, chairman of the Board." Dr. Amos pointed to a well-dressed man in his early thirties. He chuckled. "From his last name, you can tell his family has played an important role in the history of the hospital." Wes smiled in acknowledgment, while Brannan stood and shook his hand.

"Next to David is Dr. Emil Flagg, the medical staff's representative to the Board." Dr. Flagg, a pathologist in his early sixties, had a dyspeptic smile and smelled vaguely of formaldehyde. Stretch wrinkles radiated from the single button of the white lab coat that struggled to corral his rotund torso. Flagg glowered as he scrutinized Wes from head to toe and then nodded abruptly.

"Helen Ingersol, president of Ingersol Construction is next," Dr. Amos continued. "This is Helen's first meeting with the committee." Helen Ingersol, a strong administrative type with short brown hair and brown eyes that flashed intelligence, smiled acknowledgement.

"And last, but not least, is Ed Wycoff. You already know Mr. Wycoff." Wycoff motioned for Wes to take the empty chair next to him.

"The tragic events of the weekend have forced us to make some difficult decisions," Wycoff said, his lips compressing tightly. "As this will affect your consulting contract, we felt that we should involve you in today's discussion."

Wycoff paused. "Before addressing the issue, however, we have one other item of business. Dr. Amos, would you call Roger Selman in?" As Dr. Amos left the room, Wycoff turned to Wes. "Roger is the hospital controller," he explained.

Wes worked for his grandfather the summer before college, herding sheep in the mountains high above his Wyoming ranch. Sometimes dark thunderheads appeared on the horizon, churning their way toward the summer pasture. Even though the air was deathly still, uneasiness always preceded the pyrotechnics soon to come. The same atmosphere filled the room as Dr. Amos returned with Roger Selman. They took their seats—Dr. Amos next to Wycoff and Roger Selman at the end of the table.

Except for the drumming of Wycoff's fingers on the cold marble table, the room was silent. Wycoff studied the concerned face of each Board member. Satisfied that he had their attention, he removed the hospital's financial report from a manila folder and placed it on the table. He gazed at it for a moment, withdrawing his hands for dramatic effect.

"Ladies and gentlemen," he said, "Mr. Selman has provided us with an unusual document. In my twenty years as a financial analyst, I have never seen anything like it!" He paused for emphasis. "You are to be congratulated, Mr. Selman!" he said, clapping loudly.

Wycoff's sarcasm was not lost on Selman, who squirmed in his chair. He smiled uncomfortably.

"Mr. Selman, when you joined the hospital five years ago, we had a successful business. No debts—one million dollars in the bank." Wycoff took a drink of ice water and wiped his mouth with a handkerchief.

Beads of perspiration formed on Selman's forehead. With a thin forefinger, he tugged on his collar, loosening the knot of his necktie, which seemed to tighten as Wycoff spoke.

Wycoff's eyes narrowed. "The report given this morning shows a substantial reversal," he said glacially. Still staring at Selman, he methodically flipped—one by one—through the pages of the report.

"During the previous twelve months," he continued slowly, "we generated a loss of three million dollars. Monday morning, our borrowing reached *two million dollars,* taking us within $150,000 of our credit limit. With less than $150,000 of cash in the bank, we are perilously close to not making payroll. Why, Mr. Selman," he said with callous sarcasm, "you and your associates have put us on the verge of bankruptcy!" The room was silent.

Helen Ingersol spoke. "I'm not an accountant," she said, addressing David Brannan, "but this is the first time I've seen the hospital's financial statements and there are a couple of questions I need answered before I decide if I'm going to stay on the Board."

"Shoot," Brannan said.

"Mr. Selman," Helen said, addressing the controller, "your financial report shows the hospital's volume is up, but so are its losses. Your costs haven't increased dramatically. In my business, this would signal a pricing problem. How do your prices compare with those of your competitors?"

"We aren't sure," Selman replied, avoiding Helen's gaze. "No two customers pay the same price. Insurance companies all have their own contracts. Most are given discounts. It's difficult to get the prices of the hospitals with whom we compete."

"What about your costs?" Helen asked. "How do they compare with the competition?"

"Don't know." Selman replied with an embarrassed shrug. "That information is too confidential."

Wycoff interrupted. "That's understandable," he said. "What isn't understandable is why we don't even know our own costs."

"Is that true?" Helen asked incredulously.

Selman nodded ruefully. "Without a good accounting system in place, we have to … guess."

Wycoff cut him off. "The problem isn't accounting!" he replied sharply. "The problem is management. You don't plan. Instead, you spend all of your time putting out fires."

"Actually, Mr. Wycoff…" Selman countered, breaking in.

"Don't interrupt me!" Wycoff snapped, pounding his fist on the table. "The reputation of the hospital is plummeting. Employee morale is low, productivity is lower, and service is rotten. I can't attend Kiwanis without being deluged with complaints about service. I'm fed up with it!" he shouted.

"Eighteen months ago," Wycoff continued more calmly, "I opposed bidding on the Mountainlands Insurance contract without cost data. Hap Castleton moved ahead anyway—on your recommendation!"

"If we hadn't bid the contract, we would have lost the business to competitors." Selman replied desperately. "I don't know if we could have survived the drop in volume."

"There's a lot you don't seem to know," Wycoff replied dryly.

From the expression on their faces, it was apparent the Board was not comfortable with the caustic approach Wycoff was taking. Still, no one spoke.

Roger Selman took a deep breath. "It's been a difficult year," he acknowledged, "but I think the worst is behind us. Yes, we've lost money but the problem can be fixed. That's why Wes Douglas is here, isn't it?"

Breaking Wycoff's gaze, Selman shot a plea for help to David Brannan. He had always been more sympathetic than the rest. "Give me three or four months," he said, "and you'll see a dramatic reversal of our position."

Wycoff slammed the table. "We can't survive that long! For the past three years, we've seen a steady decline in financial strength. Although we can't hold you solely responsible, your inability to provide cost information has significantly affected our ability to operate this hospital."

Wycoff's voice lowered as he circled in on Roger Selman for the final kill. "Mr. Selman," he said, "with the death of Hap Castleton, we have decided to reorganize the Administrative Council. As a part of the reorganization, we are asking for your resignation." Wycoff forced his lips into a glacial smile. "If you don't resign," he continued, "you will be fired."

Selman gasped as though he had been hit in the abdomen. He scanned the faces of the Board, searching for any sign of support—but none was offered. Denied a reprieve, he settled back in the large leather chair. In a minute or so, the lines around his mouth relaxed as fatigue replaced shock.

Roger Selman was sixty-two years old—and he was tired. He was tired of fighting the administration and the Board. He was tired of operating a department with few resources. Most of all, he was tired of the hours it took to straighten out the problems created by the well-meaning, but inefficient, Hap Castleton.

His emotions surprised him. He was no longer angry; he was relieved. *Without Wycoff, I might live another ten years. The money isn't important. I can find another job; maybe retire. I might start enjoying life again.*

Selman turned to Wycoff, who watched the transformation with quiet curiosity. Selman decided to give a speech he had rehearsed, but never before had courage to deliver.

"The world has changed, but the Board is still living in the 1960s," he started. "Healthcare is no longer a charitable enterprise—it's a business. For five years I've told you we need a new accounting system—something that will allow us to bid intelligently on insurance contracts while controlling our costs."

Selman continued, drawing a bead on Wycoff. "It's the Board's responsibility to provide direction and control. Mr. Wycoff, you have provided neither. You failed to act and the hospital has reaped the consequences.

"The physicians complain about inefficiencies," Selman said, turning to Flagg. "But most physicians haven't got a clue about what it takes to run a profitable hospital. The medical staff can't even agree on the routine matters.

"The hospital *is* in trouble," Selman added. "But firing me isn't going to fix that. The hospital needs to adapt, but that won't happen so long as you dinosaurs are in control." Wycoff sat up abruptly, insulted.

Roger Selman straightened himself with dignity. He folded his papers and stuffed them into the large envelope he had carried into the meeting. Standing, he shook his head in quiet disgust at Wycoff, then crossed the room. "Welcome to the twenty-first century," he said as he shut the massive walnut door behind him.

The room was silent as Board members studied each other, uncertain how they felt about Wycoff's actions—or Selman's response. Before they could react, Wycoff spoke.

"Mr. Douglas," he said, "the Board has empowered me to offer you a contract to serve as interim administrator of Brannan Community Hospital—just until we find a permanent replacement. We know you're not a hospital administrator, but you understand finance—which, for the moment, is our most pressing need."

Wes looked up in surprise. *Interim administrator?* Unwilling to speak until he thought the offer through, Wes studied the Board members. In the two weeks Wes worked with the hospital on the design of the new accounting system, he lost much of his enthusiasm for Edward Wycoff. Working with him would be difficult.

On the other hand, Wes had consulted with small firms in trouble and enjoyed the challenge. His practice was small, and he did have the time. If he was successful, it might lead to future consulting jobs in the industry. Accepting the assignment would be a good way to become better known in the community.

Awkwardly, Wes cleared his throat. "If we can work out something financially, I think it might be an … interesting project."

"We'll pay $5,000 a month for six months," Wycoff said.

Wes did the calculation in his head. "That's about $30 an hour. My consulting rate is four times that."

The lines deepened around Wycoff's mouth. He shook his head with firmly. "The hospital's in trouble, Wes. We can't afford that. Five thousand a month is our offer, guaranteed for six months if you perform to our expectations—longer if it takes more time to get a permanent replacement."

Wes thought about his new accounting practice. He only billed thirty hours last month. In a week or so, he could finish the current projects and sublet the office. Once again, he turned the offer over in his mind. He took a deep breath and blew it out slowly. "I accept," he said.

Wycoff smiled smugly as he sank back into the large wingback chair. The expressions on the faces of the other Board members ranged from happiness, to relief, to despair.

David Brannan broke the silence. "I don't mean to change the subject, Ed, but I have a meeting downtown in twenty minutes. Do we have enough cash to meet the payroll on Friday?"

"I spoke with the business office last night." replied Wycoff. "They're expecting a $400,000 payment from one of our larger insurance companies. We should get it by Wednesday. With that payment and our remaining line of credit, we should be able to squeak by."

"Any chance it won't be here in time?" Brannan queried.

"If it's not here by Wednesday, I'll drive to Salt Lake City and walk the check through their accounting department myself," Wycoff said. "It wouldn't be the first time."

"If payroll is covered, then I suggest we adjourn," said Brannan, smiling with relief. "Do I have a motion to adjourn?"

"I so move," said Dr. Amos.

It was evening when Wes entered the administrator's office for the first time since assuming his interim post. He was surprised to see Hap's untouched books, journals, and memorabilia. He gazed at the personal items—family photos, a dusty rainbow trout, and a pair of running shoes—and remembered his last visit to the office. Hap's beaming personality permeated the room like the rays of sun that poured in through the French doors behind his desk.

The room was different today. The forest green drapes were drawn and, except for the light from a small corner lamp, the office was dark and tomblike. Wes turned on the lights, opened the curtains, and settled into the large green armchair facing the desk.

The administrative wing was empty. He was grateful for the silence as he reflected on the events of the day. Had Wes participated in the discussions leading to the firing of Selman, he would have opposed it. Even if Selman was incompetent, he had knowledge that would have been helpful to a new administrator. After the meeting, Wycoff explained that the action was inevitable and he decided to spare Wes the task.

Although Wycoff's intent may have been good, it clearly backfired. Selman was well liked; his dismissal, so soon after Hap's death, shocked and offended the employees. The hostility was more than evident at a meeting held later that morning when Wycoff introduced Wes as the interim administrator.

When Wycoff announced the dismissal of Selman, two employees on the front row started crying and a supervisor stormed from the meeting. Four department managers introduced themselves afterward in an attempt to be cordial, but it was obvious most blamed Wes for the release of Selman. *If Wycoff had planned to set me up to fail, he couldn't have done a better job*, Wes thought.

Wycoff was not attuned to the sensitivities of other people. The word on the street was that he was bright, but ruthless. Although this was a temporary position, Wes was starting to realize the negative effect it might have on his fledgling CPA practice.

His thoughts were interrupted as Birdie Bankhead, the secretary to the administrator, entered the room. She carried a large yellow envelope. "I thought you'd left for the day," Wes said looking up in surprise.

"I had, but our application for an accreditation visit has to be in Chicago by Friday."

Birdie's lips were drawn tight and Wes realized she was struggling with some strong emotions.

"If you'll sign the forms, I'll drop them by the post office tonight," she continued. She handed him the forms. He signed them and handed them back. Wes detected animosity that hadn't been there this morning before Roger Selman's dismissal.

Birdie's eyes glistened as they caught the picture of Hap's family on the desk. "You'll want Hap's things out of his office. I'll remove them tomorrow," she said stiffly.

"There's no hurry," he said sympathetically. "Let his family do it—at their convenience."

Birdie looked at him through the cobwebs of reddened eyes. She hadn't slept for two nights, or maybe she was still asleep; this past week had been a nightmare. From deep inside, a mournful sob shook her frame.

Wes stood up and took her hand. "Listen Birdie," he said. "I don't agree with everything that's gone on. This whole thing has been precipitous. Let's not rush Hap's family. I can work around his things for a few days."

Observing his sensitivity, the lines around Birdie's eyes softened. *I wonder if he knows what he's got himself into.* Birdie didn't understand why the Board hired someone with no experience to take the reigns from Hap. *Maybe he's been selected to take the fall—to deflect the blame from Wycoff and the Board if the hospital folds.* Her sympathy rose as she contemplated the probable consequences for Mr. Wes Douglas, for the hospital, and for employees like herself.

She took a deep breath, releasing it slowly. "I'm sorry about the reception you got at the meeting," she said, starting anew. "The employees are good people. They're still in shock over Hap's death and now with the firing of Roger Selman…" she trailed off.

Wes nodded. "I understand," he said. "I'm not happy about the way things were handled today." He shrugged and smiled weakly. Birdie smiled sadly in return.

"Is there anything I can do before leaving this evening?" she asked, pointing at the pile of mail and messages on his desk.

"I'm flying to Seattle to finish an assignment for a firm," he said. "Watch over things while I'm gone."

"When will you be back?"

"I told the Board I could start a week from Monday."

"There's a phone call from Wycoff that might change your plans." Birdie paused uncertainly, then crossed to his desk and tore a phone message from a notepad. "Wycoff called an hour ago," she said. "The bank is calling the hospital's past loans. He doesn't think the hospital can make payroll."

Wes was speechless.

"You should also look at this." She handed him the evening edition of the *Park City Sentinel.* The headline read:

Hospital Employees Threaten Walkout

Vote "no confidence" on appointment of new administrator

Wes blinked, his eyes wide with bafflement as he read the lead article. He rubbed his tired eyes and stared out the French doors at the black storm clouds gathering to the east.

"I'll cancel my flight," he said.

4

Resolve and Regret

Through an open window in his small studio apartment, Wes listened to the noise of the street below. A freight truck was backing into an alley and someone was shouting instructions to the driver in Spanish. The freight dock for the hotel next door was directly beneath his window.

He rubbed his eyes and checked his alarm—5:00 a.m. The evening news had forecast stormy weather. Wes smelled the rain before it hit the dusty asphalt below. A gusty wind snatched a newspaper high in the air above the alley as a clap of thunder rumbled in the distant mountains.

Wes stumbled to his feet and shut the window. He returned to his bed. Sinking into the pillow, he took a deep breath, held it, and slowly released it. *If only I could relax the muscles in my back.* He eyed the medicine on the nightstand, tempted for a moment to take another pill. He shook his head with firm resolve. *No more painkillers this morning. They'll cloud my mind. I need all the faculties I have to handle my second day.*

He gently straightened. It had been a year since his automobile accident and this morning the pain in his lower back was as severe as the night he was pulled from his mangled automobile. He had a vague remembrance of being lowered onto an ambulance litter before losing consciousness. Sometime later, somewhere on the turnpike, he drifted back to consciousness. A paramedic was starting an IV and someone was reading his vital signs over the radio to a nurse at the hospital.

"Kathryn? Where is Kathryn?" he asked in a panicked whisper.

"It's going to be all right buddy," the paramedic answered soothingly. The paramedic lied. Nothing would ever be right again.

Friends told him time would soften the loss. Someday life would have meaning again. As for now, the only relief was the distraction of hard work. If Wes filled his time with activity, there was no time to dwell on the past.

Even so, his mind burned with her memory. Rarely an hour passed that he didn't think of Kathryn—her slender figure, twinkling green eyes—the impish look that played around her mouth just before he kissed her. He closed his eyes, his mind an inferno of misery.

Unable to sleep, he sat up. Three months ago, he realized it was time to move on with his life; to find a new environment, new friends, and a new challenge to occupy his time. That was the reason he left Maine, perhaps even the reason he took on Brannan Community Hospital.

Erasing memories, however, was easier said than done. Often, in the slumber of the early morning, he would return to the evening of the accident. In the recurring nightmare, he felt the play in the steering wheel as the tires slipped on the wet pavement … the crushing impact of the crash … the blackness that blended the smells of burning rubber and gasoline mingled with pain and the sound of the rain as it hit the oily asphalt below.

Wes' body was heavy with fatigue as he drove to work an hour later. To focus his thoughts, he reviewed the events of the previous day. At 1:00 p.m. he met with Elizabeth Flannigan, the director of nursing.

Flannigan—a scrappy Irish woman with flaming red hair—was a tough supervisor, famous for her skirmishes with the medical staff. She ran her department with a General Patton-like efficiency, which won the affection and animosity of the medical staff. Sensing the Board's concern, Wes spent the first ten minutes quizzing her about her budgeting system and cost control. He asked if she had a plan for staffing cuts.

He shouldn't have done that — not during their introductory meeting. The nursing staff was paranoid as it was. Alarmed, Flannigan ran to Dr. Emil Flagg who confronted Wes in his office, pouncing on him with the fury of a Rocky Mountain hailstorm.

"Hell-bound financiers like Wycoff are destroying healthcare!" Flagg shouted, his enormous fists smashing a stack of financial reports on Wes' desk. "Wycoff, the miserable miscreant, thinks he can run this place like a brokerage house. This isn't Wall Street and our patients aren't stocks and bonds!"

The meeting lasted for an hour. Flagg was angry at managed care, insurance companies, paperwork, hospital administrators, and the members of the Board. Wes, in his eyes, was one with Wycoff. Wes assured him human factors would be considered in any reorganization. Flagg didn't believe it.

As his car pulled into the parking lot, Wes wondered if he made a mistake accepting the position. *No. Negative thinking never solved anything. Besides, what are my alternatives? My practice hasn't exactly taken off—this town has too many public accountants. What else could I do? I could crawl back to the managing partner at Lytle, Moorehouse, and Butler.*

Wes chortled good-humoredly. He still remembered the shock on his arrogant supervisor's face the day he resigned. *"Going West? Well, that's just ridiculous. I've never heard of such a thing,"* the smug New Englander replied on hearing the news.

I decided to accept this job. Right or wrong, I'm in this up to my ears. The jobs of over three hundred employees depend on me. This place has been here for sixty-five years. It might fail eventually—but not during my watch!

"Good morning, Mr. Douglas!" A notably more chipper Birdie Bankhead looked up from her computer and smiled brightly. The puffiness was gone from her eyes and her voice was as cheerful as the pink suit she wore. Wes was grateful for the change.

He smiled and pointed at his watch. "You're up early," he said.

She nodded. "Had a ton to finish before the phone starts ringing."

Birdie continued typing and then looked up with a start. "That reminds me," she said. "Hank Ulman, president of the Employee Council, called me at home last night. He wants to meet with you—this morning, 10:00 a.m.—downtown at the Pipe Fitters Union Hall. I wrote the address down."

Birdie reached for her purse. Retrieving a small notepad, she tore the message off and handed it to Wes. "920 South Oak Avenue," she said. "Small red building—second floor—just above the bakery."

Wes' brows pulled into a scowl as he read the note. "I didn't know we had a union."

"Technically, we don't, but there's been talk of one since Wycoff vetoed the budget. He wanted Hap to cut salaries by twelve percent. Someone leaked the story to the local newspaper. Caused quite a stir among the employees. That's when people started talking about organizing a union. Guess the issue is surfacing again," she sniffed. She returned to her typing.

"Hank Ulman," Wes said, turning the note over in his hand. "Is he one of our employees?"

Birdie nodded. "Works in Maintenance. Moonlights part time as a mechanic for a flight service in Salt Lake City. He has a reputation as a troublemaker. He ran once for city council on the American Socialist Party ticket. Got seven votes.

"Most of our employees ignored him until four months ago. When Wycoff got involved in the operation of the hospital, Hank was elected president of the Employee Council."

Quiet surprise registered in Wes' eyes. "What do you mean by—'Wycoff got involved in the operation of the hospital?'"

"He got the Board to appoint him budget director," Birdie replied. "Once he got control of the hospital's budget, he controlled the departments."

"The Golden Rule," Wes replied wryly. "He who controls the gold, makes the rules."

"Right," Birdie replied. "Hap planned to take the responsibility back. He got Wycoff to agree to transfer the title to Del Cluff." She sighed. "That was before the ... accident."

Wes' eyes scanned the floor. His thoughts seemed to be elsewhere.

"Call Hank," he said finally, "and tell him there'll be no meeting, at least not with him and not at the Union Hall. Then arrange a meeting with our employees for 10:30. Ask scheduling to pull in all on-call nurses—I want as many of our full-time staff there as possible."

"Supervisors?" Birdie asked.

"No, just employees—I'll meet with the department heads tomorrow."

Birdie scratched a note in her planner.

Energized by the completion of his first official act, Wes was hungry. "Think I'll catch breakfast," he said brightly. "When I get back, let's meet to plan the rest of the day."

On Wes' first visit to the cafeteria, he was pleasantly surprised to find it warm and cheerful. Nothing fancy—if anything, a little homespun with checkered red and white tablecloths and freshly painted yellow walls.

Canyon Elementary School decorated the south wall with crayon drawings depicting brightly colored surgeons assisted by chalk white nurses. The aroma of eggs, bacon, and coffee wafted from a spotless kitchen. A radio was playing country music and the room hummed with the pleasant chatter of fifty or so employees and visitors.

Wes selected a tray and headed for the cafeteria line, confident that few employees would recognize him as the new administrator. *A good chance for a little reconnaissance.* He grabbed a packet of silverware.

An attorney friend told him about a hospital malpractice suit his firm had handled involving a physician who severed a carotid artery during surgery. For two days, attorneys interviewed the surgeon and operating room personnel. Frustrated at their inability to crack the case, they sent two clerks to the hospital. Posing as visitors, the clerks spent three days in the cafeteria, drinking coffee and eavesdropping on the conversations of hospital employees. "Employees like to gossip," the attorney said.

In the security of the hospital's cafeteria, employees prattled over the case, condemning the incompetence of the physician and the unwillingness of the medical staff to censure him.

Having learned more from the chatter of the cafeteria than they would have gleaned in ten months of depositions, the attorneys approached hospital administration with their newfound evidence. The hospital settled out of court for two million dollars.

Wes paid for breakfast and took a table near the center of the cafeteria, not far from a group of housekeepers seated at a large round table. "Did ya hear they fired poor ol' Mister Selman?" a heavy woman in a blue housekeeping uniform said to her companions as she buttered a thick pancake.

"It was Wycoff that got him," replied a frail woman with a thin nose. "Now that Mr. Castleton's dead, Wycoff's going to have his evil way with the hospital," she predicted dourly.

Her dark eyes turned bitter. "Doc Flagg said he's been pushing staffing cuts for three months. He'll have us all on unemployment if he gets his way." The employees at her table nodded ominously.

"He don't believe in unemployment insurance neither," another housekeeper hooted. "He'll have us on the street!"

"Hap would never have stood for that," the first woman interjected, her eyes widening with resentment. She took a hearty bite of her cheese omelet and leaned forward conspiratorially. "Say, what's this new administrator like?"

"He's a real dandy," her companion replied. "Flagg says he's Wycoff's man—a guy from back east, a fancy finance fella. Doc says he don't know nothin' 'bout hospitals."

A flash of alarm exploded across the housekeeper's round face. "Good Jehosophat!" she said, rocking back in her cafeteria chair. Wes held his breath as the vintage chair—a survivor from the original hospital—groaned under her weight. Luckily, it held and a worker's compensation injury was avoided.

Wes' eavesdropping was interrupted by the cafeteria intercom. "Mr. Douglas, line four," the operator announced. Many of the employees scanned the cafeteria, trying to catch a glimpse of their new boss. After the interest died down, he quietly made his way to the hall where he picked up a phone.

"Wes speaking," he said.

Birdie was on the other end and her voice registered concern. "I have Mr. Wycoff on the line. I told him you were unavailable. He insisted I track you down," she said.

Given what he'd learned about Wycoff's inclination to involve himself in operations, Wes wondered how long it would take him to call. Wes had one message for the Chairman of the Board. *The Board sets policy, raises capital, and hires and fires the CEO. Internal operations, however, are the sole responsibility of the hospital administrator.*

"Put him on," Wes said tersely.

The phone clicked. Wycoff was on the other end. "Saw the article in last night's paper," he began, his words coming in short staccato-like bursts, "I'll be down shortly. Want to meet with the Employee Council. I've dealt with threats like this before. Don't know who they think they are, but I'll nip this thing in the bud."

"I appreciate your concern, Mr. Wycoff," Wes said politely, "but I'll handle it."

"You can't meet with them alone." Wycoff said sharply. Wes sensed the surprise in Wycoff's voice.

Wanna make a bet? If you think you're going to set the tone of my administration, you've got a surprise coming. "That's my intent," Wes said pleasantly. "Involving members of the Board in personnel problems will only complicate the issue. Let's set an early precedent, Mr. Wycoff—the employees deal with the administrator—not the Board."

"Don't be a fool," Wycoff said spitting his words out with contempt. "A good CEO uses the talents of his Board."

"Not in operations he doesn't."

Wycoff gasped at Wes' insolence. "As chairman of the Board, I'm going to meet with our supervisors on the financial crisis," he said with all the authority he could command.

Wes took a deep breath and held his ground. "As chairman of the Board, you will meet *only* with the Board. The Board will set policy. I will communicate that policy to employees," he said. "In this hospital, the administrator handles operations."

Wycoff sputtered. "I have several issues to discuss with the employees. The budget, our new organizational structure—"

"Those are operational issues," Wes repeated firmly. *Don't give in—we're setting precedent*, he thought.

Wycoff was silent. Wes knew he was angry. "I appreciate your concern," Wes continued. "If I need your help, I'll call."

Wes waved cheerfully at Dr. Flagg, who stormed by without speaking.

"Good-*bye*, Wes," Wycoff said flatly as he slammed down the phone.

Were those parting words—or a threat? Wes wondered.

It took a heroic effort by housekeeping to arrange the cafeteria for a meeting on such short notice. The breakfast line shut down promptly at 10:00 a.m.—thirty minutes early—as a team of housekeepers quickly descended on the department, removing tables, vacuuming floors, and setting up chairs. Wes had one goal for the meeting—avert a walkout.

The room filled quickly. Wes entered from the rear and walked briskly to a portable podium at the front. He stood there as the room quieted.

"I'm Wes Douglas, your new administrator," he began. "I know many of you are surprised with my appointment—none of you more than I." *A feeble attempt at humor—no one smiled.*

Wes could see the audience was divided into three groups. A small cluster standing in the back exchanged guffaws with their ringleader—a stocky maintenance man with a barrel chest and large animated arms that swung out from his body as he mimicked Wes. From an earlier description, Wes assumed the comedian was Hank Ulman—the self-appointed union steward.

A second group, scattered throughout the audience, watched dispassionately, arms folded and faces skeptical. *Convince us the Board didn't make a mistake,* they seemed to say.

The third group, ten or twelve people on the front row, were receptive. They were few, however, and seemed to be intimidated into silence by the rest of the audience.

"I'd like to start by explaining my management philosophy," Wes began. For the next ten minutes he discussed the goals he had established for the hospital, the most important of which was to put the operation in the black.

"I've had my say," he concluded. "Now, I'd like you to talk to me about your concerns."

The room was silent. Finally, an employee from the business office raised her hand. "I have a complaint," she said. "The Board never consults us, so we never know what's going on. There isn't a single employee who has ever heard of you and suddenly you're the new boss." The room hummed with assent.

"The newspaper editor knows more about what's going on than we do," the employee continued. "Hap never told us about a financial crisis." Her face twisted with skepticism. "How do we know it's real?"

"It's real," Wes replied.

"Can you guarantee there'll be no layoffs?" a nurse demanded.

"No. But, your supervisors will be consulted before we cut staff. There'll be no secrets."

A lab tech raised his hand. "There's a rumor you're an accountant. Well, I've got a complaint about finance. The employees bear the brunt of the hospital's losses, but it's not our fault—pricing's the problem. We're doing some of our lab tests for less than the cost of reagents."

"Waste is another problem," a nurse added. "Last week we threw away several hundred dollars of sterile products because they were outdated. This seems to be a problem in all units."

Wes took notes. "Helpful input," he said.

Complaints continued for another twenty minutes.

At last, Wes began summarizing. "There was a time in my career when I placed blame for poor quality and service on employees," Wes concluded. "Experience has changed my belief. I've come to realize the problem is usually poor management. Give me a few days to find out what is going on," he said, "and we'll hit the issues straight on."

His approach seemed to be working. Many employees smiled—a few applauded. As the morale of the meeting improved, Hank Ulman abruptly left the room, taking two coworkers with him.

Good riddance, Wes thought.

Wes was within striking distance of his goal. He cleared his throat. "There's one more issue I want to discuss," he said as the employees quieted. "An article in the paper reported a threatened employee walkout. The hospital has problems, but a walkout won't solve—"

A muffled explosion interrupted his words. It was followed by a loud hissing noise. A stream of boiling water, red with rust, gushed through the opening under the boiler room door and swirled over the feet of the employees. A laundry worker in low-cut shoes screamed in pain as she grabbed her ankles. A coworker grabbed her arm, but slipped on the linoleum floor and fell in the scalding overflow. Two men pulled them from the water.

Hank Ulman appeared in the doorway wearing hip boots. "A pipe to the boiler's broken!" he shouted. "Everyone out!"

The room exploded with commotion as the crowd pushed to the front of the room, knocking over chairs in their efforts to escape the scalding flow. An employee hit the crash bar to the emergency exit, setting off the alarm as workers pushed one another through the door and up the stairwell. Hank had ended the meeting.

Thirty minutes later, Wes called Hank Ulman to his office.

"Like I tol' Hap, the boiler's old—needs replacin'." Hank smiled, exposing a broken, chestnut colored tooth. "Gonna kill somebody someday." "The steam pipe came right off the wall," he continued. "Good thing I was there. If I wasn't, things might have turned out differently."

"I'm sure that's true," Wes replied flatly.

A few minutes later, on his way out of the hospital, Wes checked in with Birdie. "Got a meeting at the bank," he said.

"I've scheduled the department heads for tomorrow," she replied. "Nine o'clock."

"Got it!" he replied, recording the appointment in his planner.

5

High Noon

Arnold Wilson stood angrily. Placing both hands on his desk, he leaned forward, thrusting his jaw threateningly in the face of David Brannan. "Okay—I'll level with you, David. We've lost confidence in the hospital's ability to compete. Your controller can't even tell us where you're losing money!"

For the past twenty minutes, Wes had watched a jousting match. On the offensive was Arnold Wilson, vice president of Park City State Bank, scourging David Brannan for the hospital's poor financial performance. Wycoff, sitting in the corner, was uncharacteristically silent. Wes, the newcomer, said nothing. It was just as well—Wilson was doing his best to ignore him.

"You should've seen the response of the Loan Committee," Wilson said, throwing his hands up in disbelief, "when Selman told them the hospital doesn't even have accurate cost data on its products and procedures."

"Selman's your problem?" Brannan injected. "Selman's gone!"

"And who replaced him?" asked Wilson belligerently.

"We don't have a replacement," Brannan admitted.

"No controller? And a new administrator who's never worked in a hospital!" Wilson hooted. "No wonder your employees lost confidence in the Board. Do you expect the directors of my bank to react differently?"

"I expect them to work with us until we resolve our problems," Brannan said evenly. "For thirty years we've been a good account—a loyal customer even when other banks were offering us lines of credit at much lower rates."

Wilson rolled his eyes. "David! We're not talking small amounts of money," he said. "By your own projections, you're looking at a fourth quarter loss of $900,000."

Brannan was unimpressed. "If you call our line of credit, we won't be able to make payroll. Then our revenue stops and we won't be able to pay you the money we owe you."

"You owe us two million dollars," Wilson said, "secured by three million in accounts receivable." He snatched a thick file from his desk and thumbed to the third page. "Here it is—your total accounts receivable at the end of August were $3,078,000. We have an in-house collection agency. If the hospital closes, we'll collect the accounts ourselves. Or, we could sell the receivables outright." Wilson slapped the file closed. "A group in Ogden has agreed to buy your accounts for sixty cents on the dollar—that's $1.8 million in cash."

Brannan sputtered in annoyance. "It's $150,000 less than you'll get if you stick with us," he countered.

"It's $1.8 million more than we'll get if the hospital goes bankrupt," Wilson said. He dismissed the argument with a wave of his hand. "Besides, that's the worst case scenario."

The president of the bank stuck his head in the door. Hearing the bedlam, he had come to see if he could help. "May I join you?" he asked.

Brannan motioned for him to enter. A muscle twitched nervously in Wilson's jaw. Face reddened, he popped a pill. The bank president started to close the door, but he noticed Wilson's agitation. He motioned for him to get a drink from the water cooler across the hall. Wilson left the room while the president acknowledged Wycoff and crossed the room to shake hands with David Brannan.

"How are you, David?" he asked, pumping his hand firmly.

"I've been better," David said curtly. He gestured to Wes. "This is Wes Douglas—our interim administrator."

The president shook hands with Wes and motioned for Brannan to sit down as he seated himself in Wilson's chair. Interlocking his fingers, he leaned forward. "What seems to be the problem?" he asked with a frigid smile.

Brannan's eyes blazed—hot enough, Wes thought, to ignite the paneling on the wall. "You know darn well what's the problem!" Brannan barked angrily. "The bank's canceled our line of credit. Without it, we can't meet payroll. I want to know who's responsible!"

Wilson reentered the office, and his boss motioned for him to shut the door, as Brannan's shouting was attracting the attention of customers in the bank's lobby.

The bank president arched his eyebrows. "I'm responsible," he said. "Some people think the money we loan is our own—they think they're borrowing the funds of a group of wealthy investors who own the bank. That's not the situation, David."

He made no attempt to hide the condescending tone in his voice. "The money we loan comes from depositors—school teachers saving for retirement, young couples planning for a home, small merchants trying to scratch out a living . . . we have a responsibility to those people, David. A responsibility to see that their funds are wisely invested—that they aren't squandered on organizations unable to manage their own finances."

"Don't give me that garbage!" Brannan spat the words out contemptuously. "For twenty years, my father was a major shareholder in this bank. I know what banking's about."

The banker shook his head sharply. "But your father's not a shareholder anymore," he said, his words short and biting. He picked up a copy of the bank's annual report and shook it in the air. "This committee calls the shots now," he said, tapping the picture of the new directors on the cover. He tossed the report down on the table. "We have a new Loan Committee, David. Would you like to know the committee's criteria for new loans?"

Before David could reply, he continued. "Loans must have collateral," the president said with emphasis. "Loans can't exceed seventy percent of collateral. Borrowers must have positive cash flows. Borrowers must show their ability to *pay their loans back!*"

"Why, David," he continued dryly, "your hospital doesn't meet a single criterion. We have no choice but to call the loan."

The room was quiet as Brannan digested the information. Wes had no idea that David's father had been an owner of the bank. His withdrawal—for whatever reason—had precipitated a shift in power that David Brannan was obviously just starting to comprehend.

From the corner, Wycoff appeared to enjoy the whipping Brannan was taking. Sitting next to him, Wilson, arms folded, nodded at his boss approvingly. Brannan glanced at Wycoff, who gave no support, and then glared at the bankers. Everyone seemed to expect Wycoff to speak, but he sat silent and expressionless.

Sensing the meeting was about to end with disastrous results for the hospital, Wes jumped in. "I understand your commitment to your depositors," he said calmly. "That's why I find it hard to believe you're willing to see the community's only hospital go out of business."

"There are other hospitals in the area," Wilson said defensively. "Some firm just built a new one in Midway—eleven miles from here. It's not too far to go for healthcare."

"I'm not talking healthcare, I'm talking economics," Wes said, taking the offensive. "Brannan Community Hospital has about three hundred and fifty employees. Surely you don't believe it's to the benefit of your depositors for the community to lose its largest employer."

A question shadowed Wilson's eyes. "What do you mean?" he asked.

As Wes spoke, Wycoff's eyelids, lowered to veil his emotions, lifted slightly. He leaned forward to listen to the conversation.

"The hospital spends twelve million dollars a year on payroll. I have data showing sixty-five percent of those payroll dollars are spent locally. Every dollar of payroll generates an additional dollar in secondary spending in the community. In total, the hospital is responsible for sixteen million dollars a year in local spending." Wes paused for effect. "Are your directors willing to take this money from their depositors?"

Wilson looked annoyed. "Who said anything about taking money from our depositors?"

"Who gets the sixteen million?" Wes asked. "Your customers, the local merchants," he said, answering his own question. "Many of those merchants have loans with your bank. With this reduction in income, how many will be able to repay those loans?

"Most of our employees are customers of the bank," Wes continued. "If the hospital closes, many will be forced to leave the community to find jobs. As they leave, so will their deposits. Most of these people own homes— mortgaged by your bank. As two hundred homes hit the market, what will happen to the price of real estate in the community? What will be the effect on the bank as real estate values fall and your collateral in those homes dries up?"

The room was silent as the bankers digested Wes' message. The president bounced a questioning look off Wilson. "Is this the hospital's loan file?" he asked, pointing to the folder on Wilson's desk.

"It is," Wilson affirmed.

"Bring it with you. Let's meet in my office." The bank president stood to leave as Wilson gathered the file, and then he turned to Wes. "Give us a few minutes—we'll see what we can do."

"Gentlemen, we have a proposition for you," Wilson said when he and his boss returned. Wilson took a seat at his desk, while the bank president stood, arms folded, at the door.

"We'll continue to work with the hospital for ninety days, at which time we'll reevaluate our financial relationship," Wilson announced. "Our conditions are as follows: In thirty days you'll have a business plan showing how you'll compete profitably. In ninety days, you'll be at breakeven. Thirty days beyond that, you will reach a net income of at least three percent of total revenue. We assume you won't be able to reach these goals without layoffs and a restructuring of your entire operation," he concluded, looking up from his notes at Wes.

"And, in sixty days," he continued, "you must have an accounting system in place able to accurately report product cost. We anticipate these costs will be shown in your updated business plan."

"I think we can do that," Wes said slowly.

Wilson paused to look at his boss, who nodded for him to continue. "There's one last requirement," Wilson added. "Unless you're willing to meet this final requirement, the deal's off. We want a lien on the new MRI you purchased last January and on the land you own north of town as collateral."

Brannan sat up. "That's a little stiff," he complained. "The MRI was purchased with a grant from the Michael and Sara Brannan Foundation. We were hoping to hold the land unencumbered. Even if we can't build a new hospital now, there's a partially complete doctors' office building on the property."

"Those are our requirements," Wilson stated with finality.

Edward Wycoff, who was taking notes, looked up. "I have an alternate suggestion," he said, speaking slowly and deliberately. "I don't know how the Brannan family would feel about a lien on the MRI the foundation gave the hospital. They've contributed significantly over the years—it would be a shame to turn our backs on that support."

David Brannan gave Wycoff a look of disbelief mixed with gratitude—it was the first time David could remember Wycoff speaking favorably of the Brannan family.

Wycoff continued, addressing the bank president directly. "Your last requirement closes the door on several options our new administrator might need to turn the hospital around. I think there's a better way."

"I'm listening," the banker said cautiously.

"What if I were willing to guarantee the line of credit up to two million dollars? The bank would still have the loan—collateralized by the accounts receivable. All the requirements you stipulated would remain, except the liens on the equipment and the property."

"I think the Loan Committee might approve something like that," The president responded. "What do you think, David?"

"I think it's a gracious offer," Brannan responded gratefully. "I'll have the hospital's attorney draw the note up right away."

"My attorney will insist on doing that," Wycoff interrupted. "The note would be guaranteed by stock I've set up in a family trust. My attorney is an astute businessman. I've discussed matters like this with him and he has stipulated the trust must hold the liens.

"The trust doesn't want to own an MRI or one hundred acres of land," Wycoff said reassuringly. "But an arrangement of this kind would serve as an incentive for management to take the actions needed to put Brannan Community Hospital in the black."

Brannan was silent. The gratitude vanished from his eyes. Wycoff was the smarter of the two and he knew it. Still, David Brannan was unable to guarantee the note himself and, for his family's sake, he didn't want to see the hospital close. He pondered the situation momentarily and then nodded his agreement.

Wilson's boss grinned broadly. "Good! I'll arrange for the bank's attorney to meet with your trustee," he said, holding his hand out to Wycoff. "Hopefully we've happened on an agreement that will assure the hospital's continued operation, while protecting the bank."

"I'm sure it will be to our mutual benefit," Wycoff replied smoothly.

Although the weatherman predicted rain, the sun was shining through scattered clouds as Wes left the bank, grateful for the help offered by Edward Wycoff. *I misjudged Wycoff,* he thought. *Few board members would be willing to risk their own money to save a community hospital. There's more at stake here than I thought.*

Alone in the bank's conference room, Wycoff placed a long distance call. "I need Mr. Devecchi ... now," he said when a secretary answered. She put the call through immediately.

"Devecchi," he said. "Ed Wycoff here. They bought it! Yeah, I gave Wes Douglas just enough rope to hang himself. No, I don't think Brannan suspects anything. Yes, we've got the liens. They have ninety days ... and then we've got 'em."

6

Never Give Up

Wes thought often about his grandfather, Admiral Wesley Douglas, a naval engineer with degrees from Annapolis and the Massachusetts Institute of Technology. As much as anyone, Grandfather shaped the beliefs and attitudes Wes carried into adulthood.

In 1983, Grandfather encouraged Wes to join the local Boy Scout troop. He realized fourteen-year-old Wes needed a better outlet for adolescent energy than girls and skateboarding. Wes quickly climbed to the rank of Life Scout. At sixteen, he was ready to tackle the rank of Eagle.

As Wes was interested in the environment, he proposed a restoration of a nature trail in a state park not far from his home for his Eagle project. He would clear the trail of weeds and garbage. In addition, he would construct a park bench every quarter mile and a small pavilion at the three-mile mark.

Grandfather Douglas, an engineer by training, reviewed Wes' proposal. He thought it was too large. Wes knew better, or so he thought, and submitted the proposal as written. In later years, Wes would learn to take counsel from those older and wiser.

Wes started the project June 1st. He planned to finish by July 1st. By the middle of July, however, he had only reached the halfway mark. Part of the problem was the park ranger. Ranger Morris believed in quality. If Wes didn't do the job right the first time, he made him repeat it. While Wes' friends spent their summer swimming, earning money, or chasing girls, Wes spent his clearing weeds, hauling rocks, and building benches. By August 1st, he was ready to quit.

He complained bitterly to his father, who encouraged him to see the project to completion. Certain he would find an ally in Grandfather, he bicycled to his home one evening. Grandfather Douglas listened patiently, his eyes emotionless, as Wes explained the difficulty of the project. When the boy finished, the admiral spoke quietly, but firmly. "You've made a commitment that's going to be difficult to fulfill," he acknowledged. "Before you renege, however, you need to think about the consequences."

Wes' body stiffened. "Consequences?" he asked.

Grandfather nodded sympathetically. "Consequences. The park ranger has invested a lot of time in planning and supervising your project. Because of your promise, he persuaded the Parks Department to buy lumber for the benches and pavilion."

Wes shook his head in denial. "The project's too much work," he protested.

"Maybe . . . but you're the one who designed it."

"Grandfather, it's ruining my summer!"

"Better your summer than your reputation."

"I don't care what others think," Wes replied flippantly.

"I do—you share my name."

Wes was silent, shamed by the truthfulness of his grandfather's logic.

"A reputation is an important thing," Grandfather continued. "It is based on character. Character is formed by habits, and habits are formed by actions." The admiral's gray eyes softened as he placed a hand on the boy's shoulder.

"This isn't the first time you'll face a task that's bigger than you, Wes. Quit now, and you'll set a precedent. The next time you bump up against a problem, it will be that much easier to retreat. Give up a couple of times and you'll form a habit. Habits are hard to break. Reinforce it, and soon you'll lose the strength to finish anything that challenges you."

For the rest of the summer, Grandfather drove Wes to the state park. They finished the project just as school started. In later years, Wes would reflect on that summer as one of the turning points of his adolescent years. It taught him the meaning of perseverance.

Twelve years after the death of his grandfather, Wes returned to the trailhead at the top of the park. With permission from the Parks Department, he placed a small plaque where the trail ended. On it was a quotation by Winston Churchill one a wise grandfather branded into the soul of young Wes Douglas.

"Never give up," the plaque said. *"Never, never, never give up!"*

Wes called an afternoon meeting of the hospital's supervisors to formulate a plan to put the hospital at breakeven in ninety days. "What obstacles do you face in running your departments?" he asked as the meeting started.

Jeff Lee, director of the laboratory, spoke first. "Most problems relate to our losses. For many years, the hospital made money. Some departments were profitable on less volume than they're running now." Lee shook his head in confusion. "I've heard the problem is managed care. I don't know what that means. Wycoff tells us managed care has created a new environment—one requiring us to manage our departments differently. No one has told us how."

Wes wrote on the board:

Managed care—training and management

Elizabeth Flannigan, director of nursing, spoke next. "Our budgeting system stinks," she said bluntly. "The forms we're asked to fill out each year are impossible to understand and there's no one to answer questions."

The laundry manager agreed. "Some of us spend weeks preparing forecasts and budgets. When they come back, management has cut them without our input or consent. It's stupid to hold us accountable for budgets we didn't prepare," he said, his face flushing red.

"This isn't a recent phenomenon," Flannigan added. "The controller's office has never been open to our needs. The accountants there think we work for them—in reality, it's the other way around."

Wes nodded, writing on the board:

Poor budgeting system

Unresponsive controller's office

"Most of the time we can't understand what those accountants are talkin' about," the laundry manager chimed in. "They have their own language—they do. Why . . . they're harder to understand than the docs."

Flannigan nodded in approval. "We don't get reports that are useful for making decisions," she said.

"Financial reports aren't timely," complained Jeff Lee. "What good are January's reports in May?"

Turning to the board, Wes wrote:

No service orientation

Poor communication

Reports—unacceptable format and untimely

"Other problems?" Wes asked.

The room was silent. "Those are the big ones," Flannigan said finally. "Give us the tools we need to run our departments and we'll fix our own problems."

"You'll get 'em," Wes replied.

7

Cultural Diversity

The Park City Rotarians met every Wednesday for lunch at The Prospector, a small café on Main Street. Wes joined the organization when he moved to Park City to meet civic leaders and raise his visibility in the community. The lunch routine was always the same. Introductions by the president, "fines" for harmless transgressions like having your picture in the paper, or being bald; then lunch. As club members ate, someone spoke. Wes slipped on a pair of sunglasses and discreetly slept through a presentation on zoning.

Today the speaker finished early. After the obligatory applause, a waiter handed out dessert—*Death by Chocolate*. Wes calculated how many miles he would have to run to burn it off and sighed. Since he left Maine, he had gained ten pounds.

Across the table, a young professional made eye contact. He rose and extended his hand. "I am Rajendra Ramachandran," he said with a crisp English accent. "My friends call me Ray."

The table was too wide to shake hands from a sitting position. Wes snatched the napkin from his lap with his left hand and rose, extending his right hand in greeting. "Wes Douglas," he replied. They shook hands, and Ray motioned for him to sit down.

When Wes joined the club, the president asked each member to stand and introduce himself. From the brief introduction, Wes remembered Ray. Born in India and educated in England and the United States, he joined a small law practice on Main Street two years ago. His language was elegant.

"You are the new hospital administrator," Ray said in a tone conveying polite regret.

Wes responded with a curious nod.

"You have many problems at your hospital," Ray said. He shook his head with solemnity. "Many, many problems."

The conversation in the café quieted as several people turned to listen. Wes smiled. A friend told him being a hospital administrator in a small town was like being a fire hydrant in a pack of mad dogs. It was impossible to attend a public function without having someone bend his ear about the hospital. It didn't do any good to be defensive—most of the complaints were about events that occurred before his watch.

"I met my wife in England," Ray continued. "We have lived here in the United States for ten years, in Park City for two." He nodded to himself. "We understand the culture and are comfortable with our new home."

Ray's face softened into deep sadness. "Recently, my father-in-law, a merchant in Kanpur, died. We returned home for the funeral. Then, at my wife's insistence, we brought her mother to the United States. She will live with us until she joins her husband." His eyes narrowed speculatively. "Of course we do not know how long it will be, but she is not in good health.

"One month ago, she suffered a heart attack," he continued. "We took her to the hospital and she was admitted to the Intensive Care Unit." Ray shook his head. "I must report that she had a bad experience.

"Park City is a small town," Ray continued. "The people are good, but isolated. My mother-in-law also has not been exposed to other societies. Her religious and cultural beliefs are strong, and were violated—I'm sure more through ignorance than intention." Ray studied his hands, folded in his lap, and then looked directly at Wes. "You must do more to educate your employees on the beliefs and cultures of patients from other cultures. If not, they will go to other hospitals."

For the next thirty minutes, Ray explained the culture of India. He discussed its dietary practices, beliefs about the origin and treatment of illness, and preferences on personal space. Wes listened and took notes and they parted friends.

When he returned to his office, Wes Douglas asked Birdie to see if Elizabeth Flannigan was available to meet with him. A few minutes later, Flannigan knocked and entered his office. As she took a seat across from his desk, he spoke.

"Do our employees get diversity training?" Wes began.

Flannigan was in a foul mood. Two nurses had quit; to meet staffing requirements she worked their 11:00 p.m. to 7:00 a.m. shift. She needed a shower, her feet hurt, and now Wes Douglas was asking stupid questions.

"Right now they're not receiving any training," she said, the irritation flashing in her eyes. "When Edward Wycoff cut the heart out of our training budget, our inservice director quit. I talked to you about replacing her, but you've placed a cap on hiring new employees."

Wes ignored the jab. Most of the managers were feeling intense pressure from employees and patients alike as continued losses depleted the resources they needed to keep their departments operating. One of his roles was to keep things on an even keel.

"I got a complaint today from a family member of one of our patients," he said evenly. "He felt our staff is not sensitive to cultural differences in some of our patients."

Flannigan shot him a skeptical look. "Who complained?" she demanded.

"A young attorney by the name of . . ." Wes pulled the young man's card from his shirt pocket and read the name, "Ray Ramachandran."

Flannigan gave a curt nod. "Oh. I remember him," she snapped. "It was his mother-in-law wasn't it? Didn't speak English, so we had to communicate through the family. Belonged to an Eastern religion—couldn't eat pork, had a lotta strange ideas. I don't buy that stuff."

"We don't have to adopt the beliefs of the people we treat," Wes said. "However, we do have to be respectful and, where possible, accommodate religious or cultural beliefs."

Flannigan stiffened. "Foreigners," she muttered. "If they don't like it here, they can leave."

Wes quietly studied the defiance on Flannigan's face. Unless her attitude improved, he would have to fire her. This was not the time, however. The nursing staff had seen enough disruption.

"The name Flannigan is Irish isn't it?" he asked.

She looked up, startled. "Yes, I think I told you that once."

Wes nodded. "You also told me about how your great-grandfather emigrated from Ireland. He came in through the port of Albany, as I recall."

Flannigan smiled as she remembered the stories about him. "Yup. Tough old codger who never took guff from anyone."

"You told me when he first came to America, he had trouble finding work."

Flannigan nodded. "There was lots of prejudice against the Irish then, some of it against Catholicism."

"I believe he finally found a job working for the railroad," Wes said.

"That's how the family got to Utah," Flannigan affirmed.

"Now wasn't there a supervisor who gave him a rough time—an Italian, if I remember correctly?"

"Your memory's good," she replied. "The Italians and the Irish didn't get along. The railroad had to separate work crews to stop the fist fights."

"The conflict wasn't religious was it?" Wes asked. "Many Irish and most Italians of that era were Catholic."

Flannigan scowled. "No, it was about culture. The Irish and Italians had different languages, different customs, ate different foods … it created animosity." She smiled at the foolishness. "To his dying day, Great-grandfather wouldn't sit at the same dinner table with an Italian."

"How *do you* feel about the Italians?" Wes asked.

"My son-in-law's Italian," Flannigan answered. "Good kid." She squinted. "Are you saying I'm prejudiced against Italians?"

Wes shook his head. "Obviously you're not. I'm just wondering why, given what you've told me about your grandfather."

Flannigan shrugged. "Guess as we got to know each other, the differences weren't all that strange."

Wes was silent for a moment, hoping Flannigan was listening to her own words. "Then one difference between bias and acceptance is knowledge?" he prompted gently.

Flannigan nodded slowly. "When people know more about each other, they become more respectful, more trusting, less disapproving." She shot him a knowing look. "I get your point," she said.

"We live in a multiethnic country," Wes continued. "Walk down Main Street. There are people from all over the world. If we are to serve them, we must understand their beliefs, especially as they relate to healthcare."

Flannigan was silent as she digested the message. "What do you want me to do?" she asked.

"I'd like you to have one of your supervisors put a presentation together on cultural sensitivity. Find someone who's interested in the topic. I'd like to review it before it's presented to the staff."

Two days later, Elizabeth Flannigan was back in Wes' office with Marie Juarez who volunteered to give the presentation. Juarez, a petite Hispanic woman in her mid-thirties, was a night supervisor on the obstetrics floor. At age seven, she emigrated from Mexico with her parents. At eighteen, she entered college, graduating with a four-year degree in nursing. She was a registered nurse and, from all reports, a good employee.

As they entered the office, Marie looked doubtful. This was their first meeting and many people were still hesitant about accepting the new administrator.

Wes smiled reassuringly. "Thanks for taking the assignment," he said. "The more we educate our staff, the better they'll be at meeting the needs of our patients."

"I've scheduled Marie's presentation for next Thursday," Flannigan reported. "Do you want the whole presentation, or just a summary?"

"A summary is fine."

Marie moved to a whiteboard on the far wall. "I'll start with a few definitions I copied from an old sociology textbook," she said.

On the board, Marie wrote:

- **Culture**—*social, artistic, and religious belief structures and manifestations that characterize a specific society. Values and traditions are handed down from one generation to the next.*

- **Ethnicity**—*the unity that arises from a common religion, belief, language, and/or culture.*

- **Race**—*a classification system based on genetic characteristics such as the color of skin and the structure of hair.*

- **Cultural Blindness**—*a situation where a person assumes cultural differences do not exist.*

As Wes studied the definitions, Marie explained that race and ethnicity are not synonymous. "There are over seventeen subcultures in the Hispanic group alone," she added. "My purpose will be to educate our staff on differences that must be considered when treating patients from different ethnic groups." She continued writing. "These include:"

Cultural Differences:

- *Food*

- *Gender roles*

- *Beliefs about illness, personal space, touching, and communication*

Marie pointed to the first topic. "In healthcare, food has cultural as well as therapeutic significance," she said. "One has to consider not only what is eaten, but how it's prepared. For example, Puerto Ricans believe it's important to maintain a balance of hot, cool, and cold foods. By that, they mean types of foods—not temperatures.

"Some of our patients are vegetarians," she continued. "Those of the Muslim, Jewish, and Seventh-day Adventist faiths have prohibitions against eating pork. If a patient isn't eating," Marie summarized, "their culture could be the reason."

Wes nodded encouragingly.

"Gender roles differ from culture to culture," Marie continued. "In some cultures, the mother is the dominant decision-maker—the one who must be consulted when asking permission to treat a child. In others, it is the father. Sometimes parents share the role equally.

"Culture affects one's belief about the origin and treatment of illness," Marie added. "Our culture takes a scientific approach. We focus on trauma, pathogens, diet, and exercise. That's not true of all cultures. Some, for example, think illness is a punishment from God.

"And personal space differs from culture to culture," Marie continued.

"Define the term," Wes requested.

"Personal space is the area a person regards as his own—the distance from other people he or she needs to feel secure," Marie replied. "Arabs and Africans stand closer when speaking than those of European descent. Violating personal space can cause discomfort, or worse—anger.

"Cultures have different beliefs about parts of the body that can appropriately be touched by others. There are cultures, for example, that believe a person's head contains the spirit. To touch the head is a grave offense."

"How do you remove bandages or clean head wounds, then?" Wes asked.

"Before giving personal care, communicating what you're going to do before you do it, and explaining why it is necessary will help.

"Communication is a part of a treatment plan. In communicating with a person from any cultural group, a nurse or allied health professional should..."

Marie wrote:

- *Speak clearly*
- *Show respect*
- *Never yell*
- *Verify that the patient understands what is being said*
- *Use gestures*
- *Summarize*
- *Find an interpreter (maybe a family member) if the patient doesn't speak English*

"Aren't you going to say anything about body language?" Flannigan asked abruptly.

"I am," Marie affirmed. "Eye contact is considered impolite, even aggressive, by some groups including Native Americans, Asians, and Arabs. Hasidic Jewish males are taught to avoid eye contact with women. For Muslim-Arab women, it's considered immodest to look into a man's eyes."

Wes' brow furrowed. "Useful information."

Marie nodded. "Finally, we'll discuss stereotyping and how professionals can overcome bias."

Marie returned the marker to the white board. "Do you have any questions?" she asked.

"Nope," Wes said. "Sounds great. Good luck on your presentation to the staff. Let me know how it goes."

8

A Dynasty Falls

Perched high on a hill overlooking the small resort town of Park City was the Brannan Mansion. Constructed in 1896 in a Victorian Gothic style, its high Venetian tower mirrored the arrogance and energy of its builder, Mike Brannan—an Irishman who struck it rich in the silver mines of Park City in the late 1880s.

Ornate wrought iron doors—added more for decoration than protection—guarded an outdoor vestibule. Beyond those gates stood large double doors of carved oak and beveled glass. Beyond those doors were waterfall staircases and paneled nooks, warmly lit by stained glass.

Deep within the bowels of the mansion was the library. Roughly thirty feet square, the room was interlaced with loggias and balconies, its formal design contrasting sharply with the Gothic asymmetry of the other rooms of the nineteenth-century mansion.

David Brannan hadn't been in this room since he left for college—he preferred his condominium high above the Stein Erickson ski lodge overlooking Park City. Today, however, he had to come to sign documents that would dissolve a financial empire built by three generations of the Brannan family.

It was 3:30 in the afternoon, and David poured another drink. Replacing the bottle on the heavily carved walnut desk his great-grandfather imported from Italy, he toasted a portrait of the old goat that hung high above the hand-carved marble fireplace.

Michael James Brannan immigrated to the United States in 1882 from Ireland. Arriving through New York, he and his brother Patrick remained long enough to visit some cousins and buy supplies before heading west for the gold fields of California. They never reached their destination. Stopping in Salt Lake City for supplies, Mike fell in love with a Mormon girl named Sara, married, and never left Utah.

For a time, Mike and his brother tried farming. They failed miserably. Mike wasn't a Mormon and he wasn't a farmer. Rumors of the discovery of silver on a spur not far from Dayton Peak soon drew him to the ledges and peaks of the Rocky Mountains east of Salt Lake City.

The American Lode was the first mining claim in the district. It was not until the discovery of the Ontario mine in 1879, however, that Park City started to flourish. Purchased in 1872 by George Hearst, father of William Randolph Hearst, the Ontario Mine would produce fifty million dollars in silver ore. Later mines—the Pinion, the Walker, the Webster, the Flagstaff, the McHenry, and the Buckeye—would create a dozen or so family fortunes, including the Brannans'.

As David studied the portrait, his eyes shimmered with genuine curiosity. He wondered what the old guy would think if he could see the family today. Gone were the silver and coal mines, the bank, the newspaper, and the hotel. All that was left was the stock in a small software firm, which would provide enough money to fund a small trust for David's mother. He took another gulp, wiped his mouth with the back of his hand, and set the tumbler on the table.

Part of the family's financial disaster might have been avoided if his father, James Brannan, had not insisted on running the business late into his eighties. In James' time, much of the family income came from coal mines in Carbon County.

David's father resisted modernization, pumping money into highly speculative ventures, including the software company. These needed huge amounts of cash, jeopardizing the family's liquidity. Facing the possible loss of his investment, he turned around and spent six million dollars on improvements and mining equipment. The market for coal was depressed, however. Strapped for cash, Brannan Inc. collapsed like a house of cards.

Unable to cope with failure, James suffered a massive stroke in February, dying early in March. David Brannan inherited the family business, along with some of the blame for its collapse.

David's eyes flashed with anger as he studied the photograph of his father on the desk. With a violent sweep of his arm, he knocked it off, the glass shattering as the sterling silver frame smashed into the stone mantle of the ornate fireplace and bounced onto the marble floor. He studied it for a moment—broken at his feet—and then poured another drink.

David was not like his father, or his father's father, or his father before him. He hated the family business as much as he hated his father. Given a choice, he would have chosen a professorship in history or literature at some small Ivy League college.

He wasn't given a choice, however. Free agency wasn't a part of the Brannan family vocabulary—not where children were concerned. James enrolled his son in engineering at the Colorado School of Mines, believing one day David would take over the family's operations. David took two quarters of math and flunked out. Later, with financial help from his mother, he finished a degree in American Studies from a small college on the East Coast. He taught at a college in Minnesota before returning home to settle his father's estate.

David was grateful to his mother—she was the only buffer between him and the unpredictable wrath of his father. For his mother's sake, he did his best to save what remained of the family's fortune. There wasn't much left to save, however, and he didn't know how to save it anyway.

His thoughts were interrupted by voices in the parlor. His mother hosted the Women's Auxiliary of the hospital the last Wednesday of every month. She was not fully aware of the family situation. Her home was paid for, and David hoped to get enough money from the sale of the remaining businesses to maintain her in a reasonable way for the rest of her life. At seventy-two years of age, she deserved better than this.

David's shoulders rose and fell as he sighed deeply. Studying the documents on the desk, he slowly picked up a pen and signed the declaration of bankruptcy. The hospital wasn't the only organization in the community with financial difficulties.

9

Why Are Costs So High?

The first snow of the season was blanketing the foothills as a navy blue Accord broke out of Parley's Canyon east of Salt Lake City on Interstate 80. Wes Douglas caught a glimpse of the valley.

In the distance, a cluster of skyscrapers, majestic and tall like the lofty mountains, surrounded the granite towers of the Mormon Temple—a landmark that had dominated the skyline for many years. To the north, high on a hill, the State Capitol stood guard over the valley, its copper dome reflecting a history of mining and mineral exploration—an important counterpoint to the ecclesiastical history of the state. Originally settled by Mormon pioneers in 1847, later joined by prospectors and soldiers, and home of the 2002 Winter Olympics, Utah was as diverse as its scenery.

The purpose of Wes' trip was a meeting with the hospital's auditors in Salt Lake City. With a ninety-day commitment to reach breakeven, he needed to understand more about hospital accounting and finance. The public accounting firm that prepared the hospital's financial statements was a good place to start. Wes took the Sixth South exit downtown. Parking in the basement of Parkside Tower, he caught an elevator to the tenth floor, where he introduced himself to the firm's receptionist, then took a seat.

In less than a minute, Karisa Holyoak, managing partner, appeared. She was tall and slender with a bewitching smile that faintly reminded him of Kathryn. Her eyes sparkled with enthusiasm and intelligence.

Karisa led him to a small conference room. "This is your first week on the job," she said, taking a seat directly across from Wes at the conference table. She looked at him with wide and curious eyes. "Usually it takes me longer than that to get in trouble with a new client. How can I help you?"

"I'm the one in trouble," Wes murmured. "I'm trying to understand how a hospital that charges $1,800 a day can run at a loss."

Karisa smiled—she'd considered the question. "Our firm's had the hospital account for twenty years," she informed him. She opened the audit file and laid it on the table. "For many years, the hospital was one of our most stable clients."

Karisa thumbed through several reports, opening the most recent audit. "About three years ago, the hospital's financial position started a downward spiral," she continued, reading from her notes. "Although volume went up, revenue went down. We concluded the problem was managed care."

"Why is managed care a problem?" Wes asked.

"Well, it's an approach to cost control that has changed the way administrators have to manage. Your hospital seems to be having more difficulty than others are. We tried to do an analysis to determine where you're losing money, but the data simply isn't available thanks to a lousy accounting system."

Wes nodded in agreement. "I need better data to run the hospital. I feel like a pilot flying without instruments."

"Good analogy," replied Karisa. "And you're running out of fuel. Unless things change, you'll be out of cash in two to three months."

Wes sighed. "It might not take that long. Do you have any suggestions on how to proceed?"

Raising her eyebrows, Karisa leaned forward. "May I be candid?"

"Please," Wes nodded.

"You're a nice guy, Wes, but you're out of your league. You're an accountant. You don't know the first thing about hospitals. By the time you learn the rules, the game'll be over."

Wes agreed. Five days on the job convinced him hospital administration was different from anything he'd previously experienced. The assumptions were different, even the terminology was new. The departments in the hospital were like separate kingdoms—each with its own language and customs.

"What do you suggest?" he asked.

"Find another job . . . or find a mentor."

"I can't quit," he said. "There's too much at stake."

"For you or the hospital?"

"Both."

Karisa nodded thoughtfully.

"Can you suggest a mentor?" Wes asked.

"I don't know anyone with all the answers, but I can put you in contact with someone who might get you started. We occasionally use the services of a health economist at the University Hospital—a fellow by the name of Herb Krimmel," Karisa said, retrieving his address from her computer. "Dr. Krimmel has an interesting background—he's a physician with a degree in health economics. He teaches at the University Hospital. Coincidentally, he lives in Park City."

Opening her day planner, Karisa wrote a note. "Let me give him a call," she said. "I think he'll be willing to talk to you. You might ask him to introduce you to the controller. He has an impressive system for controlling costs. Maybe you can borrow some of his ideas."

Karisa gave him a dazzling smile, stood, and held out her hand. "Hope I've been helpful," she said.

Wes took her hand and shook it warmly. "Thanks. I'll be in touch."

Thursday evening, Wes got a phone call from Karisa telling him she had spoken with Krimmel. "As it works out, his car's in for service," she said. "Since he's a neighbor, he wondered if he could catch a ride to the hospital with you tomorrow morning. He promised to set you up with the people who can explain what's happening in the industry." She paused. "You'll find him a little eccentric, but I think you'll like him."

10

A Lesson in Medical Economics

Krimmel's home, a two-story farmhouse, was three miles north of Park City. The doctor was waiting for Wes at the curb. "I'm Herb Krimmel," he said as he opened the door. Climbing in, he brushed the residue of what looked like cornmeal from his tweed coat onto the floor. "Breakfast is always a mess."

Wes looked at him oddly. "Yours?"

"No, the chickens!" Krimmel replied. "We run a small farm. The wife would like me to sell 'em, but I wake up early—old age you know. It gives me something to do before she gets up." His eyes twinkled. "Besides, the chickens are the only ones around here who listen to me."

Krimmel laughed. Wes couldn't help but laugh too as he studied his odd traveling companion. Short and chubby, Krimmel had curly dark hair, a large Roman nose and round horn-rimmed glasses that looked like small fishbowls as they magnified his eyes in a peculiar sort of way. Wes turned onto the highway.

"You're new on the job?" Krimmel asked.

"It's my second week," Wes admitted.

"And no experience?"

"Not in hospitals."

Krimmel raised one eyebrow. "You've chosen an exciting time to enter the field. How's it going?"

Wes nodded his head up and down, then left to right as though he couldn't agree with himself. "Good ... actually, not so good," he confessed.

Krimmel didn't say anything, but studied the cornmeal at his feet. "Ought to vacuum your car more often," he mumbled.

"I'm told our medical director's an old friend of yours," Wes said.

"Who's that?" Krimmel asked.

"Dr. Emil Flagg."

Krimmel chuckled. "An old friend? Wouldn't go that far. We were classmates in medical school. Courted the same girl. I won, of course." He smiled, obviously pleased with himself. "Always felt he was a bad sport," Krimmel said with a grin. "How do you get along with him?"

A look of uncertainty settled on Wes' face. "Don't know—I've only talked with him once. Didn't go well—more of a confrontation than a meeting. Dr. Flagg thinks medicine's too commercial, he thinks there's too much emphasis on the bottom-line. Blames businessmen like Edward Wycoff, for the trend."

"Who's Edward Wycoff?"

"Our Board of Trustees chair, a retired banker. He thinks I'm his ally."

"Are you?" Krimmel asked.

"I'm not sure." Wes looked hopefully at Krimmel. "That's part of the reason I came to see you."

"Emil and I were in the same class in medical school—the class of 1964," Krimmel said. "It was a different era—one in which healthcare workers stressed quality but paid little attention to cost. One reason was costs were low. When Emil and I graduated, the room rate at the University Hospital was $40 a day—total costs including x-ray, lab and pharmacy were about $80."

"What are they today?"

"Twenty-five hundred bucks."

Wes whistled softly. "That's a lot of money!" he said. "Why so high?"

"Technology. Construction costs for new hospitals can exceed one million dollars per bed, including the investment in medical equipment."

"Is there anything hospital administrators can do?"

"They can be careful not to overbuild," Krimmel replied. "Duplication's expensive. When I was a medical student at the University of Colorado Medical School in Denver, there were twenty-two hospitals in town. All were operating at sixty percent occupancy, and most of them were building."

"Why build if you aren't full?" Wes asked.

"Several reasons," Krimmel replied. "Prestige, salary, a desire to give the medical staff the latest technology and job security. Physicians and patients alike seemed to share the *"bigger-is-better"* syndrome. Patients often equate size with quality."

"What's size have to do with salary?" Wes asked.

"Hospital administrators' salaries usually correlate with number of beds. The larger the hospital, the larger the paycheck."

"What about job security?"

"It's difficult to fire an administrator in the middle of a building project," Krimmel replied. "A three-year building project provides three years of added security for an administrator in trouble with their Board."

"You sound cynical," Wes said.

"A little." Krimmel's face softened. "In all fairness, however, that's probably the least important reason. The biggest issue is technology."

"Isn't technology good?"

"Yeah, but it has to be used efficiently. After graduating, I did my residency at St. Joseph's Hospital in Chicago—a fine facility. While I was there, Presbyterian Hospital—which was directly across the street—installed a two-million-dollar piece of equipment for use in their cancer treatment program. Shortly after that, the Board of Trustees at St. Joseph's announced they planned to build a similar treatment unit."

Krimmel shook his head in disbelief as he remembered the experience. "One afternoon, we confronted St. Joseph's administrator in the hall. We asked her if she thought about the impact this would have on cost. One community would be paying for two machines, each worth two million dollars, and each operating at thirty percent of capacity. It doesn't take a rocket scientist to realize duplication raises costs and someone has to pay the bill.

"I'll never forget her answer! *Young man,* she said, *when it comes to patient care, cost is not an issue. At St. Joseph's we don't compete on cost, we compete on quality!*"

Krimmel swore under his breath. "It was a bunch of bull, of course. Presbyterian was St. Joseph's main competitor. If their doctors went to a competing hospital, they might like it better and not come back. The administrator's concern was loss of volume.

"In 1964," Krimmel continued, "there were few incentives for hospitals to control costs. Specifically, there was no price competition."

"They didn't compete on price?"

"Right."

"Why?"

"Know anything about economics?" Krimmel asked.

"I took a course in graduate school—didn't like it much."

"You're typical," Krimmel quipped. "I teach the subject. Majored in economics before medical school.

"When you took the course," he continued, "you probably learned that to have price competition you need a free market. Remember what that is?"

"I think so, but go ahead and explain it."

"A free market," Krimmel said, "exists where private individuals—as opposed to the government—decide what products will be made, how many will be made, who will make them, and for whom they will be made. Prices in a free market are usually established by the interaction of demand and supply."

"It's starting to come back," Wes said.

"Your professor probably taught you the conditions for a free market to exist," Krimmel said. "Do you remember what those are?"

"I think so. A free market requires a consumer ... who makes the decision to buy ... shops on quality and price ... and negotiates an arm's-length purchase price."

Impressed, Krimmel raised his eyebrows. "That's pretty good," he said. "I'll have to invite you to speak to my class."

Wes looked at Krimmel warily but said nothing.

"Let's talk about how market forces work in most industries. Then let's compare that with what happens in healthcare."

From the animated expression on Krimmel's face, it was apparent he enjoyed this topic. Despite a couple of kinks in his personality, Wes suspected he was a pretty good teacher.

"You're driving a new car," Krimmel said.

"A new Honda," Wes confirmed.

"Fine . . . let's talk about how the market works in the auto industry. Who decided you needed a new car?"

"I did."

"How did you decide that?" Krimmel pressed.

"The second transmission fell out of my Nissan."

"Okay, you're a consumer who can identify a need for transportation."

"That's right," Wes said. "I met the first requirement for a free market."

"What did you tell me was the second?"

"The consumer must shop on the basis of quality and price," Wes answered confidently.

"Did you do that?" Krimmel asked.

"Yes."

"How?"

"I read the automobile reviews in *Consumer Reports*. I also talked to people who owned models I was interested in."

"Was price a consideration?"

"Yes."

"Did you negotiate?"

"Yes."

"How?"

"Visited a couple of dealers—bargained with the salesmen."

"You're sure price was important to you?"

"Absolutely," Wes said.

"Let's say the price for a new car was $50,000. Would you have bought one?"

"Probably not."

"What if the price was $5,000?"

"I might have bought two—a car for work, and a light truck for the mountains."

"So, as price goes up, demand goes down," Krimmel explained. "We call it price elasticity."

Wes was beginning to catch on. "Car manufacturers compete with each other on the basis of price. This gives them an incentive to keep their costs as low as possible. Therefore, market forces work well in the auto industry."

"You're good," Krimmel said in mock amazement.

"Now let's talk about the traditional healthcare industry," Krimmel continued. "Assume you wake up one morning with a pain in your belly." Krimmel poked him in the stomach. "You palpate your abdomen, run a few tests, and decide you need a cholecystectomy—right?"

"What's a cholecystectomy?"

"A gallbladder operation. You don't know much about medicine," Krimmel observed.

"Right."

Krimmel studied Wes thoughtfully. "So we've identified we're missing the first requirement of a free market."

"An informed consumer," Wes confirmed.

"Right. So who decides if you'll purchase a lab test or an operation?"

"My doctor."

"And who provides the product?"

"My doctor."

"Who prices the product?"

"My doctor."

"You're repeating yourself."

"I noticed," Wes said.

"Why delegate all that to your doctor?" Krimmel asked skeptically.

"He understands medicine—I don't."

"That's right. The doctor has information you don't have. This puts you at a disadvantage."

Wes nodded.

"Do you think the lack of consumer knowledge is a greater problem in healthcare than say in the car business?" Krimmel asked.

"Probably."

"What if things were set up so it was the auto salesmen who decided when and if their customers bought new cars?"

"Good deal for the salesman, maybe not so good for the consumer," Wes speculated.

"Why?"

"Salesmen make money by selling products. They'd have an incentive to sell them something they don't need."

"Maybe that's the situation in healthcare," Krimmel said.

Wes' eyes widened with recognition. He was starting to understand the economic power the physician has over the consumer.

"Okay," Krimmel continued, "we've determined the healthcare industry fails the first test of a free market—the consumer doesn't make the decision to purchase. Now, once the decision to buy has been made, does the consumer shop on the basis of quality?"

"It's hard for patients to judge quality," Wes answered. "They don't have the background."

"That's right," Krimmel affirmed. "Studies show patients judge the quality of a hospital's care by its *hotel services*—the cleanliness of the room, the friendliness of the staff, and the quality of the food.

"How about price. Do you think a patient who needs open heart surgery shops on the basis of price?"

"Nope."

"Why?"

"Prices aren't usually available," Wes said. "I've never seen a price list on the wall in a doctor's office."

"Neither have I," Krimmel volunteered. "Let's say prices were available … do you think it would make a difference?"

"Not much. I can't imagine someone asking a friend *Do you know where I can get a cheap heart operation?*"

"Doesn't happen," Krimmel agreed. He cocked his head to one side. "Do you know why?"

Wes turned the question over in his mind. "People equate low price with low quality. No one wants a shoddy operation."

"*And…?*" Krimmel prodded.

Wes grinned. "Who wants to drive a hard bargain with a doctor who's going to cut you open tomorrow?"

Krimmel laughed. "I never thought about that," he remarked slapping himself on the knee. "Good! Seriously though, let's talk about price elasticity. If you were healthy, and a surgeon ran a special on cholecystectomies—a complete operation for $1,225—how many would you buy?"

"None."

"What if the price were lowered to $200?" Krimmel asked.

"If I were healthy, I wouldn't buy one," Wes responded.

"What if your daughter had a brain tumor, and the cost of the life-saving surgery was $125. How many brain operations would you buy?"

"One, of course."

"What if the price was $10,000?"

"I would still just buy one operation."

"A million dollars?"

"For my little girl—I'd try to find a way."

"*Aha!*" said Krimmel. "So price *doesn't* influence the quantity of healthcare goods and services purchased—there's little or no price elasticity."

"For many products and services, that's probably true," Wes responded.

Krimmel was silent as he collected his thoughts. "When consumers fail to shop on price, incentives for cost control by suppliers disappear," he said. "That's one of the reasons healthcare costs are so high.

"While we're on the subject of cost incentives," Krimmel continued, "there's one other factor I should mention. Patients aren't the ones who select the hospital. The physician usually makes that decision. Because of that, many hospitals view the physician, and not the patient, as their primary customer." Krimmel looked out the window, lost in thought.

"I hadn't thought of it that way," Wes said, beginning to see the difficulties of Brannan Community Hospital in a new light.

"Let me tell you a story," Krimmel said. "When I was doing my residency at St. Joseph's, I moonlighted in the Emergency Center at Presbyterian. One day, Presbyterian hired a new administrator, a woman who felt she needed to do something to reduce the cost of healthcare.

"Since physicians control about seventy percent of hospital costs," Krimmel continued, "she decided to focus on the medical staff first. The first thing she did was tell the physicians they were no longer going to purchase excess medical equipment. If one group of physicians wanted Sony heart monitors for surgery and another wanted Sylvania, the two groups would have to get together and agree on one brand. They would no longer duplicate equipment just to keep people happy. The hospital also looked at the 'freebies' the doctors were getting—free meals in the cafeteria, free laundry, free treatment and drug prescriptions for family illnesses, and so on. Cost control was the new administrator's focus.

"St. Joseph's hospital administrator took a different approach," Krimmel continued. "He told me it was his philosophy to keep the medical staff happy. 'Give the physicians what they want' was his motto."

Dr. Krimmel gave Wes a searching look. "Guess who got most of the patients?"

"Probably St. Joseph's," Wes replied. "Because they gave the doctors whatever they wanted."

Krimmel gave him a thumbs-up. "You've got it," he crowed. "A study conducted in 1975 showed many hospitals were operated to maximize physician income," Krimmel continued. "One way to do that is to provide excess capacity. Under fee-for-service, a physician's income is a function of the time he or she spends treating patients. A physician waiting in line for an operating room or piece of equipment isn't earning money."

Krimmel looked directly at Wes. "When I first joined the staff of University Hospital, most of our surgeons were screaming for more operating rooms. Operating rooms are expensive to build. The administrator looked at the surgical schedule and found the operating rooms were only being used sixty percent of the time. Couldn't figure it out. What he failed to realize, however, was, despite the low use, there were still times when more than one physician needed the same operating suite at the same time. When an emergency arose, someone was bumped from the schedule or had to wait to get into surgery. Downtime is costly for a physician."

"Then the ideal situation from the physician's standpoint would be to have one operating room, staffed, equipped, and on-call at all times, for every surgeon?" Wes asked.

"Yes. Remember, the physician didn't make any more money if the hospital was operated efficiently than if there was excess capacity. The physician didn't share in the costs of inefficiency.

"Please don't misunderstand me," Krimmel continued, "I'm not saying medical people are dishonest—some of the finest people I know are physicians. It's just people respond to financial incentives—and the incentives of the old system were wrong."

"Interesting," Wes responded. "I've never had it explained that way before. Are there other factors influencing costs that I should be aware of?"

"There are," Krimmel replied. "I've set up appointments for you later in the week with other members of the faculty and staff I think can best explain them to you."

Wes was elated as he drove back to Park City. He was starting to understand how healthcare differed from other industries. Hard work was good therapy. There were periods of up to a full day now in which Wes didn't think of Kathryn. That too was a good sign.

He built a special room in his heart that she would always occupy, carefully walled off from everything else. From time to time, he would open the door to see if she was still there. In his mind, she smiled on those occasions, giving him reassurance that all would be fine. His new job, difficult as it was, was giving him a new sense of purpose. Even the back injury was improving. He was seeing an orthopedist in Salt Lake City. The doctor gave him exercises to strengthen the muscles in his back and they were working. The pain was noticeably less. The healing process had begun.

11

Amy

It was noon when Wes returned to the hospital. Birdie Bankhead was leaving for lunch when he met her in the employee parking lot. "There's a few messages on your desk," she said, fishing in her purse for her keys. "The bank called. You left your copy of the note in Arnold Wilson's office—they'll mail it to you."

"The bank has renewed the note on the condition that the hospital be at break-even in ninety days," Wes replied. "I need to get with our department heads to put together a plan."

Birdie looked at him sympathetically. "Won't be easy," she said. "Budgeting never was one of Hap's strengths. I anticipate you'll meet with some resistance from the staff."

Wes shrugged.

Birdie's eyes widened. "That reminds me," she said. "Hap's daughter, Amy, came by this morning to clean out his office. She's still there. You'll enjoy meeting her."

Wes nodded and headed for the employee entrance. By now, everyone recognized him as the new administrator. Just navigating from the parking lot to Administration was a difficult chore, as physicians, supervisors, and employees collared him to voice complaints and give advice. It took twenty minutes from the time he entered the building to the time he arrived at Administration.

By the time he reached his office, his arms were full of three-ring binders with past minutes of the Credentials, Infections, and Tissues committees the secretary of the medical staff asked him to review and sign. Nudging the door closed, he leaned against it and caught his breath. He dropped the binders on Birdie's desk.

With the interruptions, he had forgotten about Amy Castleton. He was surprised when, through the door of Hap's old office, he saw her reading from a stack of papers on the massive walnut desk. Her head was turned gently to one side, exposing a slender white neck. She had long, amber hair that glowed softly in the sunlight that poured through the French doors leading to the patio. Mute, he stared at her as she read from a letter she picked up from Hap's desk. Hearing Wes enter, she looked up, startled.

"Hi," he said, "I'm Wes Douglas."

Pursing her lips, she studied him for a moment—then her eyes lit with recognition. "Wes Douglas—of course ... Father's new financial consultant," she hesitated, "and now his replacement." She smiled sadly and held out her hand. Wes crossed the room and shook it gently, then sat down in the chair next to hers.

"Dad was pleased with your decision to consult with the hospital," she said. "I'm sorry you didn't have more time to work together."

"I'm sorry too," he said softly.

A shadow crossed Amy's face and her brown eyes filled with tears. Looking down at the letter she was holding, she bit softly on her lower lip.

As Wes watched her, an unfamiliar intensity overcame him. It was the first time he'd felt clumsy around a girl since he fell in love with Carol Reimschussel in the sixth grade.

It took a moment for him to realize he was still holding—squeezing actually—her hand. She looked at their hands and then into his face. A questioning look stole across her eyes. Blushing, he released her hand. Anxious to start anew, he cleared his throat and pointed to a painting on the wall above the credenza. "Interesting picture," he said. "I noticed it when I first met your father—is it yours?"

Color touched her cheeks. She smiled and nodded. "I painted it nearly twenty years ago—when I was five years old," she stated. "Dad framed and hung it in his office … I was so proud."

Her eyes, soft and sentimental, slowly surveyed the room. "Some of my happiest hours were spent here on Saturday mornings," she recalled. "Mom was taking a class at the university, and Dad would bring me with him while he opened the mail and caught up on correspondence. I'd read, or draw, or paint."

The picture, painted with acrylics, was six by eight inches and framed in walnut to match the paneling of the office. A drawing of a large man holding three balloons dominated the picture. At his side was a small girl holding a flower. A huge tree, the sun, flowers, chipmunks, and stop signs, in all their profusion of color, filled the remaining white space.

"Those were all the things I knew how to draw at that age," she explained, an impish smile playing at the corners of her mouth.

"Dad wasn't given much to worrying," Amy said thoughtfully as she surveyed the office, "but during the last few weeks of his life things changed." Her eyes narrowed as she searched for the right words. "He acted like something was wrong, but he wouldn't talk about it. Six weeks before the accident, he took out a life-insurance policy."

"People sometimes have premonitions," Wes said gently.

"We hoped the fishing trip would restore his enthusiasm," Amy said sadly. "He seemed so tired—" Neither spoke as she examined the belongings she had removed from his desk.

"I was just finishing when you came in," she continued briskly, wiping her eyes. "In a few more minutes I'll have all of Dad's things, or I can finish later if you need the office."

"Take your time," he said. "I have some other errands to run."

Amy's eyes softened as she took his hand and smiled. "I hope you will visit us sometime," she said. "I know Mother would enjoy meeting you."

He nodded and turned to leave her to her task. As he did, her hand gently brushed his shoulder. As Wes walked away, he wondered if there was something else Amy wanted to tell him.

Wes Douglas had settled into a routine. Often, in the evenings he would visit the nursing stations. It was a good chance to meet employees and talk to patients. Both were a good source of suggestions.

One patient asked for a clock in the room so she would know when to take her medications. Wes got her one. If he ever built a hospital, he decided, there would be a clock in every room.

The food carts were noisy early in the morning when most patients were trying to sleep. He talked to the dietary director about training the transportation aides to be quieter.

"Could you invent a modest hospital gown?" a young executive asked. It was a good idea. From his own experience as a patient, Wes remembered having to hold his gown together to keep from exposing his backside when he walked.

"I was cold when they wheeled me to radiology for tests," a patient reported. From then on, patients were gowned and covered with cotton blankets when transported through the halls.

"Ever take a ride through the hospital on a gurney?" another patient asked. "You'll see things people don't see standing up." Wes' curiosity was piqued. He tried it. The next morning he directed Housekeeping to wash the ceilings and remove the cobwebs.

A sociologist from the University of Wyoming was admitted after a hiking accident. "Your hospital has a way of dehumanizing people," the professor said, "of stripping them of their personal identity. You replace their clothes with a generic gown. Anything that differentiates them from others, including jewelry, is impounded. It's insulting not to be called by your name. I'm not *the broken ankle in room 247*, I'm Robert Hansen!"

Wes took notes. If he survived the financial crisis, he would find ways to humanize the hospital experience.

One evening Wes was visiting patients on the second and third floors. As he exited the elevator, he bumped into a ten-year-old boy in a wheelchair. The kid wasn't seriously injured, but obviously had done something bizarre. Both legs were in casts, his hands were bandaged, his hair was singed, and most of his eyelashes were missing.

Wes smiled. He remembered how easy it was to get in trouble at age ten. One of these days, he'd have to apologize for the anxiety he and his younger brother put their parents through.

"What did you *do?*" he asked the boy curiously.

"Climbed a power pole to catch a bird," the boy replied. His face sobered. "When I touched the pole," he said slowly, "I stayed in the air . . . but my body dropped. I watched it fall . . ." His singed eyebrows rose in astonishment. "When it hit the fence," he said, "I went back into it."

The boy looked as though he expected Wes to answer a question he wasn't old enough to put into words. Wes was silent as he studied the boy quietly, not exactly sure how to respond. Finally, he nodded. "Well," he said, his voice soft but upbeat, "We're glad you're back!"

Down the hall, in room 352, was a sixteen-year-old boy with a bright blue mohawk, a tattoo, and three body piercings. Since his admission, the young man oscillated between ominous silence and violent rage. A drug user, he was admitted the previous evening with his second case of hepatitis from a dirty syringe.

"Keep this up," his physician said sternly, "and your next visit will be to the morgue."

"I don't give a -----," the youth screamed, his face twisted with rage. The doctor ordered a psychiatric consult. Wes visited only once. The young man blew him into the hallway with a volley of profanity. Wes continued down the hall, hopeful someone would help the poor kid before it was too late.

In the next room, in a circle electric bed, was a young police officer from Heber, Utah. His name was Don Hemphill. Initially, there was a problem with his insurance. The hospital was at fault. Wes resolved it and apologized. Since then, Wes visited whenever he was on the floor and they had become friends.

Hemphill was thirty-two years old and had a wife and two little girls, one four and one six. They visited each evening. Tonight they were there in bright red dresses that matched the valentines they were giving their father—never mind that it was October.

"God has been good to me," Don told Wes earlier that evening. "I'm going to beat this, you know." Wes admired his optimism, but Don was wrong. A few minutes later the doctor told Connie Hemphill that Don had an ependymoma—a cancer of the spinal cord. He would be dead by December. Connie returned home and retrieved the love notes his daughters had made but were saving for Valentine's Day—hence, the valentines in October.

Wes paused outside the doorway, not wanting to interrupt. His expression was still and serious. *I don't understand. Down the hall, we have a teenager who has given himself hepatitis—twice. He's throwing his life away, says he doesn't care if he lives—but he will. And here, we have a young father who wants so desperately to live—but won't.*

Wes continued down the hall. As a hospital administrator, he was being confronted with issues for which his business degree provided little, if any preparation.

12

Gaming the System

It was 9:00 a.m. as Wes' automobile turned onto Medical Drive. As Dr. Krimmel had a meeting, the doctor asked Wes to drop him at the main entrance. Before leaving the car, he gave Wes directions to the office of Dr. Allison Lindberg, dean of the School of Medicine. Dr. Lindberg, an oncologist by training, was waiting for Wes in her office. Wes guessed she was in her mid-fifties. She had shortly tapered silver hair and wore a white lab coat over a finely cut gray wool suit.

"You're here to learn about healthcare cost," she noted, as she motioned for Wes to take a seat.

Wes took a chair next to a large window overlooking the Huntsman Cancer Center. "Yes," he replied. "I'm especially interested in incentives, or the lack thereof, for cost control."

"It's interesting you should mention that," Dr. Lindberg said. Her eyes narrowed as she focused on a report on her desk. "I just got a memo this morning from our director of reimbursement—it's an interest of his as well."

Dr. Lindberg thumbed to the second page. "One of the fastest-growing components of healthcare costs," she said, "is diagnostic services—things like lab and x-ray tests. When properly used, they're great. There's concern, however, that a few doctors may be using them to increase their income.

"An actuary in Salt Lake City," she continued, "did a study on doctors who own lab and x-ray facilities. They use twice the tests per patient visit of doctors who don't. Her findings are consistent with studies conducted in parts of the country where there are a surplus of physicians. Contrary to what economists project, increased competition doesn't reduce physician income."

"I think I know the reason," Wes said. "Physicians can generate demand. They decide what tests are ordered. Lab and x-ray tests can be a good source of additional income."

"I think you're right," Dr. Lindberg affirmed. "An Eastern economist studied the phenomenon. Concerned with the variation he found in the number of laboratory tests ordered by physicians of the same specialty in the same hospital, he was able to isolate only one variable that statistically accounted for the variance."

"What was that?" asked Wes.

"Volume—the lower the physician's patient volume, the greater the tendency to order unnecessary tests. The root of the problem is consumer ignorance. The patient can't judge if a test is needed or not."

She continued, as Wes scribbled notes into his notebook. "Lab and x-ray tests are not the only areas where consumer ignorance supplies an incentive for physicians to provide excessive or inappropriate services. Several years ago, there was evidence we were performing too many elective surgeries. Also, for many years, there were places in the country where the hospital length of stay was longer than necessary. Ideally, the number of days a patient stays in the hospital should be solely dependent on the patient's medical condition.

"For many years, hospitals were paid under a cost reimbursement payment system. Whatever their costs, they received full payment from Medicare, Medicaid, and most insurance companies. Some payers added a small markup for profit."

"Why would a non-profit organization need a profit?" Wes asked.

"To pay for inflation. If you buy a piece of equipment for $10,000, chances are it will cost more when the time comes to replace it."

Dr. Lindberg continued. "Under cost reimbursement, factors other than the patient's medical condition influenced how long the patient stayed in the hospital."

"Such as…?" Wes asked.

"Hospital occupancy," Lindberg replied. "I did my residency at Community Hospital in St. Louis. Whenever occupancy rates dipped, our hospital administrator would catch physicians in the hall as they did their morning rounds. He'd say something like *'Doctor Smith, remember the new piece of equipment you've been after me to order for the lab? It's in! It cost $360,000.'*

"The doctor, of course, would express appreciation. Then our administrator would mention that the day's occupancy rate was fifty-three percent. *'It's hard to justify expensive equipment with half your beds empty,'* he'd say as they parted."

Lindberg smiled conspiratorially. "Guess what? In a few hours, the hospital's census would mysteriously start climbing. Patients scheduled to go home would be extended another day. Some patients who could safely be treated in outpatient settings would be admitted to the hospital."

"There weren't many incentives for cost control," Wes affirmed. "So what's the answer?"

"Some think it's incentive reimbursement," replied Lindberg.

"What's that?"

"An incentive reimbursement is a payment that gives a physician or hospital an incentive to control costs," Lindberg answered.

"How does it work?"

"The answer to that question can best be given by Larry Ortega, our director of reimbursement," she said. "He's expecting you."

13

Adverse Incentives

The director of reimbursement's office was in the basement not far from the hospital laundry. The director, Larry Ortega, was not there when Wes arrived. His secretary explained he was in negotiations with a health insurance company downtown. He called, she said, to say he'd be a few minutes late.

Wes took a seat and, for the next fifteen minutes, thumbed through a copy of *Healthcare Financial Management*. Ortega arrived shortly after 10:00 a.m. The Weather Channel forecasted a heavy midmorning storm. From Ortega's appearance, the storm had arrived. At fifty-six, Ortega had a lean frame, wore a crew cut, and had a no-nonsense manner about him.

"Sorry to be late," he said, shaking the rain from his umbrella. He unbuttoned his coat, unwrapped his muffler, and motioned for Wes to follow him into a small office that Maintenance had built out of a laundry linen room. The hospital was full and office space was at a premium.

He motioned for Wes to be seated. He checked his phone pad for messages and then looked Wes squarely in the eyes.

"Herb Krimmel said you wanted to talk to me about hospital reimbursement," he began.

Wes nodded. "I've learned that many incentives to control costs in other industries don't exist in the healthcare industry. Some have suggested incentive reimbursement can help. I'm told you're an expert on the subject."

Ortega nodded as he considered the question. "How much do you know about the history of hospital reimbursement?" he asked.

"A little."

Ortega rose from his desk and retrieved a coffeepot from a hot plate on the small credenza behind his desk.

"Coffee?" he asked.

"No thanks."

Ortega poured a cup and returned to his desk. "During the 1970s," he said, "when hospital inflation was taking off, many legislators felt the best approach to cost control was regulation. Consistent with that view, they enacted laws setting up agencies to review requests to build new hospitals or purchase expensive hospital equipment. Without prior approval, hospitals would not be reimbursed for the cost of the building or equipment." He paused to fan his coffee. "In some states, agencies were even established to approve hospital charges."

"Like room rates?" Wes asked.

"That was certainly part of it. They also reviewed charges for supplies, drugs, laboratory tests, and so on."

"It sounds like the model the government uses to regulate utilities," Wes remarked.

"I think that's what they had in mind," Ortega replied.

"It works for electric companies; how well did it work for hospitals?"

"Not well," admitted Ortega. "Utility companies have one product—natural gas for example. Hospitals have thousands. There are over 60,000 products and services at University Hospital.

"Two patients with the same diagnosis can require totally different care depending upon their age, the severity of illness, and other illnesses the patients might have. The complexity is unreal."

"You're telling me central planning didn't work for healthcare for the same reason it didn't work for Eastern Europe and the former Soviet Union," Wes volunteered. "The economy is too complex for one central body to administer."

"That's right," replied Ortega. "There's little evidence that regulation did anything to control cost. If anything, it raised costs by creating a new level of bureaucracy."

Ortega shook his head. "When it didn't work, some concluded the answer was incentive reimbursement. Payment systems encourage doctors and hospitals to consider cost when evaluating treatment alternatives."

"How does incentive reimbursement work?" Wes asked, taking notes.

"It makes the healthcare provider share in the cost of waste and inefficiency. Before 1984, many insurance plans paid hospitals and doctors by cost reimbursement. Do you know what that is?"

Wes nodded. "Just learned about it," he said. "Hospitals were reimbursed for actual costs, with a small markup for profit."

Ortega smiled cynically as he placed his coffee mug on his desk. "It doesn't take a rocket scientist to find that the easiest way to increase profits is with a cost-plus contract."

"Increase cost!" Wes said incredulously.

"That's right. While I don't think anyone purposefully raised cost only to increase profits, strong incentives to hold the line on cost didn't exist." Ortega leaned back in his chair as he stared out the window. "When I retired from the military in 1980, I was hired as director of purchasing at Long Beach Memorial Hospital in California. I wish I had a nickel for every time an equipment vendor said: *Don't worry about the price—it's cost reimbursable under Medicare.*"

Wes' eyes showed bewilderment. "Cost reimbursement is not a common payment system," he said. "About the only other place I've seen it is in the defense industry ... oh, and in some segments of the construction industry. Why was cost reimbursement the payment system of choice in healthcare?"

"The answer lies in the history of the health industry," Ortega responded. "The first insurance company in the United States was Blue Cross. This organization was formed in the 1930s by Justin Ford Kimball, a university administrator serving on the Board of Trustees of Baylor Hospital. As the story goes, Kimball started Blue Cross because he was concerned about the number of professors who were not paying their hospital bills.

"In the 1930s, most hospitals were nonprofit corporations run by charitable organizations—organizations Kimball thought should be protected from financial risk," Ortega explained.

"When the time came to select a payment mechanism," he continued, "Kimball chose cost reimbursement. As other insurance companies entered the healthcare market, they followed suit. That decision cost consumers billions of dollars over the next several decades."

"You're telling me the nonprofit status of early hospitals influenced the selection of a payment mechanism," Wes stated.

"That's right."

"Then I guess my next question is—why were hospitals nonprofit?"

"Because they evolved from poor houses," Ortega said. "In the early part of the twentieth century, people who had family or money died at home. The paupers died in charitable institutions, the predecessors of today's hospitals.

"Early hospitals were not the high-tech facilities we have today," he continued. "The first hospital in Salt Lake City was established by the Sisters of the Holy Cross to care for the large number of silver miners in Park City who were dying of lead poisoning. It was an epidemic of significant proportions. Want to know how they solved the problem?" he asked.

Wes shrugged. "Scientific breakthrough?" he guessed.

"It was a breakthrough, all right—although I'm afraid it wasn't very scientific," Ortega answered, a smile lighting his dark brown eyes. "They got the miners to wash! Physicians finally found that if miners would bathe more than two or three times a year, they wouldn't absorb lead from silver ore through their skin."

Ortega smiled sympathetically. "I tell that story simply to illustrate how far medicine has come. In the early part of the twentieth century, patients had a better chance of dying if they were admitted to the hospital than if they stayed home."

Wes processed Ortega's message. Hospitals were different in history and incentive from the manufacturers he had worked with. He understood now why Karisa Holyoak felt he needed a better understanding of healthcare if he were to succeed in his new assignment.

"Okay," said Wes. "I understand why most hospitals were nonprofit organizations, and how this influenced insurance companies to adopt cost reimbursement. I also understand how reimbursement destroyed incentives for cost control—incentives that exist in other industries. My next question is—what's the alternative?"

"Some think it's incentive reimbursement," replied Ortega.

"Is that the same as prospective payment?" Wes asked.

"That's one form of incentive reimbursement." Ortega replied. "A prospective payment system is one where an insurance company negotiates a fixed price with a doctor or hospital before the patient is treated. Using terminology from the construction industry, it's a fixed-price contract."

Wes nodded. "I understand the terminology. When I was in college, I worked part time as an accountant for a building contractor. Some of his projects were built under fixed-price contracts; others he built on a cost reimbursement basis."

"Do you think he managed them the same way?" asked Ortega.

"Probably not. There is more incentive to control cost under a fixed-price contract than under a cost reimbursement contract."

"Why?" Ortega asked.

"Fixed-price contracts place the contractor at risk; cost reimbursement contracts don't."

"That's right," replied Ortega. "Most people are less careful when spending other people's money than they are when spending their own. The same principle holds true for healthcare," he continued. "Physicians had little to lose if hospital resources were used inefficiently, and since hospitals were reimbursed for inefficient care, hospitals didn't have much to lose either."

Ortega leaned back in his chair as he studied Wes Douglas. *Wes is a bright enough fellow but he still has a lot to learn*, he thought. "I think the best person to explain how prospective reimbursement can change physician behavior is Charles Stoker, the director of our new HMO. He's out of town today, but he'll be back later this week. I'll set up an appointment if you'd like."

"That would be great, thanks," Wes said gratefully.

14

Is There a Solution?

Charles Stoker stood five-foot-eight and had a salt and pepper Van Dyke beard. His full head of wavy hair, silver with a few black highlights, gave him a patrician-like appearance. A former hospital administrator, Stoker was hired to organize the hospital's first health maintenance organization, more commonly called an HMO. It was Wes' second day of meetings at University Hospital and he hoped to learn more about hospital cost control.

"I've seen three revolutions in the healthcare industry in my lifetime," said Stoker. "The first one occurred in the 1970s with the consolidation of hospitals into corporate chains. It was a difficult time for many hospital administrators who had grown accustomed to the autonomy and, in some situations, the lack of accountability of the old system." Wes took notes.

"The second revolution," Stoker continued, "took place in the 1980s with the introduction of prospective payment systems. Cost reimbursement placed little risk on healthcare providers and encouraged waste and over-utilization. It was difficult for administrators, who grew up in a no-risk environment, to change the way they did business.

"The third revolution occurred in the 1990s as more providers assumed an insurance role, bypassing insurance companies and contracting directly with employers for health services. Some hospital chains even formed their own insurance companies."

Wes shot Stoker a questioning look. "Why would a provider willingly assume the economic risk that starting an insurance company entails?"

"Two reasons," Stoker replied. "Market share is the first. Prospective payment placed a limit on the growth of hospital revenue. It capped payments and limited the length of stay. The only way for hospitals to increase revenue was to capture more patients," he explained.

"Captive health plans allow hospitals to do that by dictating to employees which physicians they must use to get maximum discounts," Stoker continued, "and by controlling hospital admission patterns of participating physicians."

"And the second?" Wes queried.

"Cost control."

"Are health maintenance organizations a recent development?"

"Yes and no," Stoker replied. "The first HMO was formed in the 1940s by an industrialist named Henry Kaiser. Kaiser negotiated a contract to build ships for the war effort. To recruit employees without violating wage controls, he offered his employees health benefits. His program used a prospective payment system called capitation payment."

"What's that?" Wes asked.

"Capitation payment is a fixed payment a hospital or doctor gets each month to provide healthcare to a specific population. The provider gets the same amount per month, whether or not the patients use the system."

"How does that control costs?" asked Wes.

"It provides an incentive to keep the patient well," Stoker said. "And if the patient becomes ill, it encourages the provider to use the most cost-effective resources to get him or her better. There are still incentives to treat the patient: the threat of malpractice and the ability of employers to shop for other health plans if their employees are not satisfied."

Stoker studied Wes. It was obvious he didn't understand. "Let me give you an example I often share with employers when I'm marketing our plan," Stoker continued. "Role-play with me. Assume you are an obstetrician at Brannan Community Hospital. Last Friday, one of your patients came in and you delivered her baby. It's Monday morning and you're up on the floor doing rounds. As you are writing her discharge orders, she says something like this:

Dr. Douglas, we really appreciate the way you run your practice. We have used you for all three of our deliveries and we have referred several of our neighbors to you.

"You smile appreciatively—it's nice to have satisfied patients—and continue writing the discharge summary. Then she hits you with a request.

Dr. Douglas, I have a problem. As you know, I have a kindergartner and a preschooler at home. For the next few days, it's going to be hard to take care of them and a new baby. My husband works full time. My mother is flying in from Seattle to help, but she works and can't get off until Wednesday.

How about letting me stay in the hospital until then? My husband works at the steel plant where he's insured by Blue Cross's traditional indemnity plan—it will pay all of the additional cost."

Wes wrinkled his brow. "What's an indemnity plan?" he asked.

"An indemnity insurance plan is one that places no limit on hospital length of stay, has no utilization review, and pays the hospital under cost reimbursement."

Stoker stroked his beard philosophically. "You're the doctor, Wes. If you say no to her request, what do you have to lose?"

"Her goodwill," Wes replied. "She might change doctors. Worse still, she might bad-mouth me to her neighbors or friends, which would cause me to lose more patients."

Stoker nodded in agreement, "That's right," he said. "What if you say yes, what do you have to lose?"

"Not much, I'm not paying the bill."

"Okay," Stoker replied. "What about the other stakeholders in your decision? Let's start with the hospital. Remember, this is a traditional insurance program—hospitals are still under cost reimbursement."

"Well—the hospital administrator will probably be happy," Wes said. "A longer length of stay increases costs, which increases hospital reimbursement."

"That's right," said Stoker, his eyes flashing with approval. "How about the insurance company?"

"I'm not sure," Wes admitted.

"In the 1970s, they didn't care," said Stoker. "Most health insurers felt their role was intermediary, or bill payer. Insurance companies simply passed the added cost to the employer in increased premiums. Rarely did they question utilization or provider charges."

"What about the employer?" asked Wes. "He couldn't be too happy about a physician's decision to leave a patient in the hospital two days longer than necessary. Eventually, the employer would have to pay the bill through higher premiums."

"That's true," said Stoker, "but he was so far removed from the decision, he had little to say in the matter."

"Cost reimbursement didn't do much to control costs," Wes observed.

"That's what I'm saying," said Stoker. "Now let's talk about economic incentives under a capitation payment system. Let's assume you're a physician who has been hired by an organization that receives a capitation payment—an HMO." Stoker paused to collect his thoughts as he developed this scenario.

"Let's say I'm the medical director of the organization," he continued, "and this is your first day on the job. First thing in the morning, I call you into my office and say something like this:

Dr. Douglas, welcome aboard! Your references are excellent and we're happy you accepted our offer of employment. I think you'll find this a good place to work.

Before you begin seeing patients, however, there are a few things you ought to know. This isn't fee-for-service; here you get a salary plus bonus. Your bonus is paid in December, and may run anywhere from zero to two hundred percent of your salary, depending on how much money our HMO has left at the end of the year from the premiums we collect.

We receive $125 a month for every enrollee in our HMO. For this $125, we provide all the health services the patient requires, including office visits, laboratory and x-ray tests, prescriptions, physical therapy, and hospitalization. If the patient uses no services during the month, we get $125 from his or her employer. If the patient uses $100,000 of healthcare services, we still get $125.

Bonuses come from the premium pool left after expenses are paid. Our physicians get eighty percent of these profits; the remainder is retained by the HMO to buy equipment, provide working capital, etc."

Stoker continued. "Now let's go back to that fictitious maternity patient. This time let's assume she's insured by our HMO." Stoker issued a challenge. "Now, tell me how you'd react."

Wes' eyes narrowed. "I'd be reluctant to grant her request," he said thoughtfully. "If not medically required, I'd want her out of the hospital."

"Why?"

"Two added days of hospitalization would reduce year-end profits, reducing my year-end bonus."

"That's right! What about the hospital administrator—how would he or she feel about the decision to leave the patient in the hospital longer than medically needed?"

"If the hospital's being paid under capitation payment, there is no incentive to increase patient days—to the contrary, there's an incentive to get the patient out. More days means more costs, which results in less profit."

"Why?" Stoker asked.

"Because the hospital gets the same payment, whether the patient stays two days or twenty."

"And the insurance company?" Stoker asked.

Wes shrugged. "You tell me."

"As health costs have increased, employers have become price conscious. Insurance companies quote rates once a year. If their rates are higher than competition, they lose business. Today, insurance companies are aggressive in monitoring hospital costs."

"Okay," Wes said. "Then the insurance company wouldn't be happy with an extended stay either."

"What about the employer?" Stoker asked.

"He would be happy with the whole system because, for the first time, there would be an incentive for the healthcare provider to make cost-effective decisions," Wes answered.

"True."

Wes shot Stoker a skeptical look. "Sounds good in theory—but are HMOs really more cost effective than traditional insurance programs?"

"There's evidence that they are," said Stoker. "One of the principal components of healthcare cost is hospitalization. Local studies show participants in indemnity plans generate three hundred to four hundred patient days a year, per one thousand enrollees. HMOs generate two hundred and twenty. Some companies estimate they've reduced employee healthcare cost by as much as twenty-five percent since enrolling in HMOs."

"If HMOs work so well, why didn't they take off back in the 1940s when Henry Kaiser invented the model?" Wes asked. "Before 1985, I'd never heard of an HMO."

"For many years, medical associations were effective in shutting them down," said Stoker. "When I was a healthcare administration student in Seattle, there was a physician in the inner city who started charging his patients on a capitation basis. The Washington Medical Association tried to get him thrown in jail for violating state insurance laws—laws they helped draft, laws designed to keep HMOs out of the state.

"One of the most aggressive medical associations in the country was the Oregon Medical Association," Stoker continued. "It persuaded the legislature to pass a law stating HMOs could keep none of their surpluses but had to absorb all of their losses. It was a law designed to force HMOs into insolvency—which it did.

"In other parts of the country, doctors prohibited physicians who worked for HMOs from joining state medical associations. They then modified hospital bylaws to prohibit doctors who were not members of local medical associations from joining hospital medical staffs. It worked great. HMO doctors couldn't admit patients to hospitals. They were effectively precluded from practicing medicine."

"What changed?" Wes asked. "They obviously practice in hospitals today."

"In the early 1980s, the Federal Government passed legislation overriding the anti-HMO laws that state legislatures passed through the years. The impact was astounding. Hundreds of HMOs formed throughout the country."

"Are HMOs the wave of the future?" Wes asked.

"For a while we thought they were. However, patients don't like the restrictions, and medical associations have been effective in creating the impression that HMOs give substandard care. At the moment, many cost control features of HMOs are being overridden by legislatures and by public opinion. For better or worse, enrollment in HMOs is on the decline."

"Does anyone else use prospective reimbursement?" Wes asked.

"Medicare has developed a system called DRG reimbursement. It has been copied by some Medicaid and Blue Cross groups."

"What's DRG reimbursement?" Wes asked.

"It stands for Diagnosis-related Group reimbursement."

"A mouthful," said Wes.

"Sure is," replied Stoker. "DRG payment is a form of prospective reimbursement. Under capitation payment, the hospital gets a fixed payment for every enrollee every month, regardless of the services given. Under DRG reimbursement, it gets a fixed payment per Diagnosis-related Group."

"So what's a Diagnosis-related Group?" Wes asked.

"It's a disease classification. When a patient is discharged from the hospital, he or she is assigned a DRG, which is determined by the diagnosis.

"In 1984," Stoker continued, "Medicare classified all diseases into 380 or so Diagnosis-related Groups."

"How did they decide what diseases to put in each group?" Wes asked.

"According to the type of illness, the anatomical system involved, and the amount of money it takes to cure the illness. In theory, all diseases in DRG 200, for example, cost about the same to treat.

"In explaining their new system to hospital administrators, Medicare administrators said something like this:

In the old days, we paid you under cost reimbursement. Now we are going to pay you under a fixed price system. Every DRG has a fixed price. For example, every time you admit a patient with a DRG of 186, we will pay you $3,850. We will pay you that amount whether you keep the patient in the hospital three days, or thirty. We will pay you $3,850 whether you feed him steak or bread and water; whether you give him anesthetic or hit him with a rubber hammer. We expect you to get our patients well, but we don't care how much you spend—you'll only receive $3,850 in reimbursement.

Stoker gave Wes a quizzical look. "What do you think that did to hospital length of stay?" he asked.

"It probably reduced it."

"It did," replied Stoker. "Before the introduction of DRG reimbursement, the national average length of stay was about thirteen days. In Utah, it was about seven—we have a younger population and didn't have as many excess hospital beds to fill. When DRG reimbursement took effect, the national average dropped to seven days. Utah's dropped to three and a half."

"Thirty percent of the admissions at Brannan Community Hospital are Medicare patients," Wes said. "How do we survive under DRG reimbursement?"

"By controlling costs," Stoker replied.

"What keeps the hospital from providing less care than needed to get the patient well?" Wes asked.

"I'm not sure I have a complete answer to that," Stoker replied, shaking his head. "The threat of a malpractice suit plays a role. Also, if discharged patients are readmitted within a short period, the hospital receives no reimbursement for the second admission. There's an incentive to do it right the first time."

"It sounds like it's a new era for hospital management," Wes said. "I feel sorry for those who can't adapt."

"So do I," said Stoker. "Shortly after managed care was introduced, thirty percent of the hospital administrators in the country lost their jobs because they couldn't adjust."

"Let's see if I understand," Wes said in summary. "Under cost reimbursement, hospitals made money by admitting lots of patients and giving them lots of services."

"True," Stoker replied.

"Under DRG reimbursement, they make money by admitting patients, but giving them less services."

"That's right."

"But under capitation payment, they make money by not admitting the patient at all," Wes clarified.

"You've got it. Capitation payment provides a strong incentive to keep the patient well, or to get him well as soon as possible, once admitted."

Stoker continued with a warning. "Hap Castleton and his medical staff were still operating on cost reimbursement assumptions and it almost killed the hospital. If Brannan Community Hospital is to survive, it will have to change the way it does business. Your task will be to pull it off without getting canned."

Driving back to his apartment that evening, Wes reflected on what he learned about healthcare costs and the steps being taken by government and industry to stem the tide of inflation. His conversation with Stoker on the prospective payment system clarified the issues raised in his first meeting with the Board.

Hap and his administrative team had not anticipated the dramatic way prospective payment would influence the operation of their hospital. Wes now understood why physicians like Dr. Flagg felt threatened by the changes taking place in the healthcare industry. Under the old system of cost reimbursement, physicians who admitted many patients, kept them in the hospital for long periods of time, and used high quantities of ancillary services were heroes to the hospital administrator.

With the adoption of prospective payment, however, high-resource consumers suddenly became villains. Retraining physicians in the new model would be difficult.

In many ways, the economics of incentive reimbursement made sense to Wes. Still, there was an issue that bothered him—quality. *"Under capitation payment, what's to prevent physicians from providing too little care or too few services?"* Dr. Flagg had asked Wes. *"We've got obstetric patients being discharged the same day as the delivery—I'm uncomfortable with that practice."*

There were other quality issues as well. Dr. Flagg was concerned that the current environment was causing hospitals to cut staffing to levels that jeopardized the safety of hospital care. With the pressure to meet budget, Wes understood how this could happen.

Maybe Flagg's behavior is understandable. He was raised in an era that rewarded independent thought and action. That wasn't all bad. But HMOs—with their pre-certification, utilization review panels, and salaried physicians—have changed the equation.

Wes heard rumors of hospital systems that were bullying physicians into selling their practices. *"Sell your practice and join us as an employee,* they were saying, *or we'll build a clinic across the street and put you out of business."* In the old days, private-practice physicians were the hospital's valued customers. In a staff-model HMO environment, they became the competition.

Wes shook his head as he thought about the conflicting forces he would have to contend with as the new administrator of Brannan Community Hospital: physicians who wanted more equipment, a Board that wanted lower costs, and patients who expected the hospital to save them at any cost, but not bill them. It was easier being a CPA.

15

The Robbery

Sergeant Pete O'Malley rubbed the scruff of his morning beard with the back of his hand. "Whoever broke in must have known what they were after," he said, wishing hospital security hadn't called before he had a chance to shower and shave that morning.

O'Malley was an old-time cop—one who made an effort to know everyone on his beat. Park City was a safer and friendlier place because of O'Malley. With his red curly hair and large beer belly, he looked like a character from a Norman Rockwell painting.

The sergeant's eyes, a curious shade of green, swept the room for additional clues. "Whatever they wanted, it wasn't money. The cash drawer's intact—the safe wasn't even touched." He shook his head as he studied an old desk in the corner next to a large window. "What they wanted was here," he said with a sweep of his arm.

Moving to the desk, O'Malley removed a small magnifying glass from his shirt pocket and examined the broken lock on the file drawer. The surface had been dusted for fingerprints—none were found. Finished, he tucked the magnifier back into his pocket. "Prints were wiped clean," he sniffed. "Who does the desk belong to?"

Emma Chandler, a student volunteer with the Health Occupation Students of America (HOSA), stepped forward. "It's Del Cluff's desk," she said, her eyes wide with wonder.

This was the most exciting thing that had happened at the hospital since Emil Flagg left the emergency brake off his pickup truck and it careened through the lobby.

"Did he have any valuables in it?" O'Malley asked.

"I doubt it," she said softly, "he didn't have any valuables." Several employees laughed. Del Cluff came to work looking like a Bavarian peasant; the ill-fitting suits covering his lumpy body were Goodwill specials. He lived in a rented room two blocks from Main Street and drove a battered old Volkswagen bus.

Emma's smoky blue eyes sobered as she studied the battered desk. "It hasn't been opened since the accident," she continued looking up at O'Malley. "Mr. Cluff's still in a coma at the University Hospital—he has the only key."

O'Malley looked at the desk. It certainly was open now. Someone had used a crowbar to pry the lock off the file drawer. The contents were scattered on the gray linoleum floor. O'Malley was silent as he completed an incident report attached to his clipboard.

"With no suspects, and no idea of what—if anything—was taken, there's not much more I can do," he said. He signed the report with a flourish and handed it to Lexi Cunningham, the new acting controller. "Initial here and I'll file a report with the department."

Roger Selman's replacement, a twenty-nine-year-old with bright aquamarine eyes, short, dark hair, and a cheerful, yet business-like manner, signed the form and handed it back to O'Malley. The detective examined the desk once more, shot a glance at Wes, who had come for his 9:00 a.m. appointment, and shrugged.

"This is the first time you've had a burglary—and all they got were some old files," O'Malley said. His stern expression relaxed into a smile. "At least they didn't get the payroll—that's all this new administrator here would have needed," he said, motioning to Wes. There was a ripple of suppressed laughter. By now, the entire community was aware of the administrator's precarious situation.

Satisfied the investigation was over, Lexi Cunningham retrieved an armful of folders from the floor and dumped them on Del Cluff's desk. Others followed suit.

While the employees straightened the room, Lexi motioned for Wes to follow her into the hall. They had been scheduled to review the hospital's financial reports. "If you still want to meet," she said, "we can use the conference room."

"I've got a better idea," said Wes. "I need your signature on a note at the bank. Let's take care of that. While we're out, you can show me the property Wycoff wants the lien on. Any additional agenda items we have can be covered as we drive."

The paperwork took less than five minutes to finish. The bank president was so happy to have Wycoff assume financial responsibility for the hospital's two-million-dollar line of credit, he almost offered Wes free checking on his personal account. Instead, he gave him a plastic ballpoint pen with the bank's name and his picture printed prominently on the side.

Five minutes later, Wes' Honda was turning north on the old highway leaving Park City. Thinking of the previous controller, Wes turned to Roger Selman's replacement. "What happened to Selman?" Wes asked as they merged with traffic.

Lexi's aqua eyes reflected surprise at the question, but she answered with no hesitation. "He got caught in the middle," she explained. "Hap didn't like him because he was too conservative with the hospital's finances. Edward Wycoff didn't trust him because he wasn't conservative enough. The issue came to a head during negotiations for the new hospital.

"Hap realized the competition would eventually capture his market if he didn't replace the outdated hospital. He was too ambitious, however, wanting to build too many beds—to grow the business too fast. Wycoff recognized prospective payment would limit the hospital's ability to recover new capital spending. He was unwilling to approve a large outlay without a clear understanding of how the debt would be repaid. Either view, taken to an extreme, could have spelled disaster. Selman tried to play the middle ground and alienated both sides."

"Old Chinese saying—*Man who walks in middle of road gets hit by cars going both ways,*" Wes said.

Lexi smiled and nodded. "Astute observation. Anyway, Hap didn't value Selman's judgment. Hap was an optimist and didn't like what his controller was telling him. Nevertheless, Selman remained loyal to Hap, even when it hurt his relationship with Wycoff."

"Why?" Wes asked curiously.

"Well, I heard that three years ago, Selman's wife was diagnosed with cancer. Selman was so upset he didn't pay attention to his work. It was the end of the fiscal year, and the hospital was changing its funding mechanism for the employee health insurance plan, converting from a fully-insured to a self-insured plan. Over ten years, it accumulated $600,000 of savings, held in a special fund by the company. Since it was a mutual insurance company, the hospital was technically entitled to eighty percent of the fund. In the new contract, the insurance company nullified the hospital's right to the money. Selman signed without noticing the clause. It cost the hospital almost $500,000."

Wes winced. "Painful mistake."

Lexi nodded. "Wycoff found out about it and went through the roof. He stormed to the Board and demanded Selman be fired. Hap, aware of Selman's personal turmoil, stepped in and took blame for the mistake himself.

"Hap was more popular with the Board back then," Lexi continued. "Wycoff didn't have the political power to oust him. Roger Selman kept his job and he never forgot the favor."

Wes' eyes darkened. "That explains why Wycoff moved so quickly in firing Selman after Hap died," he said. "He was settling an old score."

Lexi gave Wes an appraising glance. "You're probably right. You have to understand Wycoff does many right things, though often for the wrong reasons. He's brilliant, but ruthless—people don't mean anything to him.

"Hap, on the other hand, did many things that didn't make sense from a business standpoint. But, there was never a doubt about his loyalty to the patients or his employees. He was stubborn, sometimes even prideful—but he cared about people and the employees loved him for it. Even in a managed care environment, he believed hospitals should act like charitable institutions."

A shadow of annoyance crossed Wes' face. "When the public started demanding a bottom-line approach to hospital management," he said, "the industry lost some of the characteristics that made it special."

Lexi sighed. "It's a different game today. In the old days, the objective was to heal the patient, regardless of cost or the patient's ability to pay. Hospitals were often inefficient and sometimes outright wasteful, but they cooperated with each other in achieving that goal. Today, the goal for many administrators is to cut costs and save money, even when physicians, employees, and patients are treated less than honorably."

"It's a tough balance between efficiency and empathy," Wes remarked.

Less than a mile north of Highway 40, Lexi motioned for her boss to stop the car. Wes pulled off the road. About six hundred yards up a hill, a chain-link fence enclosed the abandoned site. The construction equipment was gone. All that remained were the footings and a pile of bricks.

"That's all there is?" Wes asked in surprise.

Lexi nodded. They left the car, climbing the hill quickly.

"Our property runs from the fence to the top of the hill," Lexi said, pointing east. "One hundred acres in all, purchased in 1996. There were to be three construction phases. Phase one was the physicians' office building; phase two: the outpatient building; phase three: patient rooms and support departments.

"The building project was to be financed by industrial revenue bonds guaranteed by Park City State Bank. Back then, the bank was owned by the Brannan family. The Michael and Sara Brannan Foundation pledged an additional one million dollars."

"Neat package. Too bad it didn't work," Wes said.

"Unfortunately, when the Brannan empire unraveled, so did the new hospital," Lexi replied.

Although there wasn't a building yet, Wes was impressed with the land. The property was easily accessible from the freeway and already had power and water. "How much of the land was needed for the hospital?" he asked.

"The three phases would have occupied thirty-five acres," Lexi responded. "The rest was for future development. Rumor has it a group from back east would like to buy the property for a hotel complex. If we sold it, we could get triple what we paid for it. A better option, however, would be to build a new hospital."

A black Lincoln Continental crested the hill and stopped. Two men exited. One of them pointed to a barbed-wire fence that bordered the property on the north. "Looks like Wycoff's car," Lexi said, eyes widening in surprise.

Wes opened his car door and retrieved a set of binoculars from under the seat. "It is," he confirmed. "Who's with him?"

Wes passed the glasses to Lexi. Lexi was silent as she adjusted the focus. "Tony Devecchi," she said. "He's a retired businessman from Arizona. Owns a chain of nursing homes. He's been kicking around town for a couple of weeks. Probably looking for a place to retire."

"What's he doing with Wycoff?" Wes asked.

Lexi shrugged. "Want to ask him?"

Wes considered the question. "No, it's time to get back to the hospital. If he's got money, Wycoff's probably hitting him up for a contribution."

Wes was quiet on the drive back to the hospital. The discussion about Edward Wycoff and his relationship with Roger Selman re-alerted him to the power struggle within the Board. Wes was aware of the conflict when he accepted the job. Then, he believed the issues were black and white. Now, he was starting to see gray.

Hap Castleton, Edward Wycoff, David Brannan, and the medical staff were at war. Hap was gone, but the other players remained. In the beginning, Wes thought the battle was over efficiency—the good guys were for lower cost and higher quality care; the bad guys were for inefficiency and the status quo. Wes now saw the stakes involved more than money and power. Issues of quality, compassion, and integrity had muddied the waters. The more he learned, the more difficult it was to identify exclusively with either side.

Wycoff understood finance, but was oblivious to the fact that healthcare was about people. Hap had good intentions, but his hostility to accountants and efficiency experts hampered his ability to control costs.

What value is high-quality care if no one can afford it? Wes didn't blame Hap for not cutting costs in areas that would reduce accessibility or quality. He did blame him, however, for refusing to adopt efficiencies that could have avoided the crisis Brannan Community Hospital now faced.

Wes frowned. *Then there's Wycoff—what's he up to? Is he trying to help a hospital nurtured for a generation by the philanthropy of the Brannan family, or does he have other motives?* Wes believed the former, but the skepticism from the medical staff made him wonder.

When Wes returned to the hospital that afternoon, there was a note on his desk that Emma Chandler, the HOSA volunteer assigned to the business office, wanted to see him. He called and asked that she come down.

Emma smiled with satisfaction as she entered his office. "I think I know what the robber took," she said handing him a folder. "This was on the floor along with all the other stuff from Del's desk. It's empty now, but it wasn't when Mr. Cluff had me type the label."

Wes took the folder, the label read: *Internal Audit—Pharmacy.*

"Did you read what was inside?"

"Nope, just typed the label. When I saw it on the floor, empty and all, I thought it might be important."

"Might be," Wes affirmed.

16

The Hospital Carnival

It was 10:00 a.m. Saturday. *Time for a break*, Wes thought as he stretched the knots out of his back. Inhaling deeply, he pushed the chair away from his desk, piled high with reports. Crossing his office, he locked the doors. He was exiting to the lobby when he heard a familiar voice. Turning, he saw Amy Castleton.

"A little higher, Niels, and to the right," she said, motioning with both hands. Three feet above, on a metal ladder, sixty-one-year-old Niels Svendsen, senior custodian, obediently re-hung a poster on the freshly painted wall.

Wrinkling her brow, she studied the new location and smiled with satisfaction. "That'll do it!" she said brightly.

"Finally," Niels gasped good-naturedly. Removing a roll of tape from his worn coveralls, he attached the poster securely. It was a reminder for the volunteers' carnival to be held later that afternoon in Canyon Park.

Petite and flower-like, Amy wore a pink cotton volunteer's uniform that defined the narrowness of her waist. As Niels teased her, she laughed, tossing her head to the side so that her thick auburn hair bounced on her shoulders. Turning to take another poster down the hall, she ran headlong into Wes. "Excuse me!" she gasped. "I didn't know you were there."

She stepped back, embarrassed; he struggled not to blush. It was not every day a beautiful girl ran into his arms. Tongue-tied, he pointed at the poster. "Must be the volunteers' carnival today?" He was immediately embarrassed by the stupidity of his statement. *Of course the volunteers' carnival is today, it's been advertised for the past two weeks and I've approved the newspaper ads!*

Her brown eyes danced with laughter at his awkwardness. "It starts at noon." Cocking her head to the right she sized the new administrator up. "If your executive responsibilities aren't too pressing," she teased, "the hired hands could use a little help."

Wes smiled. "I've been reading old minutes of the Joint Conference Committee," he said. "Guess I could pull myself away. What do you want me to help with?"

With a finger on her cheek, she wrinkled her brow as though trying to solve a puzzle. "There's two dozen cakes in the Pink Shop with no one to load them. And, in the employee parking lot, there's a hospital van with nothing in it." A mischievous light sparkled in her eyes. "Think you could figure something out?"

"Manual labor?" Wes said in mock protest. "That's not in my job description!"

"It's probably more productive than anything else you've done today," she replied with an impish smile.

He didn't mind the mirth, even if the humor was at his expense. "Sounds like you've been visiting with the Board."

She took a quick breath to speak, but he interrupted her by holding his hands up. "Don't comment," he said. "Just show me the way." She pointed at the Pink Shop and then at the exit. Wes complied.

"Niels," she said turning to the custodian, "we have two more posters to hang downstairs."

"Yeah. We better get to it," Niels said looking at his watch. Niels and Amy took the stairs to the basement.

As he drove the hospital van to the park, Wes admired the incandescent hills that surrounded Park City. The aspen trees were painted in shades of cinnamon, crimson, and gold and the crisp, late fall air was invigorating.

Amy and Niels followed in the hospital pick-up. When they arrived, she gave orders and Wes obeyed. He hauled cakes, refilled soft drinks, and emptied garbage cans.

The affection of the employees for Amy was obvious. Most had known her since she was a young girl. To Amy, the employees were extended family and she returned their affection with warmth and attention that charmed young and old alike.

The carnival was well publicized by the local newspaper and radio. In addition to employees and medical staff, over four hundred people from the community turned out for the gala fund-raising event. There were pony rides for children and art exhibits for adults. Park City's local country singers, the Benton Family, provided entertainment. The bake sale raised enough money for a newborn ICU ventilator and the five-dollar sack lunches raised enough money to pay off the auto-analyzer in the lab.

For most, however, the highlight of the day was the *Dunk Your Boss* event. The Pink Ladies brought an apparatus that looked as though it had been borrowed from the dungeon of a medieval castle. There was a gallows-like platform with a chair that dropped into a tub of ice water when a baseball hit the target. Employees were charged a buck a throw—members of the medical staff, three. Wes was the first to be offered the seat of honor and everyone cheered when Dr. Flagg hit the target and Wes dropped into the frigid water.

Someone was thoughtful enough to bring dry clothes—a gray cotton uniform from the laundry. It was four sizes too big, so Amy fashioned a belt from a rope. Wes looked ridiculous, but was happy with the response it elicited from the employees. Wes was still breaking down the barriers created when Wycoff fired Selman.

By late afternoon, the crowd had left and Amy was directing the cleanup. As the last car pulled out of the park, Wes loaded the sound equipment into the van. Niels had driven the hospital truck back to maintenance, so Amy climbed into the front seat of the van, holding the only cake not sold.

Wes climbed in next to her and turned the key. Silence—

He frowned. Once again, he tried. The engine didn't budge. Wes just sat there, his eyes wide with disbelief.

When he didn't move, Amy spoke. "Aren't you going to check under the hood?" she asked curiously.

"Wouldn't do any good—I don't know a carburetor from a crankshaft."

Amy studied the expression on his face, then smiled with amusement. "You're not one of those macho mechanics?"

"Hardly," he sighed. He blinked, then focused his gaze on the empty parking lot. "Where are all the people?" he asked. "Doesn't anybody but the hospital use the park?"

"It's kind of remote," she replied. "Besides, in the evening it gets chilly up here. We're at 7,000 feet you know."

Wes nodded dubiously.

"There's a phone at Country Corner," Amy volunteered. "It's about four miles down the canyon. It'll give you a chance to walk off dessert," she said, smiling and patting him on the tummy. "I'll walk with you!" Amy said brightly.

Wes tried the engine one more time and again nothing happened. Turning to Amy, he studied the cake she was holding—chocolate with green icing. Sliced bananas on the top spelled *"Buy Me!"* The heat had turned them a repulsive brown. "What are we going to do with that?" he asked, raising an eyebrow.

Amy studied the gastronomic monstrosity with mock seriousness. "Do you think there's a reason it didn't sell?"

Wes nodded emphatically. "I suggest we donate it to the dumpster."

Once they were on the road and had established a consistent pace, Wes started the conversation. Someone told him Amy interrupted college to return for her father's funeral.

"So what's next?" he asked. "School? Work?"

"Mom still needs support. I'll stick around for a year."

"After that?"

"Probably return to the university."

"What do you want to be when you grow up?" he asked.

She gave him a sidelong glance and smiled. "English teacher. I'm majoring in comparative lit." The soft canyon breeze stroked her auburn hair. She turned and studied him thoughtfully, her eyes dancing with curiosity.

"And you, Mr. Douglas? What do you want to be when *you* grow up?"

"Alive," he said.

"Come now, things at the hospital can't be that bad," she sparred.

His face twisted into a contemplative frown. "My job lasts only until they find a permanent administrator. If my credibility is still intact, I'll probably return to my accounting practice. If I botch the job then I'm not sure what I'll do … maybe pull up stakes and return to Maine. There's a downside to the visibility this job has in the community."

"Is Maine your home?"

Wes nodded.

"Why did you leave?" she asked.

Wes sighed. "Well, I worked for a regional firm in Portland…I hated my supervisor and I got tired of the city."

"That's all?" Amy pressed.

There was another reason and she sensed it.

"I lost a loved one," he said quietly. "It was an automobile accident … I thought a change would help."

"Sweetheart?" she asked.

"We were engaged to be married," he said softly.

"I'm sorry," she said. "How long were you engaged?"

"Three years."

"A long time."

"Too long," he said. "I was waiting until we were financially secure." He gazed at the mountains, silent and deep in thought. She didn't interrupt and they walked with the crunching leaves underfoot the only sound.

"There's no such thing," he said presently.

"No such thing as what?"

"Security. You can plan your life to the smallest detail, but something always throws a wrench in the works."

Amy nodded, thinking of her father.

"When I was younger, I believed there was some grand plan," he continued slowly.

"Not now?" she asked.

"It's just a game of dice…" His voice trailed off.

"You sound like my mother," Amy said.

"She's not doing well?" he asked.

Amy shook her head. "She's pretty shattered. Her faith is teetering."

"And you?" Wes stopped walking and they stood face to face. Her face softened as her eyes reflected a gentle optimism.

"I think there's a plan," she said. "It isn't ours," she continued, "and sometimes it's hard to see, but it's there. The key, I think, is patience." She turned back to the path and continued walking. Wes followed.

"Do you like the hospital?" she asked, changing the subject.

"It's interesting."

"Interesting? Is that all?"

"Most of the issues are new to me."

"Have you ever worked in management before?"

"Yeah, but not in healthcare. Hospitals are a different breed of animal."

Amy raised her eyebrows in simple question as Wes continued. "In most firms the goal is simple—maximize profit," he said. "In hospitals, things get a lot more complicated."

"How?"

"You're dealing with people's lives. In manufacturing, we don't replace equipment that still works unless it will reduce costs or increase productivity. The carnival just paid off the new auto-analyzer, which met neither criterion."

"Then why did you buy it?"

"It's faster. That's important when the paramedics deliver someone to the hospital unconscious. The sooner the doctor gets an answer, the better chance he or she has of saving the patient. It won't happen often and the revenues will never cover the costs, but, occasionally, it will save a life.

"Financial models," he continued, "like return on investment and internal rate of return are a great help in manufacturing." He shook his head soberly. "They don't work very well in healthcare."

"Sounds like something Dad would say," Amy said softly.

"Before I took this job, I blamed high healthcare costs on inefficiency. I'm beginning to realize it's more complex. Thursday morning I was visited by a delegation from obstetrics. We have a small nursery, as you know. Right now it's not staffed. The nurses have to monitor it from the nursing station across the hall, watching the babies through a large window.

"Our average occupancy is less than three babies a day," Wes continued. "Justifying a full-time nurse for that volume is difficult, especially when you remember we're talking three shifts a day—seven days a week. It would take four full-time employees to fill that slot.

"I did the math," he said. "Full coverage would cost $126,000 a year—that's $230 for a two-day stay. I told them I didn't think the nursery could absorb that.

"Thursday afternoon," he continued, "I was on the floor and happened to look in on the nursery. There were two newborns—twin boys—one of them was blue. The baby had thrown up and aspirated. I called the nurse and she rushed in and got him breathing again.

"She looked at me like I was Ebenezer Scrooge," he continued. "*That's why we need full-time staffing coverage in the nursery!*' she snapped as she returned to the nursing station. By that time, several nurses had gathered around the nursery window. They looked at me like I was an idiot.

"They were right. All weekend I thought about what it means to have a twin brother. Playing together in preschool, venturing off arm in arm on their first day of kindergarten, double-dating in high school, serving as each other's best man at their weddings. Contrast that with the other scenario—*I had a twin brother, but he died several hours after we were born.*"

Wes shrugged. "Suddenly cost doesn't seem very important."

Amy looked up into his eyes and a bolt of electricity passed between them. With the back of his hand, he touched her cheek softly. Her mouth softened and her lips parted slightly. Without thinking, he kissed her and then gathered her into his arms as she buried her face in his shirt.

17

The Model

Edward Wycoff smiled as Tony Devecchi studied the architect's model. Wycoff commissioned it to raise capital and it was doing its job. Jaxon White, the youngest architect of Denver's most prestigious architectural firm, waited at his side, his mouth twisted tight with expectation. Two of Devecchi's business associates watched from the sidelines.

Devecchi, wearing a black shirt, white tie, and alligator shoes, circled the model like a shark eyeing its prey. Placing his hands on his knees, he bent over for a closer look, his small rat-like eyes greedily drinking in every detail. He swore softly, then nodded in approval.

"It looks different in three dimensions than it did on paper," he said, grinning broadly. "I like it! I think our young architect has done a commendable job."

Wycoff agreed. "Tell him about the project, Jaxon."

Jaxon took a deep breath and released it slowly. "The project will be called Wycoff Square," he said, pointing to the model. "It will consist of a hotel, condominiums, a retirement home with three levels of care, a hospital, physician offices, and a shopping center."

Devecchi nodded approvingly. "Ambitious project."

"You don't make money by thinking small," an investor said.

Wycoff nodded. "It's a self-contained community. Except for the hotel, the project is similar to retirement communities you've done in Arizona."

"It is," Devecchi said, fishing a cigar from his shirt pocket. He bit the end off and spat it into the wastebasket. "But, your design is better. After seeing what you've done with the concept, I think my other projects need a new architect." Devecchi nodded at Jaxon, who beamed proudly.

"You're lucky to have a good location," an investor commented. "Since the Olympics, property in Park City is hard to come by."

"The project will be built on one hundred acres, south of Park City," Devecchi replied, turning to his associates. He pointed at the model with his cigar. "Wycoff's got the lien and assures us he'll have clear title to the property within ninety days."

"The hotel will be leased to a major chain and will open within a year," Wycoff said. "Consolidated Healthcare will run the medical center."

"And you gentlemen have the opportunity to provide the funding for the shopping center, that is, provided you still want in."

"We're in," an investor said. The others nodded. "Just see that there's no complications in getting the title to the land."

A sanguine smile cracked the cold lines of Wycoff's aging face. "Gentlemen," he said with characteristic self-assurance, "it's in the bag."

Wycoff was alone in the first-class section of Delta Flight 766 from Denver to Salt Lake City. He checked his watch—4:30 p.m. The Boeing 737 sat isolated at the end of runway 32, waiting for final clearance for takeoff.

As Wycoff peered out his window, he noted the day, so full of promise that morning, was fading fast. At the airport, the temperature was dropping. To the north, a pack of gray clouds streamed across the sky, driven by an impatient westerly wind. Wycoff felt the cold dampness in the joints of his hands.

A voice came over the intercom. "Ladies and gentlemen, this is the captain speaking. We apologize for the delay. We are twelfth in line for takeoff."

Wycoff shrugged. *What's the hurry?* he thought. His entire life he'd been impatient—anxious to arrive at some glorious future destination. He looked out the window at the darkening sky. *Is this all there is? The cheerless gray of old age?*

In a rare moment of introspection, Wycoff reflected on the decisions of his early life. He had decided then that he would avoid close personal relationships. It was a decision based on practicality—wealth and power were jealous mistresses; they wouldn't allow time for anything else. As a young man, he equated wealth and power with love and security—things he knew little of as a child. Wealth was his surrogate for security and love—*except it wasn't a true surrogate,* he thought bitterly.

Edward Wycoff had a wife and family, but the warmth of those relationships died years ago, strangled by ambition that starved the affection from their marriage and choked the love from his children. He had three sons—two attorneys and a physician. A fourth child, a daughter, took her life at age sixteen.

The boys were polite, more out of deference to their mother than affection for their father. Their children never called him Grandfather— something he took pride in during their younger years, but now disliked.

I don't need people, Wycoff shrugged. *Friends come and go—only enemies are forever.* He was silent for a moment, then smiled sadly at his own self-deception. It was a good try. Denial worked well sometimes—today it didn't. At age sixty-nine, Edward Wycoff concluded there were only two tragedies in life: those who don't get what they want … and those who do.

Fifteen minutes later, Edward Wycoff gazed quietly out the window as the flight was cleared for takeoff. As the plane lifted off the runway, he thought about his childhood.

Born the fifth son of a prosperous family, his father, Jeremiah Wycoff, was a successful merchant from Rexburg, Idaho. In 1923, Jeremiah met Peter Brannan who proposed that he provide half the capital for a new bank.

At that time, the Brannans operated two banks, one in Park City and a second in Rexburg, Idaho. Both were successful operations. Although Jeremiah knew nothing about banking, the Brannans did, and he invested.

The bank in Rexburg prospered for six years, investing heavily in the farming community. The depression of 1929, coupled with a series of crop failures from 1930 to 1933, severely dampened southern Idaho's economy, causing the bank to fail in 1935.

Although the Wycoff family blamed stress caused by the bank failure on the subsequent death of Jeremiah, they had nothing but praise for Peter Brannan. Brannan arranged for the purchase of the family's assets by a Nevada bank, including the bank stock, although at ten cents on the dollar.

Edward Wycoff's older sister, Alice, was even offered a job in the Brannan household, providing domestic help for Peter Brannan's wife, who was in failing health. Inspired by Brannan, Edward Wycoff went east to get his schooling. Working his way through college, he got a degree in finance at New York University and took a job on Wall Street.

In 1943, a second tragedy struck the Wycoff family. Alice died giving birth to an illegitimate child. Edward Wycoff was told the father, a man by the name of Ramer, left town shortly after learning Alice was with child. Once again, the Brannans came to the Wycoffs' rescue by arranging for the child to be raised in a home operated by the Order of Elks in Claremont, California.

Twelve years later, the fairy tale unraveled. In 1965, while researching a possible bank acquisition, Wycoff discovered that Peter Brannan owned the Nevada bank that purchased the Bank of Rexburg. The person the family thought was their greatest benefactor had profited from the family's financial difficulties.

Ten years later, at the deathbed of his mother, he was shocked to learn that his nephew, Ryan Ramer, was none other than the son of Peter Brannan. The Ramer story was concocted to spare the Wycoffs and Brannans the scandal the pregnancy would have caused both families.

A rancorous palsy shook Wycoff's frame as he thought of Peter Brannan. Since that day in 1975, he dreamt of nothing but avenging his family. A caustic smile broke Wycoff's lips.

The chance came in 1996, while he was still on Wall Street. Word came that a small family-owned bank in Park City was for sale. The owner, a man by the name of Brannan, had invested heavily in a software company that failed, consuming the family's fortune and placing them on the edge of bankruptcy.

Further investigation showed other family assets, including a local newspaper, could also be purchased for a small fraction of book value.

Wycoff organized a group of investors who bought the bank, the newspaper and the mortgage. Wycoff was a silent partner—not even his wife was aware of his ownership interests in Park City.

Although the initial motivation was revenge, the fact that Park City had won the bid for the 2002 Winter Olympics made the transaction unbelievably profitable. And now he also held the note on the hospital's property, on which he and Tony Devecchi hoped to build their hotel, shopping center, and retirement complex.

Cautious about his partners, Wycoff had hired a private investigator to learn more about Devecchi. Originally a Philadelphia slumlord, Devecchi made most of his money through hostile takeovers. At the height of his career, he had an ownership interest in more than fifty companies. Usually, he put himself on the payroll as CEO. This provided him with annual paychecks that made him one of the highest-paid executives in the country. He then systematically looted each company.

Wycoff knew he would have to watch his back. He couldn't trust Devecchi. Devecchi, however, had the money, contacts, and resources necessary to build the complex.

Wycoff's hate for the Brannan family returned, choking off any thoughts of loneliness or remorse for the way he lived his life. For over thirty years, two goals had dominated his life. The first was a desire to make money—a lot of money. Money could buy security; it could buy respectability; it could buy power. The second was revenge—retribution to the family responsible for the death of his father and the disgrace of his family. With one transaction—the purchase of the Brannan estate—he was close to achieving both.

18

Rachel

Rachel Brannan hummed softly as she polished the teapot from the sterling silver tea set her mother-in-law gave her the day she married James Brannan. She paused, holding the teacup under a light. It was as beautiful and lustrous as the day Mrs. Brannan gave it to her.

Studying her reflection, she smiled. Unlike the tea set, she had aged. The chestnut brown hair that Jim had run his fingers through the night he proposed was now a pale gray, and the dark Welsh eyes he gazed into so lovingly now reflected the toils and trials of a life of hard work and service.

The older she got, the more she reminded herself of her grandmother, Elizabeth Price. Elizabeth immigrated with her husband in 1880. They came from the coal mines of Wales to the silver mines of Park City. Grandmother raised her after the death of her own mother. From Elizabeth, she learned the art of hard work—and work hard she did, even into her sixty-eighth year.

Rachel studied the sterling silver tea set. For thirty years, it served as the centerpiece at the annual governing board and medical staff reception, always held at the Brannan mansion. Hosting the event would be different this year with Jim gone.

Rachel turned and gazed lovingly at her husband's photograph on the desk. Jim had always provided direction in areas where she felt uncertain. Rachel's oldest son, David, resented Jim's dominance. For Rachel, however, the granddaughter of a coal miner who never felt comfortable in the presence of the rich or famous, Jim's self-confidence provided comfort and security.

A knock at the door interrupted her thoughts and her domestic helper, Hanna Brunswick, bustled into the room. Hanna carried a large linen tablecloth folded over her left arm. In her right hand, she held a large envelope, which she handed to Rachel. "David dropped this off this morning," she said. "It's a list of those who confirmed they'll be at the reception."

As Rachel opened the envelope, Hanna laid the tablecloth on the desk. "I inventoried the linen closet this morning," she said. "This is the only linen large enough to cover the serving table."

Rachel gently caressed the linen tablecloth. Like her small hand, it was frail and delicate. "The tablecloth belonged to Jim's mother," she said. "It's a shame it's getting old, but aren't we all?" She looked up at Hanna with brown eyes that still sparkled. She nodded. "It will be fine," she said softly. Hanna reclaimed the linen and marched out of the room dutifully.

Rachel turned her attention to the guest list. Sixty-five people, including spouses, would attend: forty-five from the medical staff, twelve from administration and eight from the Board. *How the hospital has grown*, she thought as she contemplated the size of the medical staff.

As a child, she attended the groundbreaking for the building replacing the original Miner's Hospital. Jim's father presided at the ceremony. The Brannan family had given the funds for construction. Through the years, whenever the hospital needed a new wing or major piece of medical equipment, the family foundation provided the funding.

Rachel turned her attention back to the guest list, scanning the names of those who would be attending. David would be there with his wife, as would her son Matthew. Matthew—now *Doctor* Matthew Brannan—had recently finished his internship and was a member of the medical staff.

Matthew was twenty-eight years old, fifteen years younger than her first child, a daughter who died at childbirth. Rachel was proud of Matthew's accomplishments. Dyslexic, he struggled with reading, so much so that many of their friends scoffed when Jim announced that Matthew was planning to become a physician. Matthew proved them wrong. With his education finished now, all he needed was a wife.

Rachel smiled thoughtfully. Matthew would be bringing Amy Castleton to the reception. Matthew had been a member of Hap Castleton's scout troop. He attained the rank of Eagle his senior year of high school. As a college student, he served as Hap's assistant scoutmaster. Not, Rachel suspected, because he loved scouting, but because he loved Amy.

Outside, Matt Brannan had begun the annual ritual of winterizing the thirty-room mansion. The job had fallen to him because David was too impatient for the job and the hired help was now too old. Matt began by replacing the weather stripping on all exterior doors and moved on to installing the storm windows.

He decided to tackle the most difficult part first: an oval window on the Venetian tower. Matt studied the tower and shook his head. The window was on the third floor. *Would have been nice if the carpenters had given some thought to energy conservation.* The original structure had no insulation and single-pane windows. In 1880, coal was cheap. What's more, the man who built it—Great-grandfather Mike Brannan—owned the coal mines. Mike, and the era in which he lived, had energy to burn.

Mike's son, Peter, replaced the coal furnace and blew six inches of insulation into the attic. The heating bills were still too high, so he went shopping for storm windows. Modern aluminum windows wouldn't do, they would distract from the architectural integrity of the building. Peter hired a cabinet-maker and glazier to build wooden frames, consistent in style with the arched Italian windows. They were pretty—but a bear to install.

Screwdriver in one hand and pliers in the other, Matt gazed in awe at the garish old house. He tried to imagine the shock on the faces of their conservative neighbors, when Mike Brannan unveiled the original color scheme: maroon walls, green trim, orange window sashes, and olive blinds. Three stories high, the Victorian mansion dwarfed the modest homes of the early miners. Atypical of nineteenth century Utah, the house was very typical of its builder. Mike Brannan was larger than life – so was his house.

Matt inherited his great-grandfather's features, but none of his genius. Standing in the shadow of the mansion, Matt felt small and inconsequential.

19

The Plan Takes Shape

Saturday evening, Rachel Brannan hosted the yearly medical staff reception. Wes Douglas used the opportunity to learn more about the medical staff's perceptions of Brannan Community Hospital. Many were concerned about the vacuum created by Hap's death. Some physicians feared Wycoff would use the void to push for deeper cost cuts.

Dr. Emil Flagg bent Wes' ear on the dangers of corporate medicine. For thirty minutes, he extolled the virtue of hospital administrators who were unwilling to subject the medical staff to the "dual degradation of budgeting and managed care." Flagg was especially critical of health maintenance organizations that dictated which physicians the patients were allowed to use.

"Some of our docs spent twenty years building their medical practices," he said. "They aren't worth a nickel now. The HMOs own the patients.

"The older docs feel betrayed," he continued, "disconnected from the healthcare system they helped build. The people who run HMOs are nothing more than bookies. They hire statisticians to study the probability of somebody getting sick, then figure ways to make a profit by shifting the risk to doctors and hospitals."

Dr. Ashton Amos, president of the medical staff, took a more moderate view. "I agree with the need for market forces. The old system wasn't good at involving all the stakeholders, but managed care isn't solving the problem either. We're substituting cost efficiency for quality. It's a scary trade-off when you're dealing with human lives.

"Since insurance companies pay the bill," Dr. Amos continued, "they think they can dictate how doctors should practice medicine. Managed care has become a huge bureaucracy."

The evening brought other revelations. Amy Castleton accompanied Dr. Matt Brannan to the reception. Wes noticed how he worshipfully followed her around the room as she visited with physicians and their wives. Wes developed an instant dislike of Dr. Matthew Brannan.

Monday afternoon, Wes met with Lexi Cunningham to develop a plan to put the hospital at breakeven in ninety days. "Hospitals lose money by generating too little revenue or incurring too much cost," Wes said. "Let's focus on costs first."

Lexi brought cost and productivity information from the Utah Healthcare Association to the meeting. Of special interest were comparative data on average cost per-patient-day for labor and materials for hospitals the same size as Brannan Community Hospital. The report clearly showed that the hospital's costs were higher than any other hospital the same size in Utah.

Labor costs were the biggest problem. For some job descriptions, Brannan Community Hospital paid significantly more than competing hospitals. In other areas, it paid significantly less. There was no consistency. "It's who you know, not what you know," one employee had observed.

Wes called Karisa Holyoak, the CPA that helped him find Herb Krimmel. "I need a consultant in hospital compensation," he said. "Someone who can help me establish fair and consistent salary schedules."

Karisa gave him the name of Dr. Emily Cook, a professor of compensation at Weber State University, in Ogden, Utah. A meeting with Dr. Cook was scheduled. Wes invited Joseph Harris, the hospital's Human Resources director, to attend.

"The problem is that your compensation system was developed over many years as the hospital added new positions," Dr. Cook said as the meeting commenced. "There were no guidelines—no governing philosophies. As a result, your salary schedules lack internal consistency and external validity."

"What does that mean?" the Human Resources director asked.

"Internal consistency means the system is fair—employees get equal pay for equal work. External validity means pay is consistent with the market. Utah Healthcare Association data shows your salaries are neither."

Joseph Harris gave Wes a sidelong glance. "I suspected as much," he said. "I inherited the present system. I've never had the resources to fix it."

Dr. Cook smiled sympathetically. "Common problem," she said. "HR directors have a lot on their plate. Most don't have a lot of time to devote to compensation design. As technology changes job content, problems arise in the areas of pay, recruitment, training, and performance evaluation."

"If we hire you, what will you do for us?" Wes asked.

"I will interview your employees and their supervisors to identify what each of your employees do. I will prepare a job description for each job, listing the major tasks of that position. Using salary surveys and statistical tools, I will determine what salaries should be. From that, I will prepare a salary schedule."

Wes was pleased that Harris was receptive. "If we hire your firm, how long will it take until we have your report?"

Dr. Cook retrieved a calculator from her briefcase and punched in several figures. "You have about three hundred and fifty employees—about a hundred different job descriptions," she said. "My firm did a similar project for Memorial Hospital in Colorado Springs. I think we could complete your study in about four weeks."

Harris nodded at Wes, who turned to Dr. Cook. "Let's get started!"

20

Inadequately Trained

Except for Dr. Matthew Brannan, the medical library was empty. At a table in the far corner, he quietly read the medical record of a former patient. His eyes were wide with disbelief as he studied the lateral x-ray. *How could I miss that?* Small beads of perspiration formed on his upper lip as he re-read the notes of an emergency room physician who saw the toddler four hours after Dr. Brannan sent her home.

In Brannan's pocket was a letter from the Quality Assurance Committee, a peer-review group whose purpose was to identify substandard practice on the medical staff. The letter requested that he come to a breakfast meeting the following Monday prepared to discuss the case of Mckinzie Anderson. It charged that he misdiagnosed her case, with near fatal results.

A week earlier, a young mother, Melissa Anderson, brought her three-year-old daughter, Mckinzie, to his office. The first examination showed a barking cough and a mildly elevated temperature of 101.1 degrees. The child was drooling, a sign Brannan should have paid more attention to, but didn't— *toddlers drool,* he reasoned. Mckinzie's breathing was labored, which he attributed to congestion or a stuffed-up nose.

The lab work was normal, except for a slightly elevated white blood count of eleven. To rule out pneumonia, Brannan ordered a chest x-ray, AP (anterior, posterior), and lateral views. He should have checked for epiglotitis but didn't. Since the child's lungs were clean, he diagnosed a viral, upper respiratory track infection (URI).

"There's nothing we can do for her in the hospital you can't do at home," he told the worried mother. "Give her plenty of fluids, monitor her temperature and give her Tylenol if her temperature rises."

Three hours later, cyanotic, and in acute respiratory arrest, Mckinzie Anderson was rushed to the emergency room by ambulance. Her epiglottis, now severely swollen, was sealing off her airway. The swelling was so severe that it was almost impossible to intubate her. Three-year-old Mckinzie Anderson nearly died in the emergency room.

Today, as Dr. Matthew Brannan reviewed Mckinzie's x-rays, he saw something he missed earlier, the characteristic thumbprint sign on the lateral x-ray—a sure indicator of acute epiglotitis. Dr. Brannan finished reading and closed the medical record. This would be the second time in a year he would be called before the committee. He was fearful the committee would conclude what he, himself, now suspected—that he was inadequately trained to practice family medicine.

Dr. Brannan was tired of feeling inadequate, a feeling he wrestled with ever since his father decided he would go into medicine. "Father," he exclaimed, when the old man broke the news. "I'm a slow reader and a mediocre student!" Undeterred, James enrolled him in a university and hired the best tutors money could buy. Hard study, good tutoring—and a family endowment of one million dollars to a small medical college on the East Coast—facilitated Matt's acceptance to the class of 1997.

Medical school didn't come easy, but Matt hung in there, ninety-fifth in a class of one hundred and three students. He finished a one-year internship and was applying for a residency in family practice when the family's fortune started to disintegrate. Father suffered a stroke, and Matt was called home to help put the family's affairs in order. There was an unwritten law with the Brannans—the family came first. Matt's residency would have to wait.

The library was quiet except for the ticking of a large grandfather clock against the wall. Matt's mother presented it to the medical staff in appreciation for the care Jim received after his stroke. Dr. Brannan's eyes narrowed and deep lines of determination formed around his mouth. *Who am I kidding? I need more training.*

He studied a bookshelf on the far wall. On the second shelf was a directory listing family practice residencies in the United States. He could apply for a residency. If he still didn't feel competent, he could follow it with a fellowship.

His lips tightened. The only complication was Amy Castleton. He had given his heart completely; she had yet to do the same. He discussed marriage. She remained noncommittal and was now dating others, including Wes Douglas. If Matt went back to school without Amy, he was sure she wouldn't be here when he returned.

"Knock, knock," Helen Castleton said as she slowly opened the door to Amy's bedroom.

Amy, sitting at her vanity by the window, looked up and blinked rapidly. "What do you think of the eye liner?" she asked. It was a new color.

"Absolutely stunning." Carrying a black dress, Helen crossed the room to Amy's closet. "Picked this up from the cleaners," she said. "Thought you might like to wear it tonight. It's one of Matt's favorites, isn't it?"

Amy nodded. "I'm not going out with Matt tonight," she said, returning to the mirror. "The film festival is in town, and Wes Douglas has asked me to go with him."

Helen's eyes registered her surprise. "Wes Douglas?" she said. "The new administrator?"

Amy nodded. Her mother was silent as she processed Amy's message. Finally she spoke, choosing her words carefully. "I don't think things are going well for him at the hospital," she said. "I wonder if it's a good idea for you to date him."

"Why?"

"He's an accountant – a miniature Edward Wycoff. There are those who think he wants to change things from the way they were under your father—to run the hospital like a business, not like the charitable organization it really is."

Amy shrugged. "That might be a good idea, given their current situation with the bank."

Helen shot her daughter a withering look. "Your father would turn over in his grave if he thought you were siding with the accountants. You remember the fights he had with Wycoff?"

"I'm not siding with Wycoff," Amy said wearily. "It just seems like times have changed and—"

Helen cut her off. "The medical staff doesn't like what's going on. They're unhappy the Board didn't consult them before appointing Mr. Douglas as interim administrator. There's talk of a revolt."

Amy started brushing her hair. "Where'd you hear that, Mom?"

"Rachel Brannan," Helen replied. "She thinks they should appoint Matt as interim administrator."

Amy smiled knowingly. "I'm sure she's a competent judge." She replaced the brush on the dresser. Finished, she shook her head until her hair fell softly on her shoulders, then stood and retrieved a dress from the closet.

"Rachel says Matt has a lot of good ideas on how to run the hospital. Maybe they'd put him in permanently."

"Anybody ask Matt what he thinks of the idea?" Amy asked dryly.

"What do you mean by that?" Helen asked.

"It just seems that whenever the family makes a decision about Matt's future, Matt is the last to know."

"Rachel thinks he would be a fine administrator, and so do I," Helen said defensively. "He would carry on the tradition of the family."

"Whose family—ours or theirs?" Amy asked dryly.

"Well, maybe both," Helen sputtered. "I thought you and Matt were talking of marriage."

"Matt's talking, Mom. I'm listening."

"You do love him?" Helen asked.

"Yes, I do, Mom," Amy sighed. "At least, I think I do. It's just that I've known him since I was six, and sometimes it seems—"

"Rachel has her heart set on a Christmas engagement," Helen interrupted.

"Well, I'm not engaged yet," Amy said as she slipped into her dress. Cocking her head slightly, she smiled. "I think that's the doorbell, Mom."

Helen gave her a resigned smile. Amy inherited her father's stubbornness—and his charm. "I can see I'm not going to change your mind tonight," she said. "I'll get the door."

Amy shot her a look of warning.

"Okay," Helen said reading her message. "I'll be nice."

Actor Robert Redford started the Sundance Film Festival in 1981, hoping to create an event that would support independent filmmaking. Through the years it grew, gaining international stature. Each winter, the public was invited as hundreds of emerging filmmakers showcased their work before many of Hollywood's most talented producers, writers, and actors.

On the evening of their first date, Wes Douglas and Amy Castleton saw two Sundance films and later dined at the Olive Barrel Food Company, a small restaurant on Main Street.

"I met your mother at the medical staff reception at the Brannan's home," Wes began while they were waiting for their order.

"It was difficult without Dad."

"I noticed you were there with Matt Brannan," Wes said, watching the expression on her face. "How long have you known each other?"

"Our families have been close friends for many years. Dad worked with Matt's father on the Board."

Wes nodded and waited for her to continue.

"Rachel, his mother, and I are close. Before we moved to Park City, she and Jim lost a baby girl. Maybe I helped fill a void. I spent a lot of time in the Brannan household when I was growing up. It was only natural that Matt and I would become friends. Dad liked Jim Brannan; they were both good fishermen. Jim Brannan owned a cabin on the Salmon River."

"Hap had many friends," Wes remarked.

"He got his energy from people," Amy said, "and he was good to everyone. It was interesting to see the diversity in the people that came to his funeral. Prominent businessmen, politicians, and housekeepers alike turned out to pay their respects."

"I always admired him for treating everyone—regardless of money or stature—with kindness and respect," Amy continued wistfully. "I don't think he acted any different in dealing with a housekeeper than he did when meeting with the governor. I think everyone at the funeral considered themselves a close friend of Hap Castleton.

"One of his pallbearers spent some time with me after the service," Amy remembered. "A fellow by the name of Arthur Skyros. Dad met him when Art's mother, Marie, moved to Park City in 1985, three weeks after her husband was jailed for holding up a liquor store in Los Angeles. Marie got a job in the hospital laundry.

"The transition from Los Angeles to Park City was tough for Art. He was poorer than most of the kids at the high school. He looked different and talked different. Eventually, of course, the word got out about his father.

"Dad became aware of the situation when Marie left work one day to bail Art out of jail for shoplifting. That evening, Dad showed up at their apartment to invite Art to join his scout troop. Marie hesitated. Dad suspected it was because they didn't have the money for a scout uniform. Dad got one from a former scout and took Art to the next meeting.

"Some of the boys in the troop looked down their noses at Art because his father wasn't a physician or an attorney. Dad was tough and never allowed down-talk. Eventually, the other boys accepted Art and he became one of Dad's best scouts. When Art graduated from high school, Dad used the fact that Art obtained the rank of Eagle Scout to get a former hospital trustee to fund a scholarship for him.

"Art worked hard in college. Four years later, Dad was the second person he called when he got his letter of acceptance to medical school.

"Shortly after Art joined the scout troop, Dad moved him and his mom out of their basement apartment. The hospital owned several homes next to the physician's parking lot, which were purchased for future expansion. One of these, he rented to Marie for $150 a month. When her arthritis got so bad she could no longer work, he lowered the rent to $50.

"One day, Edward Wycoff found out about it. The small house could have been rented out for twenty times that amount during ski season. He hit the ceiling and wanted Dad censured for misusing hospital assets.

"Dad offered to pay the difference. The Board heard Wycoff out, then ruled it wasn't necessary. Marie had been a faithful employee for many years and the hospital was a charitable organization. Not everyone on the Board was as bottom-line oriented as Edward Wycoff, so Marie stayed in the home until her death."

Amy shrugged. "Dad may not have been the best businessman in the world," she concluded, "but his heart was in the right place. He was intensely loyal to his employees and most of them loved him for it."

Wes nodded in recognition of what Amy had said about her father. He was beginning to understand the motive behind many of the things Hap did during his tenure as administrator of Brannan Community Hospital.

From deep inside her down comforter, Amy Castleton arched her back lazily. Curling her toes, she rubbed her legs against the soft flannel sheets, warm in the cold morning air of her attic bedroom. Sighing comfortably, she rolled onto her back, stretching her arms high above her head. It was Saturday morning. As she stirred, she gently pulled the covers from her head.

Sitting up, she hugged her knees, blissfully happy, but not sure why. She suspected Wes Douglas had something to do with it. The morning sunlight flowed from the window above her bed, giving the room an ethereal glow. The bedroom smelled of potpourri and cedar. Situated on the second floor, the windows of her bedroom looked out into the stately maple trees bordering Grand Avenue.

When she was a small girl, Amy pretended that her bedroom was a castle tower—a place to wait for her prince. This morning, that same magic hung in the air. *Had he come?* Tilting her head, she turned the idea over in her mind.

She settled back into the bed as her eyes traced the sculpture of the heavy ceiling beams. Hap Castleton carved them himself from cedar he hauled from southern Utah. She smiled as she remembered how her father loved working with wood. To Hap, there was something sacred about the medium.

"Wood shouldn't be forced out," he said, "but shaped and fitted together like an interlocking puzzle." He took the same approach with people.

Hap built the home their first year in Park City. Carpentry served as an emotional outlet as Hap struggled to retool himself from the job of building contractor to healthcare executive. It wasn't easy, and he wouldn't have attempted it, but for the encouragement of Jim Brannan.

Hap, a Southern California contractor had built a winter home for the Brannans in the foothills high above Glendale, California. Jim Brannan appreciated Hap's honesty and work ethic. He also observed his talent in working with subcontractors with different backgrounds, temperaments, and personalities. Brannan Community Hospital's former administrator had announced his retirement and Jim Brannan was looking for a replacement.

Park City was still transitioning from a primitive mining town to a sophisticated ski resort. The hospital needed someone who could pull the ethnically and culturally diverse community together. Not long after Brannan's winter home was finished, interest rates went through the roof, and Hap's construction business folded. Jim Brannan hired Hap to manage the hospital.

The move from California to Park City wasn't difficult for Hap—but it was for Helen. She wanted a home, but it wasn't easy for a man who had filed bankruptcy to get a construction loan. With a little arm-twisting by Jim Brannan, the bank loaned the funds for the materials and Hap provided the labor for their new home.

Hap built the home of stone, brick, and redwood. It incorporated the architectural elements of a California bungalow with broad latticed eaves, open porches, and expressive uses of wood. An article in the *Park City Sentinel* called it "Japanesque." Whatever its style, the gabled, trellised, and shingled home showed Hap's personality—functional, friendly, but, most of all, unique.

Sitting up, Amy basked in the ambience of the room. There had been so many events here through the years—tea parties in kindergarten, sleepovers in junior high, primping with Mom for dates with Matt Brannan in high school.

Her eyes narrowed thoughtfully as she considered Matt. He had been a part of her life from her first day in Park City. At first, he was kind of an older brother. Later, she learned his feelings were deeper. He had followed her around high school with worshipful awe, careful not to frighten her away while he waited for her to grow up. He was always kind—always there. The relationship grew, and so did her feelings for him.

It was an effortless relationship—secure, but not exciting. Did she love him or was she merely comfortable? With dating, school, and volunteer work, her life had settled into a dependable routine, shattered now by her father's accident.

Amy cocked her head thoughtfully. *And now there's Mr. Wes Douglas—am I falling for him?* She wasn't sure. Wes was different from Matt Brannan. Amy dominated the relationship with Matt. She led and Matt followed. Stronger, more deliberate, Wes Douglas stirred her feelings. Her forehead furrowed into a deep scowl. The whole thing was unsettling.

The return address was The Department of Justice in Denver, Colorado. Sensing its importance, the acting controller's secretary pulled the official envelope from a stack of department mail and placed it in the center of Lexi Cunningham's desk where she would be sure to see it on returning from lunch.

In a few minutes, the young acting controller returned. The secretary was right — it was important. Picking it up, she crossed the office and shut the door. Returning to her desk, she opened the envelope, her fingers trembling. Hopefully, the letter would put her fears to rest.

Lexi recognized her propensity to worry. She also recognized that most of the things she worried about never happened. The thought calmed her. *Only, why had the Department of Justice waited so long to issue its report?*

Carefully unfolding the document, Lexi scanned the introductory letter, her eyes narrowing as she searched for key words. She gasped in sudden surprise. *It couldn't be right, she must have missed something—must have read it too fast.* More slowly now, she reread the letter, then read it again.

Two years ago, the hospital received its first letter from the Department of Justice requesting information on the hospital's billing methods. Eight months later, after spending $30,000 on audit fees, the hospital submitted seven years worth of information. Sixteen months passed and the hospital heard nothing.

This letter informed them they owed $749,532, not for fraud, but for an *infringement of rules.* Brannan Community Hospital followed a long-standing practice of billing for laboratory tests one at a time. Medicare wanted them bundled. This was the second infringement in a three-month period. Earlier, the hospital received a demand for the return of $1,200,000 in Medicare payments for radiology services given over a three-year period. The government claimed the hospital used the wrong billing code. Although the difference in revenue between the two codes was only $125,000, the Feds wanted *all* of the money back, claiming the deadline for rebilling under the correct code had passed.

The Federal Government was in trouble with healthcare spending and was determined to cut costs—by hook or crook. They had dramatically increased the number of FBI agents assigned to Medicare Fraud.

"It's almost a manhunt," an article in *Forbes Magazine* reported. *"With that many cops out there, they've got to justify their keep. More and more, simple mistakes and misunderstandings are being labeled as fraud."*

The article quoted J. D. Klenke, a prominent medical economist: *"The whole focus on infringement, as opposed to flagrant violation, means everybody's guilty. There are 45,000 pages of Medicare reimbursement regulations. If you violate something on page 44,391—you're guilty. Full compliance is not possible. The regulations are Byzantine,"* the article said.

Some larger hospitals in the state hired in-house compliance officers whose sole job was to read rules and regulations. Given the tight budget, Lexi had resisted increasing her staff. She frowned. *Obviously, that was a mistake, given the Justice Department ruling and the legal cost the hospital would now incur to fight it.*

Lexi wasn't opposed to going after the bad guys. With national spending for healthcare exceeding a trillion dollars a year, there was bound to be fraud. What she objected to, however, was a Federal agency whose goal was revenue, not law enforcement. She shook her head as she laid the letter on her desk. *Hospital accounting wasn't fun anymore.*

21

Ramer

"Take two tablets twice a day—on an empty stomach," groused Ryan Ramer, chief pharmacist, as he handed a prescription to the last customer of the day. It was 6:30, and his feet ached. He'd have been out of this prison if it weren't for the babbling of eighty-two-year-old Zola Wayment, a retired hospital employee who frequented the pharmacy with small complaints and stupid questions.

Zola held the bottle close to her face. Her lips moved silently as she slowly read the label. Ramer drummed his fingers on the white Formica® counter, his lips drawn tight with impatience. Satisfied the pharmacist filled the prescription correctly, Zola carefully placed the bottle in her purse, retrieved a $20 bill, and handed it to him.

Without a reply, Ramer grabbed it, shoved the change across the counter, and slammed shut the metal security window separating the pharmacy from the hall. Most evenings, the end of the shift would have been a time for rejoicing. He was never meant for the drudgery of shift work. Tonight, however, things were different.

In nine hours, he would be meeting with Barry Zaugg, a two-bit drug runner for Sid Carnavali, the main distributor of a drug lab Ramer set up two months ago. It wasn't Zaugg he worried about. He didn't have the IQ to lace his shoes properly. Zaugg's boss, however, was a different matter. Carnavali was a mad dog. He was capable of murder.

A wave of apprehension swept through Ramer. He removed a handkerchief and wiped beads of sweat from his brow. He had problems—big problems—and Carnavali could make them worse. As he started the nightly task of balancing the cash register, his stomach churned. He reflected on the course that brought him to this frightening juncture in his life.

Money was the problem—and always had been—since he'd married Betty. The daughter of a successful physician, Betty was raised to expect a lifestyle that Ramer couldn't provide. She never let him forget it. At first, he made up the difference between his income and her spending by taking money from the till. It was a slick routine.

Each evening after closing, he would destroy the master tape from the cash register, then re-ring the day's transactions. The new total would always be $200 or so less than the day's actual revenue—money he would pocket before leaving for home. The hospital's financial controls were lax, his need was great, and the opportunity was there.

Over a three-year period, Ramer embezzled $180,000 from the hospital. He'd have gotten a lot more, but an accounting student serving an internship in the business office noticed transaction numbers on the master tape didn't correspond to those shown on customer receipts. Ramer fired the student, claiming he made a pass at a high school girl who worked part time in the pharmacy.

Ramer quit re-ringing the register. When financial pressure reappeared, he started moonlighting evenings at a local nursing home, filling prescriptions for patients from the extended care center's in-house pharmacy. At Ramer's suggestion, the nursing home started purchasing its drugs through the hospital. Hap Castleton approved the practice because it provided the volume needed for volume discounts for both medical facilities.

One evening, a fire destroyed the nursing home's kitchen and adjoining pharmacy. Ramer didn't know how it started, but he took advantage of it. Returning to the hospital, he filled a predated nursing home order for $6,000 of narcotics, which he removed from the hospital and sold to a drug dealer named Carnavali. The drugs, which netted $18,000 on the street, he reported as having been delivered to the nursing home before the fire.

It was a good trick, but it couldn't be duplicated. One can't go around burning down nursing homes. One of the residents, however, was a retired physician in the late stage of mental dementia. With funding from Carnavali, Ramer established a bogus home health agency in Salt Lake City, using the physician's narcotics number to write prescriptions, which he sold to Carnavali. The practice ended a few months later when the physician died of old age.

Financial pressure returned when Ramer's son, Ronnie, announced shortly after high school graduation that he wanted to attend the same expensive private university his mother had attended. Ramer heard of a group of pharmacists in Sweden who were caught making street drugs from over-the-counter medications. With the chemistry he learned in school, and a *Pharmacopoeia*, Ramer soon duplicated the Swedish process.

Ramer's brother-in-law, Hank Ulman, owned part interest in a small flight service operating out of the Salt Lake Airport. Business was slow, so Ramer helped him get a job in the maintenance department at the hospital to supplement his income. The plan was to have Hank fly the drugs to Phoenix. Carnavali would handle the marketing.

One obstacle was the large quantities of over-the-counter medications he would have to purchase as raw materials. Large purchase orders from local distributors tipped off the authorities in Sweden. Ramer solved the problem by purchasing the medications through the hospital, and running them through the books of his home health agency. To avoid having to remove the bulky raw materials from the hospital for processing, Ramer established a small lab in a room beneath the pharmacy storeroom. It was a sweet setup.

Ramer's business was threatened, however, when Roger Selman hired a new assistant by the name of Del Cluff. Del, a former auditor, got suspicious when he saw the number of over-the-counter drugs the home health agency was purchasing. It wasn't consistent with what he knew about home health agencies. Del requested copies of all hospital purchase orders from the home health agency. Ramer could have handled the problem, but Carnavali panicked.

The evening before Cluff was scheduled to fly with Castleton to Idaho, Carnavali paid Hank to silence Cluff by sabotaging the plane. Castleton was killed, but Cluff survived, though in a coma at University Hospital.

After the accident, Hank broke into Cluff's office and stole his audit papers. A permanent solution to the Cluff problem had yet to be reached.

The cash register balanced. Ramer removed the day's receipts, depositing them in a small safe in his office. Finished with the day's activities, he turned the lights off, locked the pharmacy and headed for the employee parking lot. In nine hours he would be back—this time to meet with Zaugg.

"Get in here before somebody sees you," Ramer whispered as he pulled Barry Zaugg through the pharmacy door.

Zaugg swore. "It's three in the morning!" he protested, twisting free from Ramer's grip. "This place is abandoned." He rubbed his arm and then slugged Ramer. "And keep your wretched hands off me!"

Ramer winced. "Hospitals are never abandoned," he warned as he shut the door. "Follow me." Crossing the room, Ramer fished in his pocket for his keys and then unlocked a door to the adjacent storeroom. Zaugg followed him through the door. A naked light bulb on the ceiling lit the bile green walls. An abandoned desk, filthy with dust, stood next to a yellowed calendar from 1988. Empty cabinets covered an adjacent wall.

"This used to be the administrator's office," Ramer said, kicking his way through the boxes littering the black and red linoleum floor. "When the administrative wing was added in 1989, the pharmacy took it over as a storeroom … We don't use it much anymore, but it makes a good cover for the lab. That's why I always keep it locked," he said, waving his key.

"I don't see no lab," Zaugg said suspiciously.

Ramer stopped and rested his right hand on a wooden storage shelf. "Once there was a door here," he said. "When my brother-in-law was hired, I had him build this cabinet. It swings out," he said, "but first, you have to unlock it."

Ramer scowled as he searched for the right key on his chain. "Here it is," he said, bending over and inserting the key into a lock on the underside of the bottom shelf. There was a metallic click. Ramer removed the key and the cabinet swung open, revealing a small stairwell.

"They kept the safe down here," he said, entering the stairwell. He flipped a light switch. "I don't think anybody knows about it anymore." Ramer continued down the stairs with Zaugg following close behind. "All of the old employees are retired and I don't let any of the new ones into the storeroom."

Ramer reached the bottom of the stairs and turned on another light. "Hank Ulman works at the shop, so he got ahold of the original hospital blueprints, the ones the carpenters use for remodeling. He redrew the wall so the stairwell doesn't show. The new blueprint shows the pharmacy as being three feet wider at this point than it actually is," Ramer nervously babbled.

Zaugg followed him through the door, then stopped. Lighting a cigarette, he inhaled deeply, letting the acrid smoke trickle out of his nose as he surveyed the room. Roughly fifteen feet square, its concrete walls were bare, damp, and sour. A single frayed electrical cord dangled from the ceiling like a hangman's noose, its mustard light giving Zaugg's face a cadaver-like appearance. In the center sat an old autopsy table from pathology, cluttered with beakers, bottles, and a Bunsen burner.

"This is it?" Zaugg asked, gesturing with his cigarette. "This is the whole meth lab?"

"It's all it takes," Ramer replied, his eyes glowing with pride. "Took me a couple of weeks to figure out how it's done, another month to figure out how to get the raw materials without arousing suspicion. Anyway, I've run two test samples and now I'm ready for production."

Zaugg nodded, his eyes darkening dangerously. "Good thing," he said. "It's been two months since Carnavali paid you the thirty thousand bucks. The boys in Phoenix are getting anxious for their delivery."

"You've seen the lab," Ramer said defensively. "Tell them they'll get their first shipment a week from Friday. I leave Friday for Connecticut. I'll be gone three days—I'm visiting my boy in college." Ramer removed a picture of his son and proudly placed it on the table. "His name's Ronny. He wants to go to medical school."

Ramer wasn't sure why it was important to impress this thug. Maybe it was to let him know he wasn't a common crook, like Carnavali. "When I return Monday night," he continued, "I'll go to work. I figure in four days I'll have the first shipment—it'll pay off Carnavali and then some."

A cold silence engulfed him as Zaugg nodded slowly. "Hope so," he said. Zaugg's cold gray eyes were the color of death as he crushed his cigarette out on the boy's picture. "Carnavali don't have no patience for deadbeats. No patience at all," he intoned slowly and deliberately.

22

Direct Materials

Monday morning, Wes turned his attention to data from the Utah Healthcare Association that showed that Brannan Community Hospital had a higher-than-average cost of materials per-patient-day. For the next two days, he reviewed the materials function with Avery Spencer, director of materials management. At their concluding meeting, he summarized the following problems:

- The hospital is not participating in the Utah Healthcare Association's group purchasing contracts. Thus, it is paying more for medical supplies than most of its competitors.

- The hospital has many open purchase orders with local vendors. Authority to purchase is not clearly identified. Misuse of purchasing authorization is possible.

- The hospital has never considered a just-in-time material management system. Just-in-time is feasible as many of Brannan Community Hospital's vendors have warehouses in Salt Lake City.

- There are no economic order quantities. Some nursing stations have excessive inventory, as nurses are fearful of running out of supplies when Central Supply is closed on weekends and in the evenings.

Having received little direction from Hap, Avery was receptive to the new administrator's suggestions. Together, they prepared a plan to address these problems. Wes presented it to Lexi Cunningham the following morning.

Lexi agreed with Wes' ideas and suggested that while he was investigating the hospital's purchasing practices, he look into the practices of the pharmacy as well. It was her observation that Ryan Ramer's lifestyle exceeded his income. Lexi reported that the pharmacy lacked defined purchasing procedures and didn't make nightly deposits. This led to a discussion of other questionable practices that had never been addressed when Hap was in charge.

In May, for example, an audit showed that the hospital's maintenance supervisor built a fence at his home with materials bought on a hospital purchase order. Reimbursement had never been made. Hap was reticent to fire the supervisor, as he had worked at the hospital for twenty-five years and was two weeks away from an honorable retirement.

Lexi suspected that the business office manager had an ownership interest in the agency used by the hospital to collect bad debts, an obvious conflict of interest as the business office manager was the one responsible for determining which accounts were given to the collection agency.

At the conclusion of their meeting, Wes asked that Lexi conduct internal audits on the Pharmacy, on Maintenance, and on the Business Office. Wes hoped that audit findings would be negative and that the firing of dishonest employees would not be needed. If employee terminations were required, however, Wes planned to make them as soon as possible. *Move quickly and take no hostages,* he decided.

Fridays were slow days for the Pink Shop. Except for emergency procedures, the operating room was closed and the census was down. Fewer patients meant fewer visitors and, thus, fewer Pink Shop customers. Amy Castleton served as the secretary/treasurer of the women's volunteer organization. Fridays were a good time to work on the books. Today, Amy's goal was to reconcile the bank statements. For the third time in an hour, she picked up the August statement and then laid it back on the counter.

Her mind wouldn't focus on anything but Matt Brannan. Somehow, Matt got word that Amy was still dating the new administrator and he was livid.

"He's a CPA for heaven's sake," Matt's tone was accusatory, as though Amy was somehow to blame for his vocation. "He is cut from the same cloth as Edward Wycoff. Profits are the only thing he worries about; patients are just means to an end—they're nothing more than work-in-process."

From her own work in the Pink Shop, Amy understood the importance of running an organization profitably. Given the financial condition of the hospital, she understood the problems the hospital's losses were causing for Wes. How to solve these problems was a primary source of contention between the Board and the medical staff.

Before his death, Hap told Amy that the Board favored a managed care approach. He taught, "Managed care seeks to control hospital costs through more efficient use of resources. Some of the ways it does this are peer reviews, pre-certification, financial incentives to encourage physicians to use fewer services, and the use of gatekeeper physicians to assure that expensive specialists are only used when needed."

Managed care troubled Hap. Insurance company clerks, who did not have the medical background needed to question physician decisions, performed utilization reviews. On a daily basis, insurance companies challenged physicians with questions like, *"Is this procedure experimental?"* or, *"Is there a less expensive medication or procedure that can be used?"*

"Medicine has always been *experimental*," Hap said. "That's why they call it the *practice* of medicine. To refuse to pay for a procedure that hasn't been tried in the past is to close the door on innovation and future research. There are diagnostic procedures that are less expensive than CAT scans, but these are invasive, more painful, and often more dangerous to the patient. Specialists *are* more expensive than general practitioners," Hap had continued, "but that's because they know more. Since when do we want to *'dumb down'* medicine?"

As for incentive reimbursement, Hap recognized the problems with traditional fee-for-service and cost reimbursement, but was not convinced that forcing physicians to select treatment options based on cost rather than quality was the right approach.

He had once shown Amy a note an internist received from an insurance company about a CAT scan he had ordered. *"Approve this, and it will be your last,"* a handwritten note on the letter said. In the same envelope, the physician received a list of the insurance company's participating physicians, sorted by cost per patient per diagnosis. The physician's name was on the top third of the list. *"Expensive providers will be eliminated from participation in our physician panels unless they change practice patterns,"* a note attached to the list explained.

Amy's father was hesitant to embrace managed care—until he could be assured that quality would not suffer. Wycoff believed that Hap's reticence brought the hospital to the brink of insolvency. The medical staff believed that Wycoff's approach would destroy the purpose for which hospitals were formed in the first place—*to provide the highest quality of care to patients, regardless of their ability to pay.*

Matt was certain that Wes Douglas was changing into a young Edward Wycoff. He accused Wes of using Amy's father as the fall guy for the hospital's current financial situation. "He's slandering the administration of Hap Castleton," Matt said. "If not with words, then actions. His intent is clear; the worse Hap looks, the better Wes will appear when he *'saves the hospital'.*" Matt drew the words out sarcastically.

"Wycoff and Wes have created a crisis in the minds of the Board and the employees. It's nothing more than justification for a power grab."

Given Amy's feelings for her father and her growing affection for Wes, Matt's accusations were troubling.

That evening, Wes reflected on the events of the past seven weeks. His first priority was to get the hospital in the black. Otherwise, the bank would pull its line of credit and the facility would close. To end losses, he could lower costs or increase revenue. Since costs are easier to manipulate in the short run than revenue, he focused on reducing costs first.

Wes started by studying the reasons for the dramatic increase in costs the industry experienced. He visited with administrators and physicians at the University Hospital. He learned that a breakdown in market forces created disincentives for the proper use of healthcare resources. He also learned about *managed care*, an initiative to create incentives for physicians and administrators to control costs.

Having a better understanding of the industry, Wes then focused on specific cost irregularities at Brannan Community Hospital. He found that labor and material costs for each patient day were higher at Brannan Community Hospital than at most of its competitors.

Satisfied with the progress made, he decided that the next logical step would be to investigate the revenue side of his hospital's profit equation. Knowing that revenue is a function of volume and price, Wes decided to address the volume issue first. He heard that St. Matthews Hospital was successful in increasing its share of the market.

Wes called Sam Lister, the director of marketing at St. Matthews with the hope that he would be willing to share some insights on how he could increase revenue by increasing patient volume. He made an appointment for Friday.

23

The Revenue Equation

From deep inside the office, Wes listened to the gas turbine engines winding up on the Bell 230 helicopter. The pad was a short distance from the east entrance of St. Matthews Hospital. As heat from the compression ignited a mixture of fuel and air in the twin combustion chambers, the sleeping engines angrily awoke, shaking the building until the floors vibrated and the windows rattled.

Across the room, close up against the window, Sam Lister watched the Life Flight helicopter take off. Facing east, it hovered six feet above the ground while the pilot visually scanned his instruments. Then, smooth as a lazy Susan, the aircraft rotated 180 degrees and lifted off into the icy morning sky.

"It's a marketing tool, you know," commented Sam Lister, director of Marketing as he turned from the window. "With two helicopters and three fixed-wing aircraft, one of which is a Cessna jet, we drop from the sky capturing patients from all over the state—patients that might otherwise be transferred from rural areas to Timpanogos Regional Medical Center or to the Ensign Peak Regional Medical Center."

Lister gathered some papers and stuffed them into an overfilled folder. "We think our care's better, of course, and the flights are medically needed. But they are marketing tools, all the same," he said, littering the floor with papers as he walked back to his desk.

A tertiary care center, St. Matthews Hospital was not a competitor with Brannan Community Hospital. The marketing director was gracious enough to spend an hour teaching Wes the fundamentals of hospital marketing. Wes guessed Lister was forty-five. A closely cropped beard framed his square jaw. With his tweed coat, he looked more like a philosophy professor than the successful marketing director of a $250-million-a-year organization.

Lister tapped his pencil on the edge of his desk absentmindedly. "It hasn't been long that hospitals have had to market their services. In the old days, under cost reimbursement, our physicians were able to create demand. Prospective payment put an end to that.

"Although I haven't studied your hospital's statistics, there are probably several reasons for the decline in patient days your hospital's having.

"In Utah, DRG reimbursement reduced the average length of stay in hospitals from seven days to three days. In addition, many rural and suburban hospitals experienced out-migration as patients went to larger cities for care."

"Why?" Wes asked.

"Transportation systems made it easier for patients to travel greater distances to receive hospital care. Also, there's the 'bigger is better' syndrome."

Lister shuffled through a few papers. "The third reason is that many large hospitals have become more aggressive in marketing to rural areas. Since prospective payment systems have capped prices and reduced patient days, the only way to increase volume is by capturing patients from other facilities."

Wes was puzzled. "How do Salt Lake hospitals market to patients in Park City?" he asked.

"One way is by selling managed care programs to employers in your community that require the use of Salt Lake hospitals," Lister replied. "If your facility lost the Mountainlands contract, a significant number of patients would have been channeled by employers to other inpatient facilities."

Lister's comments were consistent with Wes' observations. On his drive that morning, he saw several highway signs advertising HMOs sponsored by metropolitan hospitals. Most were directed to employers. Although HMOs were being sold for their potential for cost savings, it hadn't previously occurred to Wes that they were also an effective hospital marketing tool.

"Then what's the solution to our declining inpatient volume?" he asked.

"There are several possible solutions," Lister replied. He retrieved a marketing report from his briefcase. "The first is to recognize that hospital patient days represent a smaller part of total healthcare cost in the current environment. Notice the decline in inpatient revenue as a percent of total revenue," he said, handing the report to Wes. "If your hospital is to survive, it must supplement its inpatient revenue with other services."

Wes took notes attentively. "What types of services?"

"Outpatient services like outpatient surgery, occupational medicine products, and durable medical equipment. For years, physicians have been skimming—building their own outpatient surgical centers to perform high profit, low-risk procedures, while leaving the high-cost, high-risk, low profit procedures to the hospital. Hospitals have to take some of that business back."

"Give me an example," Wes said.

"LASIK surgery," Lister replied. "High profit, low-risk."

"Some hospitals are selling vitamins or offering limited forms of alternative medicine," Lister continued. "That might be a new revenue source for your facility."

"What types of alternative medicine?" Wes asked.

"Meditation, yoga, acupuncture."

"Aren't there liabilities to offering alternative therapies?"

"Yes, but in some situations, no more than for traditional treatments. You have to be selective," Lister said. "I'm not advocating crystal therapy, but some forms of alternative medicine have been shown to have therapeutic value."

Lister continued. "As insurance companies place more restrictions on the procedures they're willing to pay for, many hospitals have begun to market services to self-pay patients. There are shops in malls where a person can get a complete laboratory work-up without a physician's order. The stores don't diagnose and they encourage the patient to review the results with his or her physician. Some provide diagnostic services that insurance companies won't pay for—procedures that are more expensive, but less invasive than those offered by the hospital."

"Doesn't this alienate hospital medical staffs?" Wes asked.

"Yeah, but they're already alienated. Many of your physicians are draining off your high revenue procedures." Lister looked directly at Wes. "How many of your physicians operate their own labs, x-ray machines, or outpatient surgery units?"

"I don't know."

"Check it out," Lister said. "To illustrate how innovative some providers are in marketing to the self-pay market, there are group practices that have cut out insurance companies all together. For $4,000 a year, a patient can enroll in a plan that entitles him or her to immediate telephone access to a physician, twenty-four hours a day. The patient is guaranteed a physician appointment within four hours."

"How has the public reacted to these plans?" Wes asked.

"Within two weeks of offering the plans, many group practices sold out. When reduced overhead due to the elimination of paperwork is factored into the formula, the physicians work less hours and make more money. It's strictly for self-pay patients; there is no insurance. Hospitals could do the same thing."

"Okay," Wes said, still taking notes. "What else can I do?"

"A second approach to increasing patient volume might be to educate local employers who buy HMOs on the negative impact that sending patients to distant providers has on the local economy. As patients leave, so do their dollars. Studies show that for every dollar that leaves the community for hospital services, an added sixty cents is lost in retail revenue.

"A third approach might be to increase inpatient volume by capturing a larger share of the local market. To do that, you might consider starting your own hospital-sponsored HMO. There are also a number of small rural hospitals in northern Utah and southern Idaho that can't offer the breadth of services Brannan Community Hospital offers," Lister continued. "I suggest that you make a greater effort to capture their referrals."

"Thank you for your time and suggestions," Wes said, shaking Lister's hand firmly.

"No problem," Lister said. "Good luck."

24

The FAA Report

On Monday, Dr. Emily Cook was back to present the results of the compensation study. Both Wes and Lexi were pleased with a methodology that allowed them to calculate standard cost for revenue departments such as Nursing. They called a meeting for department supervisors. The goal was to use these standards to develop flexible budgets.

Supervisors worried initially that the standards would be used punitively. Enthusiasm for the program increased, however, when Wes announced that fifty percent of the saving from tighter standards would be shared with employees through an employee productivity bonus pool.

It was early afternoon when Wes returned from his meeting with his department heads. Two men were waiting outside his office. The larger one spoke first.

"I'm Officer Kuxhausen," he said, producing FBI identification. "Mr. Smith is with the Federal Aviation Administration. We'd like to visit with you privately."

Wes nodded, and they followed them into his office where he shut the door. "You're investigating Hap's accident?" Wes asked when all were seated. "Any clue about the cause?"

Kuxhausen nodded at Smith, who produced a large manila envelope.

"We have evidence that someone tampered with the plane," Smith replied. Opening the envelope, he laid two photographs on the desk taken by the FAA of the wreckage. Wes studied them, surprised that Del Cluff could have survived the accident. The impact broke the back of the aircraft. The fire that followed reduced the fuselage to a charred skeleton.

Smith removed a pointer from his shirt pocket. "This is a picture of the right engine, taken the morning after the accident," he said, leaning over the photograph. "The cowling surrounding the engine has been removed to expose the fuel pump. Look at the nozzle that connects to the fuel hose. Note the small hole—the probable cause of the fire.

"Notice the sticky residue here," Smith continued, pointing to the fuel line. "Kuxhausen was the first to notice it—the lab tells us it's a petroleum-based electrical tape that originally covered the hole."

Wes looked up. "A fuel line repaired with electrical tape?" he asked skeptically.

"No—sabotaged. The boys at the FAA lab tell us the hole was sanded with a three-sided file. Fuel pressure in a Cessna 340 comes through the line at about thirty-five pounds per square inch," Kuxhausen injected. "Whoever made the hole covered it, knowing that the aviation fuel would soften the tape, breaking the seal and allowing the fuel to escape. From the burn marks, you can see that fuel ran back along the hose until it made contact with the hot magneto." He outlined the path with a ballpoint pen.

A menacing smile cracked Kuxhausen's face. "Clever way to bring a plane down, don't you think?"

"Not with you guys around," said Wes calmly. "Any idea who did it?"

"Nope. That's why we're here. Are you aware of anyone who had it in for Hap Castleton?"

Wes frowned. "Everyone in the public eye makes enemies sooner or later. It's no secret the hospital's got problems—big problems. Vendors haven't been paid and employees may lose their jobs, but no particular suspect comes to mind. You're welcome to interview the employees and staff."

"We will," Kuxhausen said. Removing a business card from his wallet, he slapped it on Wes' desk. "In the meantime, if you think of anything else, give us a call."

Outside the hospital, Smith and Kuxhausen visited briefly in the parking lot before going their separate ways. "Do you think he's a suspect?" Smith asked, writing in a notebook.

Kuxhausen picked at the remnants of a steak sandwich between his teeth with a plastic toothpick. "He seemed stressed," he said. "But, what would he have to gain? Anyone who'd aspire to Hap Castleton's job isn't smart enough to sabotage an airplane."

Following Smith and Kuxhausen's visit, stories about Hap's death swept through the hospital like wildfire. Rumors of motives behind the murder ranged from a crime syndicate interested in the hospital's undeveloped property to efforts of the hospital Board to cover up illegal contracts they had taken to provide services at inflated prices to the hospital. One story even postulated an affair between Del Cluff and the wife of a jealous physician. Wes had trouble seeing Del Cluff in the role of paramour, but, as with most rumors, logic was irrelevant.

Wes had no idea why anyone would harm either Hap or Del. He was aware of a growing hostility in the community in general—and the hospital in particular—regarding the financial problems plaguing the facility. The hospital had $90,000 in payables to local vendors who would not be paid in the event of a bankruptcy.

Loss of work by several hundred employees was a similar concern. Tempers flared as employees, physicians, and Board members deflected blame for what all feared was an impending financial disaster.

Though Wes didn't fear for his personal safety, he had come to the conclusion that a hospital failure would have a severely negative effect on his career. He wasn't responsible for the bad decisions that brought the hospital to the brink of ruin, but, in the community's eyes, he would share the blame as the facility's last hospital administrator. The advisability of circulating his résumé with former associates from Portland, Maine crossed his mind.

25

An Audit of the Pharmacy

With the exception of the running shoes and trophy rainbow trout, the administrator's office looked much the way it did when Hap died. Wes didn't care for the décor. It was overdone and out of date. If the hospital survived and Wes was offered the permanent position of administrator, the velvet drapes and French provincial furniture would go. For the present, however, there was little reason to change any of it.

Still, it would be nice to have a desk that worked, Wes thought as he struggled once more to open the top drawer, jammed for the second time in as many days. Grasping the handle, he jiggled it firmly to no avail and then hit it forcefully with the palm of his hand. Still, it didn't budge. Something was caught in the runner.

Pushing back the heavy executive chair, he retrieved a screwdriver from the bottom drawer, then climbed under the desk. From his position lying on his back, it took a moment for his eyes to adjust to the dark. The runners were covered by a 2' x 3' baseboard, securely attached to the side panels by four screws. Interestingly, an amateur carpenter had sawed an opening about the size of a legal envelope in the center. It was covered with a small door with two hinges and a small latch. *A hiding place?* Curious, Wes released the latch. A yellow envelope fell out, hitting him on the chin. Retrieving it, he crawled out from under the desk.

Sitting on the couch next to the door, he looked at the penciled label on the envelope. *"Ramer Investigation."* It looked like Hap's handwriting. Inside were several slips of paper. The first was a three-by-five card with the name of Randall Wynn Simmons penned on it. Beneath, also in Hap's handwriting, was the inscription, *"Twelve Percodan prescriptions, January through March 1999."*

There was an invoice from the hospital to the Lycaon Home Health Agency for pharmaceuticals—sixteen cases of Sudafed. The order included four other items, which Wes recognized as over-the-counter drugs containing methamphetamines. A notation showed that Ramer paid for these items personally.

The last items in the envelope were two receipts from the hospital, both dated February 27, 1998. The first was for a topical antibiotic for $7. The second receipt was for a prescription for a drug called Ziac for $12.52. A canceled check to the pharmacy from the account of Hap Castleton for $19.52 was stapled to the back of the second receipt. Wes studied the documents for a few minutes and then picked up his phone and called Medical Records.

"Hi, Shannon, Wes here. Have we ever had a physician on the staff by the name of Randall Simmons? … Never heard of him, huh? How about a patient? The full name is Randall Wynn Simmons . . . Yeah . . . check the files and give me a call. Thanks." Wes hung up and returned his attention to the documents. In a few minutes, the phone rang.

"Hi, Shannon. No one by that name ever admitted here? At least as far as the records go back, huh? And how long is that? Okay, thanks anyway."

There was a knock at the door and Lexi Cunningham entered. "Come in," Wes said. "I was just going to call you." Lexi crossed the room and sat down. "Ever heard of the Lycaon Home Health Agency?" Wes asked.

Lexi nodded. "I've sent them invoices," she replied. "We serve as the pharmacy for five nursing homes and three home health agencies—they're one of them. They have a post office box in Salt Lake City."

"Why do we sell them pharmaceuticals?"

"Hap authorized it four years ago. It increases our purchasing volume—we share the volume discounts."

"Who owns Lycaon?" Wes asked.

"Don't know," Lexi replied. "We just invoice them for the drugs they order and they pay their bills. We have an open purchase order from them in the file someplace."

"Why don't you pull it," Wes suggested. "I would like to see who signed it. I'd also like you to do some research on this home health agency to determine who owns it. Call the Department of Business Regulation."

"Oh, and while you're playing the role of detective," Wes added, "see if you can find out anything about a fellow by the name of Randall Wynn Simmons. He may have filled a prescription at the hospital sometime in 1999. Check these prescription numbers." He handed Lexi the card.

Lexi's blue eyes reflected her curiosity. "What's this all about?"

"I'm not sure, but it may have some bearing on Hap's death. See what you can find out, but keep it low-key, okay?" Wes cautioned.

That afternoon, Lexi pulled the open purchase order from Lycaon Home Care. A Nancy Baum had signed it. She listed herself as the purchasing agent. The name didn't ring a bell, and she couldn't find her in the Park City or Salt Lake City phone books. She called the administrative offices of the Social Security Administration and found Lycaon wasn't Medicare certified. *Strange,* she thought, *Medicare is the largest payer of home healthcare costs in the state of Utah. How do they stay in business?*

With a visit the following day to the Department of Business Regulation, she got a copy of Lycaon's business license and articles of incorporation. To her surprise, the owners were listed as Ryan Ramer and Hank Ulman. Late that afternoon, she reported that information back to Wes.

"As far as I can determine from talking to the offices of Medicare, Medicaid, Blue Cross, and several other large insurance carriers," Lexi said, "Lycaon has never billed a third-party payer for a visit. Yet they've run a good volume of drugs through the pharmacy over the past four years."

"Were we paid?"

"To the penny."

"Why would Ramer and Ulman own a home health agency?" Wes asked. "It's outside their expertise."

"Beats me! Neither one of them has ever said anything to me about it."

"What about Randall Simmons?" Wes asked.

"Oh, I almost forgot," Lexi replied. "That's an interesting story in itself. I couldn't find his name in the phone book. I started to wonder if he was still alive, so I checked out the Social Security Death Index on the Internet. He died in Fillmore, Utah, in 1999. I called Millard County and got a copy of his death certificate. He passed away in a nursing home.

"I checked the phone book for the nursing home, no listing. I called the Utah Nursing Home Association and found the place burned down in '99. I was able to place a call to the former administrator. He retired and lives in Greeley, Colorado, with his daughter. He recalled Randall Simmons; said he was a patient there for four years before his death. He told me Simmons was a retired physician from Panguitch, Utah. Practiced from 1949 to about 1989.

"Decided to call the Bureau of Narcotics," Lexi continued. "The numbers you gave me were for prescriptions signed by Dr. Simmons in 1999—class three narcotics for a patient named Darin Erickson. No one knows who Erickson is, but they were filled at a pharmacy in Salt Lake City. Simmons' license was lifted two months later because of these prescriptions."

"Why?" Wes asked.

Lexi smiled cynically. "Dr. Simmons had Alzheimer's—he didn't have clear mental faculties after 1994. I wondered if Erickson was still alive, so I ran his name through the Social Security Death Index. I found a guy named Darin Erickson who died in 1966. I checked with the Drivers License Division and found that someone using his name and social security number obtained a driver's license in 1998. Apparently, this person got a copy of his birth certificate from the data on his tombstone and used it for identification."

Wes was silent while he digested the information. "A physician with Alzheimer's who writes narcotics prescriptions for a dead man with a renewed driver's license. What do you make of it?"

"I think someone forged prescriptions and filled them using fake ID."

"Good work, Lexi. Keep snooping. Let me know what you find."

26

Facility Problems

Wes laid his glasses on the blueprint, then rubbed his tired eyes. He was perplexed. For the past two hours, he and his chief engineer, John Conforti, met with Park City's fire chief, to determine if there was a way to bring the facility into conformance with State Fire Code.

Wednesday, Wes got a six-page letter from the state fire marshal detailing the building's violations. The letter threatened to close the facility unless a remedy was agreed upon. Wes immediately called the fire chief to set up a meeting.

The chief, who had done his best to cooperate, shook his head apologetically. "My own kids were born here; we come here for healthcare. We don't want to see the hospital shut down, but it's got to meet code, Wes."

Many violations were resolved, but two remained. Wes replaced his glasses and studied the blueprint. "This main section of the building dates to 1935," he said, tapping the document with his knuckles. "What I don't understand is why the issue's coming to a head right now."

"The State Fire Code was amended in 2001," the fire chief replied. "Back then, we put the hospital on notice that the facility would have to be remodeled or closed. The Board promised they'd build a new facility. With that understanding, we gave them a variance. All that changed in September when the Board announced the cancellation of the project." He arched his eyebrows and shrugged. "No replacement—no variance."

Wes took a deep breath, then released it slowly. He understood the chief's argument; he just didn't have much money. "Okay," he said with a tone of finality. "I'll agree to replacing the sprinkler system. I hate to do it because the whole building will be torn down in a couple of years anyway, but you leave me no choice." Wes turned to Conforti. "How much will that cost us?"

"Fifty thousand bucks."

Wes whistled under his breath. "What's left?" he asked, looking at the blueprint.

"The newborn nursery."

"I can't close the newborn nursery," Wes said. "We can't survive if we get out of the baby business. Besides, Castleton just spent $30,000 recruiting and outfitting a new obstetrician."

"If we keep it, we have to get a code-approved egress," said Conforti. "The current hallway's too narrow. It's three feet wide; the code calls for ten. It met code when the wing was built, but doesn't now."

"I have an idea," the fire chief chimed in. He pointed to an area near the nursery. "You could create a new hall by removing the west and south walls of the pharmacy storeroom. That would give you a twelve-foot hallway emptying directly into the lobby—just thirteen feet from the main entrance."

First floor, Administrative Wing, Brannan Community Hospital

Nonconforming hall to Nursery

Wes nodded as he studied the blueprint. "Might work," he said. He turned to Conforti. "What do you think of that?"

Conforti shrugged. "I like it. I'd rather lose a storeroom than a nursery.

"There's one problem, though," Conforti continued. "Ryan Ramer's pretty possessive of the area. Two months ago, the director of volunteers tried to store some stuff for the Pink Shop in there. Ramer lost his cool. You'd have thought we were asking for the keys to the narcotics vault. Ask him again and you'll probably get the same reaction."

"Then we won't ask him," Wes countered. "He's gone for the weekend and the fire marshal will be here Monday. Let's get a crew in this afternoon. I'll deal with Ramer later."

Friday afternoon, Lexi reported back to Wes on the continuing investigation of Ryan Ramer. "He becomes more interesting by the day," said Lexi. "By policy, the pharmacy must deposit all funds received on a nightly basis. Ramer has always resisted, claiming he was too busy. I'm on a committee at the hospital credit union where Ramer's a member. In the past five years, he's financed some expensive things: a boat, a cabin, and a Lexus. Usually, he pays the loans off early, making sometimes two or three extra payments a week. The dates always correlate with the dates on which he makes the pharmacy's deposit."

"What do you make of that?" asked Wes.

"Well, I was puzzled by the pharmacy receipts you gave me from Hap's envelope. The prescriptions were for medications Hap was known to be taking. There was nothing unusual about them."

"So?"

"So we pulled the cash register tape Ramer delivers with the pharmacy deposits. In theory, it is a copy of the receipts from the sales for the day."

"Why do you say 'in theory'?" asked Wes.

"Because the dollar amounts for the transaction numbers found on Hap's receipt for that same date are different. My theory is that after the pharmacy closed and the other employees went home, Ramer would re-ring the tape with fictitious transactions, under-ringing the transactions by as much as $200 per day. He would then use that money to pay down his credit union loans. The cashier there said he always pays in cash."

"You think Ramer was embezzling from the hospital?"

"Yes. And there's more. I got his Social Security number from his personnel file and used it to get a copy of his birth certificate. His mother's maiden name was *Wycoff*."

Lexi pulled out printed documents. "That's not a common name," she said, "so I checked his pedigree with the Family History Library in Salt Lake City. His mom was none other than Edward Wycoff's sister."

Wes raised his eyebrows. "Ramer is Wycoff's nephew?" he said incredulously. "I didn't know that."

"No one does. It seems to be a well-kept secret," Lexi replied. "But I'm not sure why."

"That would be interesting to find out," replied Wes.

Saturday afternoon, the carpenters removed the pharmacy storeroom walls without incident, creating a hallway between the nursery and Pink Shop. The only surprise was a heavy bookshelf with a built-in cabinet attached to the east wall.

"Funny, that's not shown on the blueprints; must've been added later," said the carpenter. "Shall we tear it out?"

The supervisor studied it carefully, then shook his head. "It's not a bad-looking piece of furniture," he said. "Leave it. That new night security guard Wes hired after the burglary has been griping that he doesn't have a place for his stuff. We'll move a small desk here and it can serve as his workstation. Make sure to screw it to the wall securely. There'll be a ton of traffic through this area. We don't want a service cart knocking the whole thing over."

27

Ramer's Reversal

"Why didn't you warn me?" Ramer screamed, his rage choking him. Ramer had just burst into Hank Ulman's office. His brother-in-law had never seen him angrier.

"Warn you 'bout what?" Hank asked as he took his feet off his desk.

"Warn me they were going to knock the walls of the pharmacy storeroom out."

"Didn't know they did," Hank replied, as surprised as Ramer. "Why would they do that?"

"Made the thing into a hallway," Ramer replied. "Connects the newborn nursery to the lobby."

"I never saw a work order," Hank said defensively. "It wasn't on the schedule board when I left Friday." His eyes widened as he thought about the hidden staircase. "Did they find the door to the lab?"

"I don't know—no, don't think so. The bookshelf is still there . . . but they bolted it to the wall. Worse still, they've put a desk with a phone and our security guard in front of it—now it's his workstation!"

A tense silence enveloped the room. "What are you going to do 'bout the delivery?" Hank asked. "You promised to ship Thursday. You can't renege again. Carnavali will kill you."

A nauseating wave of fear washed over Ramer—for a moment he couldn't breathe. "I don't know," he gasped. As his eyes darted about the room, he wiped the beads of perspiration forming on his forehead.

"Our options are limited," Ramer said tensely. "We've got $55,000 worth of Sudafed down there. We can't get it out without tipping everyone off and, even if we had the money to replace it, it would take me a couple of months to do it without raising the suspicions of my drug reps. You don't order $55,000 of amphetamines without someone asking questions."

"We've got other problems here at home," Hank volunteered as Ramer evaluated his options.

"Like what?"

"An investigation. Wes is looking into the home health agency."

"What are you talking about?" Ramer asked wildly. The tension in his abdomen tightened.

"I was installing a new phone line for a computer in the business office, you know, on Friday. Heard Lexi Cunningham talking with Emma Chandler," Hank continued.

"Who's Emma Chandler?"

"High school student, belongs to a health occupations club, volunteers in the business office. Anyway, Cunningham's askin' her to pull all the home health agency purchase orders. She's calling the State Division of Business Regulation in to do an audit of the agency's prescriptions."

"Why would they do that?" asked Ramer.

"Maybe they found Cluff's work papers. Maybe they were in Hap's desk. They sure as the devil weren't in Cluff's. I searched the place for thirty minutes the night I broke into the business office." Hank shook his head. "You've got a problem, buddy."

Ramer's face hardened. "No, *we've* got a problem. If I go down, you go down."

28

Paradigm Solutions

Tuesday, Wes scheduled a meeting with David Brannan to discuss a pledge on the new facility. From reading minutes of the Board of Trustees, Wes learned that the Brannan Foundation committed an endowment of one million dollars for the new building, to be paid in four installments. The first installment was made in April of 2003. In June, David Brannan reported that the foundation was having financial problems and told the Board that more payments might not be forthcoming. Wes wondered why.

David Brannan arrived dutifully at 2:00 p.m. It was apparent to Wes that he was embarrassed by the family's default. As David took a chair in Wes' office, Birdie popped her head in to remind the administrator that he was two hours behind on his afternoon appointments. The waiting room was filled with hospital creditors, physicians, patients, and unhappy employees, all demanding immediate solutions to their problems.

Wes didn't waste time on small talk. "I met with the fire marshal," he said soberly. "The building doesn't meet code. We are making some changes, but, in the long term, remodeling will cost more than replacement. Unless we can show progress on a new facility, they plan on shutting us down.

"With the hospital's financial situation," Wes continued, "and without the foundation's endowment, we stand little chance of getting more financing. Will the foundation be able to help us with the remaining $750,000?"

"I wouldn't hold my breath," David said soberly. "No doubt you have been told of the family's financial difficulties."

Wes nodded.

"There's less than a fifty percent probability the foundation can meet its commitment," David continued. "The foundation's assets consist of 10,000 shares of Brannan Inc., a holding company," he explained. "At its peak, it owned two coal mines, a major interest in the bank, Park City's only newspaper, and Paradigm Solutions, a software development house. All that's left is Paradigm. It's not yet profitable."

"But it does have value?" Wes asked.

David nodded. "It could. I have a potential buyer. He won't commit, however, until the company shows that it can turn a profit."

As a CPA with Lytle, Moorehouse, and Butler, Wes consulted with several high-tech firms in Maine and was familiar with the industry. Many fortunes were being earned in software development. Folding his hands, he leaned forward. "Tell me more," he said.

"The company was formed in 2000 by a group of engineers and software programmers in San Diego. On their first contract, they teamed with Tandem Computer and an electrical engineering firm to develop and install a hardware and software system for the Boeing Corporation.

"Boeing was concerned about the security of its aircraft plant in Oceanside. There was a lot of union unrest—concern about industrial espionage. Boeing contracted with Paradigm for a computerized security and environmental control system. The system was to provide security, access control, monitoring, and fire protection for their entire facility.

"Employees would be allowed to access only those areas for which they were authorized. A Tandem computer would control access through the central station. One of the requirements was that it must have the ability to read and process 15,000 employee access control cards during the ten-minute period employees report to work each morning.

"It was an expensive project," David continued. "The hardware included a central command post, employee identification card readers, television cameras, monitors, and smoke and fire detectors—all in addition to the software code.

"Halfway through the project, Paradigm ran out of money. They underbid the contract. My father bought the company thinking he could save it with an infusion of one million dollars."

Unfortunately," David explained, "my father was wrong; the software had a major design flaw. By the time the contract was finished, the overrun exceeded four million dollars. Unwilling to lose his first investment, Father came up with more money from other companies owned by Brannan Inc. In retrospect, he wouldn't have bought Paradigm if he knew how much it would take to finish the contract. He bled his other companies to get the cash."

"What's the status of the contract now?" Wes asked.

"The project is finished and there are new potential customers. Paradigm is negotiating with a large hospital chain to design and install a similar security system for its hospitals. This system would also include the monitoring equipment in the ICUs and nursery."

"What else is needed?" Wes asked.

"About $800,000 for development work. I have a venture capitalist who will fund us, but he is unwilling to put the money in until we can show our ability to control cost. If I can get the $800,000, we can modify the software and get the contract."

"Okay, so you have a computerized environmental control and security system," Wes clarified.

"Right."

"And the software works."

"More or less. There are bugs, but I think they're few. The system's running in California and Washington," David explained.

"And you have customers, with money, willing to buy and modify the system, and a venture capitalist who will fund it," Wes reiterated.

"Right, and an investor that will buy the company if it turns a profit."

"What else do you need?" Wes asked.

"More sophisticated control systems—specifically job order costing."

"If I could help you put an acceptable system in place, how long would it take for you to finish the contract?" Wes asked.

"About three months," David replied, surprised at the turn the conversation was taking.

"At that time, do you think you could sell the company for enough money to cover the foundation's commitment to the hospital?"

"Yes," David affirmed.

"I've developed costing systems for defense contractors," Wes said. "I don't have much time, but we can't survive without the prospect of a new hospital. I'll give you forty hours of free consulting time. Let's see if we can get Paradigm Solutions in the black."

David's eyes lit up as he considered the possibility of a sale. "That would be great, Wes! ...Um, I need one more favor," he said, pressing his luck.

"Shoot."

"We're working on interfacing our computer with a telemetry unit that can broadcast a video signal at least seven miles to a central station. We need a place to test the telemetry component of the system in a reinforced concrete building. Could we use a room in the hospital for about a week?"

"How large of a room do you need?"

"My engineers tell me we need a room with about four hundred square feet. There has to be at least one floor above the test room and it needs to be within two hundred feet of other telemetry units, like fetal heart monitors, to test for interference."

"I'll give you the boardroom," Wes said. "Coordinate with Mary Anne."

"Ryan? Ryan Ramer, isn't it?" A large man wearing a convention nametag stuck out his hand.

"Do I know you?" Ramer asked. His lips puckered with annoyance.

"Robert Applebee. Don't you remember? The Elk's Home? Claremont, California? My wife and I are in Park City for a convention."

"I remember the school," Ramer snorted. "Don't remember you." With that, he broke off and continued down Main Street. He didn't look back.

"My!" the conventioneer's wife said. "Who was that?"

"Ryan Ramer. He was raised with me in the Elk's home," her husband replied. "No one knew much about him. He started showing bizarre behavior in the sixth grade. Became obsessed with poisons and explosives, as I recall. He was sent to a lockdown institution when the headmaster's car blew up. We never heard what happened to him after that." The conventioneer shook his head. "He was a strange kid."

"Well!" his wife exclaimed, "It doesn't seem like he's changed much!"

29

First Management Reports

Monday morning, Lexi met with Wes to review the first reports of the new accounting system. Elizabeth Flannigan also attended the meeting.

From the beginning, Wes' goal was to empower the department heads by giving them the information they needed to make decisions. He believed that Hap often made decisions that should have been made on a departmental level.

The meeting was held in the boardroom so that all the reports could be spread out for examination. Lexi laid the reports on the table and stepped to the whiteboard. "When we first met with the department heads last September," she said, "they told us they needed information for . . ."

Lexi wrote on the board:

Pricing

Cost control

Strategic planning

Measurement of the efficiency of our hospital as compared with other facilities

"I think the system we have implemented will meet the criteria. It will provide standard costs that we can use in pricing."

"What's a standard cost?" Flannigan asked.

"It's what something should cost," Lexi replied.

"Like a budget?"

"Yeah. The system will allow us to compare actual costs to standard–budgeted–costs for cost control. It will also give us the information we need for strategic planning."

"Like what?" Flannigan asked.

"It will tell us which procedures are profitable and which aren't. Then we can determine what business we want to go after. If a service isn't profitable, we can shut it down."

"Like alcohol and chemical treatment?" Flannigan asked.

"Good example."

Lexi continued. "The system will tell us how much we make or lose by DRG, doctor, or insurance company." She frowned. "The preliminary reports suggest some of our prices are dramatically lower than costs."

"I suspected as much," Wes interjected.

"The new accounting system gives us a host of new reports," Lexi said enthusiastically. "If you have a few minutes, I'll review the most important."

Wes nodded for Lexi to continue.

"Let's look at the report on profitability by DRG," Lexi said. "Here's a report on DRGs one through seven."

Brannan Community Hospital
Profit or Loss by DRG

DRG	# Cases	Actual Revenue Per Case	Actual Cost Per Case	Profit (Loss)
1	120	$8,500	$8,450	$50
2	12	$3,240	$4,200	$(960)
3	45	$1,270	$1,200	$70
4	15	$5,680	$6,130	$(450)
5	67	$3,240	$3,100	$140
6	32	$1,200	$900	$300
7	45	$980	$1,020	$(40)

Definition of Column Headings:

Column 1: Diagnosis Related Group (DRG)
Column 2: Number of cases in each group seen by the hospital for a specific time period
Column 3: Avg. actual reimbursement received by the hospital for all patients in DRG category (regardless of their insurer or the reimbursement system used by their insurer) [This is calculated by taking actual reimbursement received and dividing by the number of patients seen.]
Column 4: Average cost to the hospital per case
Column 5: Average actual profit or loss on all patients seen in this DRG category (the difference between Column 3 and Column 4)

"As you can see," Lexi explained, "we make the most money—$300 per case—on DRG 6. We lose the most money—$960 per case—on DRG 2. If money were the only consideration, we would work to increase the volume of DRG 6 patients, and phase out, or reduce the services that comprise DRG 2.

"The next report," Lexi continued, "is an analysis by insurance company for DRG 6. It's the type of data we need to negotiate with insurance companies."

Brannan Community Hospital
Average Profit or Loss by Insurance Company
DRG 6—Circulatory Disorders

Insurance Company	# of Cases	Actual Revenue Per Case	Standard Cost Per Case	Profit (Loss) Per Case
Blue Cross	13	$1,320	$900	$420
Medicare Part A	48	$800	$900	($100)
Medicaid	4	$750	$900	($150)
Aetna	15	$1100	$900	$200
Western Health	6	$1000	$900	$100
United	2	$1050	$900	$150
Security Insurance	5	$870	$900	($30)

Definition of Column Headings:

Column 1: Name of insurance company
Column 2: Total cases for the month for this insurance company
Column 3: Average amount paid by the insurance company per case
Column 4: Hospital's average standard cost (budgeted cost) per case
Column 5: Profit or loss per case for this insurance company per month, (revenue minus standard cost)

"The last report," Lexi continued, "compares the average cost of each physician, compared to standard cost, for DRG 6."

Flannigan studied the report. "Remind me once again what standard costs are," she said.

"It is what the procedure should cost."

"It's the budget?"

"Right."

"Why does Dr. Brannan have a higher average cost than other physicians?" Wes asked. "He is $950 over budget, per case."

"He has a different practice pattern. He uses more medications, more lab tests, and so on."

"How come?" Wes asked.

"Dunno—maybe he has more complications. I checked with Medical Records and found that his patients with this diagnosis have the longest length of stay of anyone."

Brannan Community Hospital Physician Based Analysis DRG 6				
Doctor	# of Cases	Standard Cost Per Case	Actual Cost Per Case	Variance
Brannan	5	$900	$1,850	($950)
Hemingway	2	$900	$700	$200
McDonald	8	$900	$890	$10
O'Reilly	12	$900	$1,100	($200)
Lee	1	$900	$1000	($100)
Samuels	9	$900	$500	$400
Allen	5	$900	$850	$50

"Interesting," Wes said. "I never thought we could pick out substandard practice through accounting data." He was quiet for a moment as he studied the report. "How do you recommend we use the data?"

"We'll code the physician names—give each doc a number. Physicians will only know their own number. For many, that will raise their curiosity enough to find out why their practice patterns differ.

"When we're sure the data is right," Lexi continued, "it might be a good idea to share it with the Morbidity and Mortality Committee. If it's correct, Dr. Brannan might benefit from a little peer review."

Thursday afternoon, Lexi confirmed the data shown in the report. Friday morning, Wes met with Dr. Emil Flagg, Chairman of the Morbidity and Mortality Committee, to review the report.

"The quality of Dr. Brannan's care has been a concern since he joined the medical staff," Dr. Flagg acknowledged. "I'm not surprised by the data. He has had more than his share of complications. It may be that he's not qualified for all the medical privileges he's been granted."

"Such as . . .?" Wes pressed.

"Obstetrics and surgery. He's not certified in either."

"Assuming he's not qualified, how did that happen?"

"A rural hospital with a poor history of peer review, a father who has funded its deficits for the past twenty years, politics…" Dr. Flagg replied.

"Where was the Board when this was happening?" Wes asked. "They have the legal responsibility for granting medical privileges."

"The Board is only as good as the information it gets from the medical staff."

"Okay, then where was the medical staff?"

"Medical staffs of small hospitals have problems with peer review," Dr. Flagg said. "Brannan's partners had to work with him on a daily basis so they didn't want a fight. The docs in competing clinics were either too busy to care, or didn't want to give the appearance of a conflict of interest. Traditionally, physicians have been reticent to criticize their own."

"What about the administrator?" Wes asked.

"He had his hands full with managed care and huge deficits. Plus, he may not have wanted to risk the relationship with the Brannans. Historically, they've bailed the hospital out when revenues didn't cover expenses.

"Also, it's hard when the medical staff isn't behind you. Hap was burned several years ago when he took disciplinary action against a radiologist. Everyone on the medical staff complained privately about him. When the administrator took formal action, however, it became '*them against us*.' The staff rallied behind the radiologist."

Wes removed his glasses and stared out the window as he collected his thoughts. "Okay, so what do we do?" he asked, weariness lining his voice.

"Dr. Brannan will be coming before the Quality Assurance Committee next week," Dr. Flagg said. "With a new administrator and a renewed resolve by the Board to fix the hospital, this may well be the time for me to push for a resolution to the problem."

Dr. Flagg looked Wes straight in the eyes. "If there's a fight among the medical staff, it won't be pretty," he said. "You'll be in the middle."

"You're smart enough to realize," Dr. Flagg continued, "that when there are problems, the hospital administrator makes a good fall guy."

"What do you mean?"

"It's unlikely the Board will take any blame. The medical staff can't be fired, so..."

"I get your point," Wes said. "No need to finish the sentence."

"Let's be candid, buddy," Dr. Flagg said. "The Board got you because they wanted a hired gun—someone who would do a quick and dirty housecleaning. To do the things necessary to save this place, you'll make enemies. The Board's not going to support an unpopular administrator. Once the dirty work's done, they'll dump you for someone who can come in and be the good guy. You're expendable."

Wes got one of those 'ah-ha' looks on his face as everything suddenly fit together. "That explains it," he said, shaking his head.

"Explains what?"

"Why the Board brought someone in from the outside." He smiled foolishly. "If I had thought about it more deeply, I probably could have figured it out for myself. It's too bad," he said almost to himself.

"Your job as administrator was offered as an interim position. You didn't want the job permanently did you?" Dr. Flagg asked.

"If you had asked me two weeks ago, I probably would have said no. Recently though, I've started to get into the rhythm of things. I like solving problems." He smiled wryly. "It's more interesting than tax or auditing."

Dr. Flagg shrugged. *The hospital could do worse.* "Well, you know what's at stake," he said eyeing the young administrator curiously. "So, what do you want to do?"

Wes thought for a moment. "Win or lose," he replied firmly, "let's do the right thing."

Monday afternoon, Dr. Emil Flagg reported back to Wes. His face reflected his surprise. "We won," he said with astonishment. "The committee recommended that Brannan's surgical privileges be restricted. I met with him on their decision this morning."

"So what was his response?"

"Disappointed—but, he'll live with it. Really, he has no choice. Things are changing around here and I think he can see the writing on the wall."

"Congratulations," Wes said.

"Thanks," Dr. Flagg said. "Quality is something we've struggled with for a long time," he remarked. "With the changes you've been making, the medical staff appears to be more open to suggestions than anytime since I've served as medical director.

"Speaking of quality control," Dr. Flagg continued, "there's a husband-wife team who do quite a bit of consulting with hospitals in the area of quality control. They've got good references. It would probably be worth our time to give them a call."

30

Improving Quality

A week later, Dr. Tom Woolsey and his wife, Dr. Joyce Eyre-Woolsey, were in Wes' office to discuss total quality management. Tom was a former professor of biostatistics at the University of Utah Medical School. Joyce taught business administration at Weber State University.

Emil Flagg was out of town. Wes had invited Elizabeth Flannigan, but she was concluding a meeting with her supervisors. While they waited for her to arrive, Wes asked Tom how he got interested in quality.

"Joyce was studying the changes that occur in industries as they mature," Dr. Tom Woolsey replied. "Much of what she was finding applied to healthcare. We decided to do a couple of seminars together and that led to consulting." Tom turned to his wife. "Why don't you tell him a little about your initial research, Joyce," he said.

"As they mature, most industries go through four stages of development," Joyce explained. "Stage one can be characterized as: '*If you build it, they will come.*' [1] Demand exceeds supply and producers don't worry much about marketing. The steel industry is a good example of stage one. When Andrew Carnegie started U.S. Steel, there were few suppliers and lots of pent-up demand."

---

[1] Berkowitz, Eric N., Ph.D. and Robert T. Kauer, Ph.D., "The Strategic Life Cycle," *The Journal of Strategic Performance Measurement,* August/September 1998, Volume 2, Number 4.

Tom picked up on her point. "The hospital industry entered this stage in the early 1950s," he said. "There was a shortage of hospital beds. The Federal Government came to the rescue with funds to build new hospitals with the Hill Burton Act."

Joyce continued. "In the second stage, supply catches and then exceeds supply. Firms start to compete in the marketplace. This is the stage of selling and competition."

"In healthcare, this occurred in the early 1970s," Tom said. "Although cost reimbursement softened the impact of oversupply, hospital beds no longer guaranteed success. Hospitals started marketing their services."

"Stage three is one of restructuring," Joyce continued. "The focus is on ending excess capacity. You can see that happening now in banking, the airlines industry—"

"And in healthcare!" Tom replied, finishing her sentence. "Thirty years ago, there were 6,000 hospitals in the country, today there are about 4,000. Even the hospitals that have survived have fewer beds than they did in 1970."

Joyce nodded in agreement. "We have even seen hospital corporations buying competing hospitals to close them—get them out of the market."

"The final stage is customer value," she continued. "To capture market share, the seller focuses on quality. That's where the health industry is today and that is probably one of the reasons you have called us here," she said, smiling. Wes looked up as Elizabeth Flannigan entered the room.

"Sorry I'm late," Flannigan said. "Problems in Pediatrics." As Flannigan took a seat, Wes began with a series of questions on the history and experience of the consulting firm.

"How long have you been consulting in quality?" he asked.

"Four years," Tom replied.

"You're no longer with the university?"

"Joyce still teaches," Tom said. "I'm now with the firm full time."

"What services do you offer?"

"We do seminars for physicians and hospital employees on TQM."

"What's TQM?" Flannigan asked.

"Stands for total quality management," Wes replied. "It's an approach to production developed by an American professor, W. Edward Demings, in the 1950s."

"Demings took his ideas to Japan," Tom said, continuing where Wes had left off. "At that time *'Made in Japan'* had an unfavorable connotation—it implied you were buying junk.

"The Japanese embraced Demings' ideas and philosophy," he continued. "Two decades later, it was the Americans who were having trouble competing. The Japanese, for example, almost put American automobile manufacturers out of business."

Wes nodded. "That's when American manufacturers decided to get serious about quality. They invited Demings back and began implementing his program.

"While TQM was originally developed for manufacturing," Wes continued, "it seems that many of its concepts have direct application to healthcare."

"Give me an example," Flannigan said skeptically.

Joyce, who had written her doctoral dissertation on total quality management, spoke up. "TQM," she said, "teaches companies to focus on their customers."

"We need to do more of that," Flannigan admitted. "We get so caught up in disease and technology," she said, "that sometimes we forget about the patient."

"TQM teaches organizations to solve problems using teams of production workers," Joyce continued.

"My first job was as a staff nurse," Flannigan contributed. "I knew a lot more about what was going on in the hospitals than those in administration. The people on the floor are the best qualified to identify problems and their possible solutions," she added.

"TQM involves benchmarking—studying the best competition has to offer and replicating it," Tom explained.

Flannigan turned to Wes. "That's essentially what we're doing with the data we get from the Utah Healthcare Association, isn't it?" she asked.

Wes nodded. "Monthly, we receive a report comparing us to other hospitals our size using the average nursing hours per patient day," he said clarifying the issue for Tom and Joyce. "It also gives us comparisons using the average number of housekeeping hours per thousand square feet of floor space and other such measures. It's been a great help in budgeting."

"We also review comparative data on morbidity and mortality. Our infection rate, for example, is one of the lowest in the state," Flannigan said proudly. Her lips settled into a questioning frown. "Everyone wants quality," she said. "In a service industry, that's sometimes difficult to define. How do you define quality?" she asked looking directly at Tom.

"Quality is meeting customer needs and expectations," he replied. "Our consulting firm helps hospitals improve the quality of the healthcare they provide by focusing on two issues—quality control and quality assurance."

"I thought those were the same thing," Flannigan said.

"Not quite," Tom replied. "Quality control takes place *after* the fact."

"Like an autopsy," Flannigan said.

"Yes. In a hospital setting, quality control is often performed by individuals or committees who review medical records to see that proper procedures were followed. Quality assurance, on the other hand, takes place *before* the fact."

"It's like preventive medicine," Wes clarified.

"Good analogy. Hospitals perform quality control by verifying that physicians are properly trained before granting them hospital privileges, assuring that proper procedures are in place to prevent infections, and so on."

Joyce continued. "One of the early attempts at quality assurance was outcomes management. Outcomes management focuses on improving quality by developing guidelines that physicians can use in treating specific illnesses. They include treatment protocols, boundary guidelines, and clinical pathways."

"What are those?" Wes asked.

"A treatment protocol is a checklist of activities that should be performed for specific illnesses or injuries. A boundary guideline defines medical practice beyond which physicians incur penalties," she explained.

Tom continued Joyce's thought. "A clinical pathway goes beyond this. It is a complete patient treatment plan designed to achieve the best outcome possible. In addition to outlining the care to be given, a clinical pathway identifies the outcomes to be achieved and their timeframes."

Wes shook his head. "This doesn't sound that innovative," he said.

"It's not," Tom replied. "The concept has been around for a long time. It just hasn't always been applied.

"The approach was first proposed in 1913 by a Harvard surgeon by the name of Emery Codman," he continued. "He called it the *'end results idea.'* It consisted of tracking surgical patients for a year to see how their treatment turned out. The goal was to determine the most likely cause of success or failure in treatment.

"Codman planned to accumulate the information into a database that could be used to improve treatment profiles. Unfortunately, his proposal to the American Medical Association was essentially ignored—it got only five hundred dollars in funding."

"More importantly—to Codman, anyway," Joyce interjected, "other physicians stopped sending patients to him and his practice suffered, so he abandoned the idea." [2]

"In 1919," Tom said, "the concept was resurrected by the American College of Surgeons. They performed a study of six hundred ninety-two hospitals with one hundred beds or more. The study showed that only eighty-nine met the minimum standards."

Tom smiled. "The response of the Board of Regents to the report was swift and uncompromising. They collected all the copies, carried them to the basement of the hotel, and burned them."

"Men of action," Wes replied wryly.

Tom nodded. "Despite its rocky beginning," he continued, "outcomes management is in the news again. One reason is the pressure employers and consumers are putting on the industry. They want some assurance that the products they're buying are of high quality."

---

[2] Many of the concepts in this section are drawn from an article by Joseph Flower entitled "Measuring Health," which appeared in the *Journal of Strategic Performance Measurement,* August/September 1998, Volume 2, Number 4.

"Patients like to think their physician's approach is based on what research has shown works best," Joyce said. "Unfortunately that isn't true. A 1992 Harvard study estimated that as many as 180,000 patients die each year from medical mistakes.[3] A 1997 Rand Corporation study of autopsies showed a thirty-five to forty percent error rate in diagnoses."[4]

Wes frowned. "Why wouldn't someone with twelve years of medical school under his or her belt follow the best practices?"

"There are two possibilities," Joyce said. "The first is they may not know what the best practices are."

"A little hard to believe," Wes said dubiously.

"That's a common reaction," she replied. "Let me read from an article in the August/September *Journal of Strategic Performance Measurement.*

> *Most practices in clinical medicine have never been tested in double-blind peer-reviewed scientific studies, or even through retrospective statistical analysis. When practice techniques have been firmly established or debunked in such studies, the knowledge often does not seem to affect clinical practice. Many physicians fail to hear of the new knowledge; others routinely ignore it, preferring to continue to practice the way they were taught in medical school."* [5]

"What's the second reason physicians don't follow the best courses of action?" Wes asked.

"Limitations of human memory. Several years ago, a prominent medical school created a computer-based decision model for diagnosing the most common medical illnesses. They asked physicians to walk through the decision tree they used in diagnosing specific conditions.

"They took the model and created a software program. A patient could sit at a terminal and answer a series of questions. At the conclusion, the software would offer a diagnosis.

---

[3] Allen, Jane E. "Doctors, Insurers Meet to Highlight Ways to Reduce Medical Errors," Associated Press, October 14, 1996

[4] "U.S. Healthcare Can Kill, Study Says," *San Francisco Chronicle*, October 21, 1997

[5] Flower, Joe. "Measuring Health," *The Journal of Strategic Performance Measurement*, August/September 1998, Volume 2, Number 4.

"The researchers then compared the diagnoses of the physicians with the diagnoses made by the computers, using the models provided by the physicians. Guess which were more accurate?"

"I'd guess the physicians," Flannigan said.

"Wrong," Tom said. "In each situation, the computer was more accurate than the physician who developed the model."

"Why?"

"Physicians are human; they get tired, they're forgetful, they aren't consistent, even in following their own model."

"So what's the lesson?" Wes asked.

"If you're truly interested in quality, encourage members of the medical staff to adopt practice protocols that have been shown to have the best outcomes," Tom said.

"Our firm has purchased decision-tree software to aid physicians in diagnosis and in the preparation of a treatment plan. You can run it on a PC computer or a palm pilot. Many hospitals are purchasing the package for their physicians," Joyce said.

"Is it expensive?" Wes asked.

"Not as expensive as poor quality," Tom replied.

"What else can your firm do?" Wes asked.

"We have programs to help you focus on improving customer satisfaction, market share, and profitability. Our people can help in identifying and eliminating activities that provide no value to the customer."

Wes was silent as he considered Tom's proposal. Finally, he spoke. "Our cash flow is tight, but quality improvement is something we can't afford to ignore. Give me a cost proposal and I'll take it to the Board."

31

Quality Assurance and Safety Practices

E mil Flagg sat quietly in the conference room off the cafeteria. In a few minutes, the Quality Assurance Committee meeting would begin. As he reviewed the minutes of the previous meeting, he reflected with pride on the progress that the committee had made this year. *The medical staff is finally cleaning up its act!*

Five years ago, Dr. Flagg escorted Dr. Marshall Kearl, an intoxicated physician, from the operating room. Connie Sieger, the O.R. supervisor, smelled alcohol on Dr. Kearl's breath when he checked in that morning. Curious, she asked him what procedure he was there to perform. When he slurred the pronunciation, she called the medical director's office.

Dr. Flagg took the incident to the Credentials Committee. Since this was the third such occurrence, he recommended that Kearl be permanently barred from the medical staff. At that time, however, the medical staff showed little enthusiasm for monitoring the care of other physicians. The Credentials Committee suspended Kearl from the medical staff for two weeks. It was a slap on the wrist for Dr. Kearl and a slap in the face for Dr. Flagg. Flagg wasn't one to forgive easily. Two years later, when Kearl was sued for malpractice, Flagg testified on behalf of the plaintiff. Kearl lost his license. Emil Flagg smiled with satisfaction at the memory.

Things changed with the arrival of Wes Douglas. From the beginning, the new administrator recognized that the hospital's credibility depended on the quality of its medical staff. Wes' experience in manufacturing gave him an appreciation of total quality management and he was anxious to apply those principles to healthcare.

One of the first things he did was change the chair of the Quality Assurance Committee. The old chair was a pediatrician with an aversion to conflict. With Flagg's coaxing, Wes appointed Dr. Christopher Slabbert, an aggressive surgeon with the diplomacy of an assault rifle. He was irritable and caustic. *Just the man for the job*, Flagg thought.

Still, Flagg was not happy with the way the committee was structured. He scowled as Dr. Henry Bozeman entered the room. Dr. Bozeman was an anesthesiologist. Flagg didn't trust Bozeman anymore than he trusted Kearl. As Bozeman's practice depended on a good relationship with the hospital's surgeons, he was reluctant to censure even the most negligent physician behavior.

Then there was Dr. Tilich, seated directly across the table, shoveling down a shrimp salad. At three hundred pounds, he was a good candidate for a gastric bypass. Tilich earned one million dollars investing in Park City real estate. Five years ago, he retired from his practice, *ten years after he retired mentally,* Flagg thought. Tilich rarely said anything; he contributed nothing to the committee. As Tilich reached for another roll, Flagg wondered why he even came to the meetings. *Probably for the free lunch.*

Wes arrived just as Dr. Slabbert was calling the meeting to order. Yesterday's *Park City Sentinel* reported that HealthGrades.com gave the hospital an unfavorable rating for quality. Today, quality was the top item on Wes' agenda.

Dr. Slabbert started by reviewing the minutes of the previous meeting and then turned to the first item on the agenda—medical staff privileges.

A new physician must apply for membership on the medical staff and hospital privileges. Medical staff membership allows a physician to admit patients, hold office on the medical staff and vote at medical staff meetings. Medical staff privileges detail the specific procedures the physician is allowed to perform. To receive privileges, physicians must document their training and experience. Medical staff membership and medical staff privileges are reviewed on a yearly basis by the Board of Trustees.

Dr. Slabbert presented the list of physicians recommended for approval and asked for a motion to forward their names to the Board. The motion was seconded and carried by unanimous vote of the committee.

"We have an application for readmission to the medical staff from Dr. James Turley," Dr. Slabbert continued. He turned to Wes to explain. "Dr. Turley was suspended from the staff three years ago for malpractice. He refused to take advice from his peers. Arrogant jerk," he added.

"He wouldn't even listen to my nurses," Elizabeth Flannigan interrupted.

Dr. Slabbert nodded. "It finally caught up with him. A nurse called his home about a patient in ICU. He wouldn't come in and the patient almost died. We threw him off the medical staff."

"Where's he practicing now?" Wes asked.

"Snowline Medical Center." Dr. Slabbert scowled as he scanned Turley's file. "Got a letter from his partner—an unhappy camper. Wants him reinstated so he can provide coverage for the patients here." He glanced uneasily at the committee. "Discussion?" he asked.

"Does anyone know where the sour cream went?" Dr. Tilich asked.

"I visited with one of the doctors at Snowline last night," Dr. Flagg reported, ignoring Dr. Tilich. "Turley intimidates most of the nurses—only the strongest will stand up to him."

"Doesn't sound like he's changed much," Wes volunteered.

"He hasn't," Dr. Flagg said. "Yesterday, the Credentials Committee met on his application. Their recommendation is that we turn him down."

"There's never enough sour cream," Tilich mumbled. "Someone should tell that to the kitchen."

Dr. Bozeman, who was monitoring the discussion, spoke for the first time, directing his comments to Dr. Slabbert. His voice was lined with concern.

"What about the ramifications?"

"Ramifications?" Dr. Slabbert asked.

"Yeah—like what if he starts doing all of his surgery at Snowline?"

"He already does." Dr. Slabbert gave him a withering look. "Remember, he doesn't have privileges here."

"What about his partners?" Dr. Bozeman asked.

"His partners?"

"Yeah—they do ten or eleven cases a week."

Dr. Slabbert shrugged. "Their office is here in Park City; it's a commute to Snowline."

"It's a risk we'll have to take," Flagg chimed in.

Dr. Bozeman's face flushed red as he turned to the hospital administrator. "What do you think Wes?" he said. "Are you willing to take a financial hit?"

"Better that than a malpractice suit," Wes said simply. "Besides, if we have to, we can always recruit a couple more surgeons."

An uneasy silence filled the room as Dr. Bozeman simmered.

"We need a formal motion," Dr. Slabbert reminded the group. Wes, as secretary of the committee, picked up his pen.

Dr. Flagg raised his hand. "I move that the Quality Assurance Committee recommend to the Board of Trustees that Dr. Turley's application for membership on the medical staff be *denied*."

"All in favor?" Dr. Slabbert asked.

Everyone but Dr. Bozeman responded 'aye.'

"I abstain," the anesthesiologist mumbled.

Dr. Slabbert retrieved a new folder from a stack of papers he brought to the meeting. "The next item on the agenda," he said, "is Dr. Matthew Brannan. He was served last week with a lawsuit. Until it's resolved, I recommend that his membership status be changed from Type I to Type II."

From reading the medical staff bylaws, Wes knew that active members of the medical staff could receive either a Type I or Type II membership. Type I members have no restrictions placed on their membership. Type II physicians are reevaluated quarterly. A Type II classification can be caused by an unfavorable peer review or a current lawsuit.

"You already suspended his surgical privileges," Dr. Bozeman said, torpedoing Dr. Slabbert with his eyes.

"Right."

"And his obstetric privileges."

"Yes."

"You've shut his medical practice down."

"No, he still has his privileges in the department of medicine. He can continue to practice medicine; we're just going to watch him a little more closely," Dr. Slabbert countered.

"Has anyone thought about the impact this is going to have on the family?" Dr. Bozeman said.

Dr. Slabbert looked confused. "The family?" he asked.

"The Brannans!"

"What about them?" Dr. Slabbert asked.

"For fifty years, they've bailed out the hospital."

Dr. Slabbert paused. "They probably won't do handstands," he admitted. "But," he continued, "they probably won't be giving us much more financial support anyway. Rumors say they're in Chapter 11."

That was news to Dr. Bozeman.

"This stinks!" Dr. Bozeman bellowed. "This whole nitpicking process."

Silence.

"Who're we trying to impress?" Bozeman continued, pointing his fork at Wes. "A two-bit administrator that doesn't know a scalpel from a retractor?"

"Don't get personal," Dr. Slabbert warned.

"We don't have money for this stupidity!" Bozeman continued. "T-Q-M," he said, drawing each letter out in contempt. "This isn't General Motors, it's *Brannan Community Hospital!*"

"The world's changing," Dr. Slabbert said, "so must the hospital."

"Drive all the doctors away and there won't be a hospital," Dr. Bozeman barked. "Since Hap … left, everyone's acting like we're the University of Utah Medical Center."

"We can't go back to where we were six months ago," Dr. Slabbert said. "If we can't compete with the big boys on quality, we have to get out of the business." He pulled an envelope from a folder. "Remember, the Credentials Committee supports our recommendation."

Dr. Bozeman's voice thickened with sarcasm. "Turley is gone, his partners may leave. Dr. Brannan's Type II until he goes back to school—I suppose I'll be next," he said.

Dr. Bozeman had issued a challenge. To his surprise, Dr. Slabbert was willing to pick it up. "Maybe you will," he said glacially. For a moment their eyes locked in a silent challenge. Dr. Bozeman blinked first. His eyes returned to the table.

"Do I have a motion?" Dr. Slabbert asked.

"I move that we recommend to the Board of Trustees that Dr. Brannan be given Type II privileges, until a review of the lawsuit by investigation by the Medical Executive Committee," Dr. Flagg said. Wes continued to take notes.

"All in favor?"

Wes Douglas, Emil Flagg, Elizabeth Flannigan, and Christopher Slabbert all voted in the affirmative. The committee turned to Dr. Bozeman who was deep in thought. He was rethinking his strategy. A week earlier, Slabbert threatened to bring in his own nurse anesthetist. If he lost Dr. Slabbert and his partners, Bozeman's practice would be down to three days a week. He cringed as he thought about the $600,000 mortgage on his new home.

"Your vote Dr. Bozeman?" Slabbert asked.

Silence.

Dr. Slabbert's voice pitched up a notch. "You with us, Henry?"

Silence—then a terse nod.

"Well," Dr. Slabbert said with a sense of accomplishment, "the only item remaining on the agenda is adjournment."

"I move we adjourn," Dr. Flagg said triumphantly.

32

The Competition

With the successful installation of a new management information system and the steps he had taken to increase service quality, Wes turned his attention externally—to the competition. One of the obvious reasons for the decline in patient volume was Snowline Medical Center, ten miles to the south. From visiting with a member of the Utah Healthcare Association, he learned Consolidated Healthcare of Arizona, a for-profit hospital corporation formed in 1985, built the facility.

The UHA representative told Wes that Consolidated Healthcare of Arizona was well capitalized and that most of its facilities were new. The company boasted that their savings came from centralizing the purchasing, housekeeping, financial, and dietary functions. Its charges were slightly higher than many not-for-profit hospitals in the state—not including Brannan Community Hospital, which had raised prices in its struggle to remain solvent.

The company was vertically-integrated, owning hospitals, nursing homes, and a health insurance company that served as the nucleus for its managed care program. The corporation recently started an aggressive program of physician practice acquisition in an attempt to control physician referrals.

Although the corporation was criticized for its aggressive marketing practices, Wes was impressed by its efficiency and financial strength. The UHA rep suggested that Wes meet Jon Einarson, Snowline's hospital administrator.

"Today's hospital employees are too expensive," Jon Einarson snarled. At age thirty-five, he stood six-foot-three and tipped the scales at a muscular two hundred and twenty pounds. His clean-shaven face accentuated the rawboned features he inherited from his Icelandic ancestors and his sea green eyes could pierce an opponent like a Viking pikestaff.

For the past two hours, Einarson had given Wes a tour of his building, highlighting efficiencies in design that allowed the hospital to reduce staffing by twenty percent. Now, they dined in the private dining room next to Einarson's office.

Einarson reached for his steak knife. "A good administrator knows how to slash labor costs," he said cutting the rim of gristle and fat from his thick steak. "That's why we axe old facilities. We design our buildings to save labor. In five years, we can pay for a new building in payroll savings alone.

"Before entering the market," he continued, "I approached your hospital with a purchase offer. Your Board of Trustees chair, Edward Wycoff, killed it." Einarson took his first bite and nodded approvingly as he savored the flavor. "It was a mistake," Einarson continued. "Park City would have been a better location for us, but your Board resisted our for-profit ownership. In the long run, his decision will hurt us both."

"Why?" asked Wes naively.

"Because there isn't a big enough population to support two new hospitals. That's why I was pleased when I heard you wanted to meet with me. Hopefully, you've come to the same conclusion," said Einarson.

"The Board will never support a consolidation," said Wes. "The community tradition is too strong."

"The tradition is wrong," Einarson retorted angrily. "Hospitals are too expensive to plop in every community along the Wasatch Front. What your Board is doing is a disservice to the community," he fumed. Taking a breath and folding his napkin more calmly, he continued smoothly. "If you want to do the right thing for Park City and yourself, you'll work with us. We can make it worth your time."

"What do you have in mind?"

Einarson swallowed and leaned forward conspiratorially, dropping his voice to a whisper. "You don't have to take explicit steps to sabotage the operations. Your hospital's a sick patient, Wes. Remove the life-support systems and it will die on its own."

"What specifically are you suggesting?" asked Wes, his eyes wide.

"We've heard about your efforts with budgeting, cost accounting, and so forth. Don't waste your efforts. Let nature take its course."

"And if I do as you suggest?" Wes asked.

"When the hospital closes, there will be a position for you with Consolidated Health at a generous salary. We'll give you a two-year contract at $150,000 a year. You won't have to do anything; use the time to rest, or find a new job."

"Three hundred thousand dollars to close the hospital," Wes mused. "What you're talking about sounds like a bribe."

"Don't get caught up in semantics, Wes. When the place falls apart, you'll need a new job. Wycoff's not going to take responsibility for the stupid things the Board's done. When he gets done with you, you won't be able to get a job in Park City waiting tables."

Wes was surprised at the boldness of Einarson's offer. Jon Einarson obviously hadn't risen to the top of his profession by being timid. Wes knew that what Einarson was proposing was a conflict of interest. Wes paused in mock seriousness as though considering the offer. "You don't mind if I discuss your generous offer with my Board?" he asked.

Einarson saw through the sarcasm and was offended. "Don't be stupid, Wes. We must be discreet. I'm doing my best to save your hide and you're insulting me."

Wes Douglas folded his napkin and placed it on the table. "Thanks," he said as he rose to leave, "but I'm not interested."

"You'll be sorry," Einarson said threateningly.

"Perhaps."

"Quote me, and I'll deny it," Einarson called as Wes left the room. Wes closed the door firmly behind him.

Thayne Ford swore—not a soft, mealy-mouth cuss like his grandmother when she burned the rolls or dropped a stitch in her knitting, but a blaspheming profanity that fermented angrily in his guts and exploded with the violence of an Irish pipe bomb. Slightly ashamed, he glanced over his shoulder to see if anyone was listening. That wasn't likely, as the newspaper office was empty. It was 4:00 a.m. He was up against deadline for the Wednesday edition of the *Park City Sentinel* and the press was broken—*again*.

He grabbed a rag from the table and wiped his hands. It wouldn't be easy to fix this time. Manufactured in 1952, parts were ridiculously hard to get and money was tight. Subscriptions were down. It wasn't enough that national papers like *USA Today* targeted rural markets. Even the statewide newspapers like the *Salt Lake Tribune* had online editions that stole readers from the smaller biweekly newspapers.

In a few minutes, he'd call Edward Wycoff, his silent partner. Wycoff would write a check to fix the press—but not to replace it. Thayne doubted he'd ever get that commitment. There would be a price, of course. Thayne would agree. If it were a question of ethics or money, he'd choose the latter. There weren't other options at his age.

33

Power of the Press

Wes was elated. All morning he'd worried about the interview, and with good cause. Since assuming the post of administrator, the local newspaper was unrelenting in its criticism of Brannan Community Hospital. In a small town, hospitals operate in a fishbowl. Whenever news was slow—which was often in rural Utah—someone at the *Park City Sentinel* started poking in the hospital's closets for a skeleton.

As Wes watched the front steps of the hospital, Thayne Ford unlocked the door to his car. He turned and waved at Wes with a smile before entering and driving off. *Won that one!* Wes thought.

Thayne disarmed Wes from the start. Contacting Wes' former employer in Maine, he checked his consulting references. "Their enthusiasm was overwhelming," Thayne reported sheepishly. "They liked your style. Said you were good at identifying operational problems and better still at fixing 'em. 'A real smooth cookie,' one reported.

"Sorry I've been so tough on you in my editorials," Thayne continued. "It's in everyone's best interest for you to succeed—at least if we want to have a hospital."

"Volume is down," Wes volunteered, "and the negative press we've been getting hasn't helped."

Thayne's eyes narrowed with regret as he stared at the floor. "The news media can get carried away sometimes."

Suddenly, Thayne's face brightened. "Tell you what we'll do," he said. "Whenever a new president is elected, the press usually gives him a sixty-day honeymoon—a period during which they lay off the negative press. Maybe we ought to do the same for you."

"That'd be great," Wes said eagerly. "I'll tell you whatever you want to know—so you don't think I'm hiding things from you. Give us sixty days to get our act together. If we haven't fixed things then, you're free to go after us."

"You're a tough negotiator," Thayne said. Both laughed.

"Okay. Now tell me what's going on," Thayne began. "Is it safe to be admitted to Brannan Community Hospital?"

"Of course," replied Wes. "We have our problems, like everyone else, but the overall quality is as good as any rural hospital in the state."

"What kind of problems?" Thayne queried shrewdly.

"We have a physician we are disciplining. The Board has temporarily suspended his privileges."

"Anyone I know?" Thayne pressed.

"I can't give the name," Wes replied, "but we're working through the problem."

"Any trouble getting the medical staff to support you?" Thayne asked while taking notes. "I've heard some doctors are reticent to criticize peers."

"You said this was off the record?" Wes verified, nodding at the notebook.

"It's just for the files," Thayne replied smoothly.

"There was resistance from some members of the medical staff," Wes said, "but Dr. Emil Flagg, Chairman of the Credentials Committee, handled the situation."

"I hear there's quite a bit of conflict on the Board."

"I don't think we want to address that publicly," Wes said warily.

"Remember the deal," Thayne said. "It's just between us."

Wes nodded, and for the next thirty minutes he answered Thayne's questions about the operation of the hospital as truthfully as he could. Topics discussed included Board politics and the problem small hospitals have competing with the resources and specialized staff of larger facilities.

He probably didn't learn anything he didn't already know, Wes thought as he concluded the interview. *Most of these problems will be fixed in sixty days; they'll be of little interest to the newspaper then.*

"I've enjoyed the interview," Thayne said as he closed his notebook. "It's given me new hope for the future of the hospital. Let's keep in touch; I need to know what's going on, but I'll support you—at least through the honeymoon period."

Standing on the steps of the hospital, Wes was elated to have found a supporter. He was about to get the shock of his life.

In the security of his office, Thayne Ford reviewed his notes. The most interesting part of the interview was the malpractice scoop—the issue that caused the medical staff to suspend *"Dr. X."* The young administrator wouldn't tell him who that was, but at about that point in the conversation, Wes was called into the hall to talk to a fire inspector.

Thayne took the opportunity to look at the notes of the Credentials Committee meeting that Wes referred to. As Thayne suspected, the name of the physician was scratched out. The patient's admission number was not erased, however, and Thayne wrote it in his notebook.

He picked up his phone and punched in the phone number of Patricia Fielding. Trish was a medical records librarian in the hospital and one of Thayne's sources. He met her in a bar on her first night in town from Brooklyn. Crazy hair, but good figure.

"Heyyy, Trish! Guess who?"

The voice at the other end of the line bubbled with excitement.

"Thayne? How ya doin'?"

"Doin' good. Got a favor though. Got a hospital admission number . . . wanna know who the patient is. Yeah, I can wait." He doodled on the notepad while she checked the files.

"Mckinzie Anderson? Seen in the emergency room, huh? What was the problem? Hmm . . . the doctor missed the diagnosis? Almost resulted in her death? Yeah, that's bad. Family plan to sue? Well, maybe they'll change their mind," he said, scribbling in a pad. "Who's the Doc? *Ah,* Dr. Brannan . . . the *Little Prince* . . . "

Thayne Ford held his notepad at arm's length as though admiring a beautiful work of art. A big Cheshire grin spread across his face. "I owe you one, Baby."

34

Anniversary Dinner

D r. Emil Flagg smiled with satisfaction as he gazed at his wife and the children that gathered around the table. It was not often that the whole family was together. Tonight they were celebrating his sixtieth birthday and everyone came for dinner at the Yarrow Inn. It was to be a surprise party and Emil played the part well. Having been married to Edith for thirty-five years, there were few surprises. Edith never forgot an important occasion. As he gazed at her, she radiated back the love that kept the family together through the good times and the bad.

Emil was not the easiest man to live with. His impatient and explosive personality often put him in conflict with his sons, who inherited their mother's aversion to conflict. Edith was the magnet that kept them together and, tonight, the boys were here for her as much as for him.

Robert, the oldest son, was an electrical engineer from Seattle and had flown in that evening with his wife and three sons. *A handsome family*, Emil thought. Seated across the table were Tommy and his fiancée, Megan. At twenty-eight, Tommy had just been accepted to George Washington Medical School. It was high time that he get married, and Megan couldn't have been a better match if Emil picked her out himself.

Tom and Megan met last summer in Hawaii. Emil was presenting a paper at the annual meeting of the American College of Pathologists and took the family with him. Tom and Megan connected at the hotel pool.

Megan's father was the president-elect of the college. Already, he had approached Emil about chairing an important committee. An honor Emil hadn't sought, it would mark an important milestone in his career.

Technically proficient, Emil was never politically wired. Some of his colleagues said it was his abrasive personality. Emil preferred to believe it was his unflinching honesty. A good pathologist doesn't use euphemisms. He wouldn't call a tumor a cyst to make someone feel better, yet that's what often happened in the world of hospital politics—incompetence was couched in softer terms in the reports of Peer-review and Credentials Committee. Emil silently scowled. *Incompetence is incompetence—spare the euphemism!*

Across the room, a tall gentleman with gray hair entered the restaurant with his wife. It was Paul Jameson, an attorney and a first cousin to Edith. *He's not here for the party,* Emil thought. Emil and Paul had not spoken for years. The distinguished couple was shown across the dining room by the maitre d' and seated at an adjacent table.

"How are you this evening, Paul?" Emil asked, startling the old buzzard. Emil even stood and shook his hand. "I'd like you to meet Tommy's fiancée, Megan."

Paul hadn't seen Emil and his family when he entered the restaurant and was surprised at Emil's cordial response. "How do you do, Megan?" he sputtered.

"I've been wanting to come by and settle that easement problem," Emil continued, before Paul could regain his balance. Paul and Edith owned adjacent cabin sites in the High Uinta mountains north of Kamas, Utah. They inherited the property from a common grandfather. Edith got the west section, near the highway—Paul got the east. Both pieces of property had water and timber. Paul's had a better view of the valley but lacked one important thing—access to the road.

If their grandfather had been an attorney like Paul, he would have divided the property north and south, or at least would have provided legal access to the road. He wasn't, though; he was just a poor sheepherder who wanted to do something special for his grandchildren.

Shortly after the inheritance, Paul approached Emil about the problem. All he wanted was a ten-foot easement through Edith's property. Emil was still smarting, however, about a lawsuit Paul's client filed against the hospital. Emil wasn't affected, but the case was without merit, and Emil told him so.

When Paul refused to drop the case, Emil took offense. An argument ensued where Paul suggested the best way to reduce malpractice suits was to eliminate incompetent doctors, and Emil countered that the ethics of attorneys was one step above that of the Mafia. For ten years, they hadn't spoken, while the property sat vacant. Paul's forehead arched suspiciously. "How much money do you want?" he asked.

Emil smiled generously as he put his arm around Paul's shoulder. "I don't want anything except to put this bitter saga to rest. Bring the papers by my office Monday. I'll sign them." Paul weighed the comment with a critical squint as he took his seat.

Emil's wife raised her eyebrows in pleased surprise. "That was nice of you, Dear," she said, when Emil was reseated. "I know his children have dreamed about building a cabin on the land for many years. I'm proud of you for putting an old feud behind you."

Emil shrugged good-naturedly. "If it makes you happy, it makes me happy," he said, placing his hand on hers.

"It's been a good year," he continued as he scanned the table. "Tommy's been accepted to medical school and has a lovely fiancée. Robert is doing well and his children are growing up to be fine boys. And, in November, we had the largest volume in pathology ever. It's time to share our good fortune."

Indeed, things were getting better at the hospital. Emil had been suspicious of Wes Douglas at first. *What did a CPA know about running a hospital?* Still—his analytical approach and never-give-up attitude were having a positive effect. Patient volume was up and cost was down—thanks in part to a new cost accounting system Wes installed. Best of all for Emil, the Board and medical staff were—at least for the moment—not at each other's throats. There was even talk of resurrecting the building program that was canceled shortly before Hap's death. Emil smiled with satisfaction.

A young man in a white shirt and black bow tie arrived at the table and nodded at Emil. "I'll be your waiter tonight," he said. "The house special tonight is chicken Jerusalem with artichoke hearts. It comes with a green salad with a light vinaigrette dressing."

Emil looked at his wife. "That sounds good to me, Dear," she said.

"I'll take the same," he replied, without even looking at the menu.

"Maybe we should build a cabin too," Edith said, as the waiter moved down the table to take Robert's order. "We'll be having more grandchildren in coming years; it would be nice to have a family retreat."

"Even if the kids don't use it, it might make a romantic getaway for us," Emil said with a wink. Edith's brown eyes registered pleased surprise—romance was not Emil's strong suit. "As a matter of fact—" Emil's sentence was cut off by a pat on the shoulder. Looking up, he saw Thayne Ford from the newspaper.

"What a fortunate coincidence catching you together!" Thayne said, nodding at Paul Jameson.

Emil studied Paul sharply, then bounced a quizzical look off Thayne.

"You two are going to be spending quite a bit of time together in the next few weeks, what with depositions and all," Thayne continued.

"What are you talking about?" Emil asked.

"Haven't you heard?" Thayne chortled. "Matt Brannan is suing the hospital for public defamation of character. Paul is his attorney. As Chairman of the Credentials Committee, you are listed as a defendant. It's here in tonight's paper." Thayne held up the newest edition of the *Park City Sentinel*. The headlines read: *Wes Douglas Spills All—Dr. Brannan's a Quack, Board's Incompetent.*

Emil gasped. He grabbed the paper, spilling ice water on his wife. She jumped up, knocking her chair over, which tripped a waiter, who spilled a large Caesar salad on Paul. Emil glared at the headlines, read the first three paragraphs of the article and swung angrily to face Thayne.

"When did Wes say this?" he snorted.

"Copyrighted article from an interview at the hospital yesterday," Thayne replied brightly. He pulled a stenographer's pad from his pocket. "Do you have a statement to make?"

"Be careful," Paul cautioned from the adjacent table. He was wiping salad dressing from his coat with a linen napkin. "Anything you say can be used against you in the courtroom."

Emil's face flushed red. Jumping up, he grabbed Paul by the coat lapels. "I'll give you a statement—you two-faced SOB!" he shouted.

"Careful," Edith pled. Emil looked at her, then shoved the frightened attorney into the buffet table, which collapsed, taking Paul to the floor with it.

Thayne Ford grinned and snapped a picture.

"Tomorrow's lead story," he said to himself brightly.

35

Last Official Act

Wes reached for the last pile of vendor checks Birdie Bankhead gave him before leaving for the evening. Unless a miracle occurred—which was unlikely—approving them for payment would be his last official act as administrator of Brannan Community Hospital.

Downstairs, the joint meeting of the medical staff and Board had begun—Wes had been specifically asked not to attend. In a few minutes, Dr. Flagg would present a resolution from the medical staff to the Board requesting that they release the hospital administrator. Edward Wycoff would read it, and then move that the Board accept the resolution. Another member of the Board would second the motion and Wes would be history.

Sighing, Wes picked up his pen and leaned back in the large leather chair that had once supported Hap Castleton. He stared at the evening edition of the *Park City Sentinel* on his desk. Not only had Thayne broken his word by immediately publishing everything, but he badly distorted what he'd been told. Wes would never call Dr. Brannan a *quack* or the Board *incompetent*. The motivation had to be more than a good story.

Wes shook his head as he started signing the checks. He was embarrassed—embarrassed for the Board that trusted him with their hospital and embarrassed for the medical staff who, despite imperfections, did their best to provide high quality healthcare. Most of all, Wes was embarrassed for the employees who deserved more than the ridicule the *Park City Sentinel* was heaping on them and their organization.

He smiled sadly. One person he would not have to be embarrassed for was Amy Castleton—she could hold her own. The evening the paper hit the streets, she cornered him in his office. Choked with anger, she read aloud Wes' derogatory "quotes" about her father. Wes tried to tell her that Thayne Ford fabricated them, but she wasn't listening.

"Dad may not have been a polished CPA," she said, her eyes glistening with tears, "but he was honest and he treated people with dignity." She slammed the door behind her as she left.

From the window, Wes watched her leave the hospital in Matt Brannan's Mercedes. Wes was in love with Amy, but it was obvious the relationship was not going to work. Wes signed the last check and placed it on top of the pile. Birdie would retrieve it and process the checks in the morning. There was nothing left to do but pack a few personal belongings.

He removed a pen set he got when he left Lytle, Moorehouse, and Butler and a book of poetry Kathryn had given him. From the locked bottom drawer of his desk, he retrieved the file he had accumulated on Ryan Ramer. He would mail it to the district attorney later that evening.

Downstairs, the meeting was heating up. He could hear the shouting all the way up the stairwell. *It's all over but the screaming,* he thought. There was no reason to stick around. If they needed him, they could reach him at his apartment before he left town.

Heavy with fatigue, he stood and snapped shut the briefcase that held the few belongings he would take with him. Picking it up, he crossed the room, and then paused at the door. Several days earlier, he found a picture of Amy that Hap apparently misfiled with an old financial report. It was taken when she was eleven, on a fishing trip with her father. He returned to the desk, opened the top drawer, and placed it in his side pocket quickly. Shutting the drawer, he crossed the office, locking the door on the way out. He would leave the keys at the switchboard.

36

Carnavali

Ryan Ramer's hands were still shaking as he unlocked the door to his Lexus at the Salt Lake Airport. He and Hank Ulman finished a meeting with Barry Zaugg, Carnavali's drug runner and hit man. Carnavali was ticked and Ramer was frightened. Carnavali had paid $30,000 for drugs Ramer had yet to deliver. Thanks to Wes Douglas, the lab and the raw materials were sealed away.

Zaugg was unsympathetic to Ramer's story. As he left, he slammed a wrench through the cockpit window of the small private plane Hank Ulman was servicing. "Worse things than this will happen if Carnavali doesn't get his shipment," he threatened.

Ramer slipped into his car and settled into the heavy leather seats, deep in thought. Problems were multiplying faster than he could find solutions to them. As he pulled out of the parking lot and onto the freeway, he realized that his life was riding on this.

By morning, Ramer had a plan. He and Hank discussed it as they ate their lunch privately in his office. "We've got three objectives," he began. "Satisfy Carnavali, retrieve the materials from the lab, if possible, and get rid of the evidence uncovered by Cluff. I still think there are work papers out there, someplace. If Lexi Cunningham hasn't found them, she will."

"Lexi is onto something," Hank affirmed. "The past couple of days she's been hanging around Maintenance, asking questions. And she knows about the home health agency."

Ramer nodded. "I've got a plan that will solve all three problems. Carnavali wants drugs; he doesn't care what kind. I've got fifty bottles of morphine and another seventy bottles of Demerol in the narcotics safe that I could give him. It's two weeks' worth of hospital inventory."

"But you get audited on that stuff, don't you?" Hank asked.

"That's where you come in," replied Ramer. "Several years ago, I was moonlighting at a nursing home in Salt Lake. One night, the place burned. I don't know how the fire started, but it provided the cover for me to process an order for drugs that I was able to sell on the streets."

"You want to burn the hospital down?" Hank asked incredulously.

"Just the administrative wing. It would destroy the pharmacy, evidence of the lab and Cluff's work papers," Ramer said.

"What about Lexi?"

Ramer shrugged. "Maybe she dies in the fire."

Hank was silent as he mulled the thought in his head. "A fire's no good," he said slowly. "But maybe I got a better idea. How 'bout an explosion? I've been tellin' administration for two years that the boiler's got troubles, that someone's gonna get hurt—or worse—if they don't fix it. It's right beneath administration and close enough to the pharmacy. It'd probably take out the whole wing if I rig it right."

"Is the boiler big enough to destroy all the evidence?"

"We've got two hundred gallons of gasoline in Maintenance for the backup generator. The fire marshal told us to get it away from the generator. I'll put it in the storeroom in the basement. If anyone asks, I'll tell 'em that Wes told me to do it."

Ramer reviewed the proposal in his head, then smiled and nodded in acceptance.

"When do we do it?" Hank asked.

"Saturday morning, a little after 7:00 a.m. It's the monthly meeting of the Board. With Wes gone, Lexi Cunningham will be representing administration."

"What about the stuff in the lab? You gonna let it blow?"

"Friday night we get it out. We either tunnel through the wall in the basement or go down through the floor of the Pink Shop."

"The Pink Shop would be easier. It will be closed. Plus, the basement is too close to the cafeteria."

"I'll meet you tomorrow night at the Pink Shop—provided that gives you enough time to rig the boiler."

"I can do it in an hour," Hank said. "One more question—what about your uncle? Won't he be at the meeting?"

"Wycoff? He's in Denver, completing the details on the closure of the hospital. We're going to simplify it for him," Ramer said with a grim smile.

The mood was sober at the Castleton household. In the four months since Hap died, a murder investigation had ensued, the hospital's financial problems were revealed, Matt Brannan's hospital privileges were suspended, and now Hap's replacement had been fired.

It was Friday evening, and Helen Castleton and Amy were finishing a quiet supper. "Your father would never have allowed things to deteriorate at the hospital like they did under Wes Douglas," Helen said, as she cleared the dishes from the table.

"Mom, to be perfectly honest, Dad *did* allow things to deteriorate," responded Amy, surprising herself with her criticism of her own father. "He did a great job for many years, but he didn't adjust his style to accommodate the demands of managed care. The hospital's financial problems aren't totally Dad's fault, but he played a role."

"At least he was never vindictive," her mother replied tersely. "After all the Brannans have done for the hospital, to single out Matt like he did . . ."

"Whatever Wes' mistakes were, they don't matter now that he's gone," Amy said sadly. "He's closed his CPA practice and has probably left town."

"Do you think the hospital will close?" Helen asked.

"I don't know. If it does, a substantial piece of Park City's history dies with it."

"Our family has a lot invested in that hospital," Helen added.

"I know. Some of my happiest childhood memories were the Saturday mornings I spent with Dad at the hospital when he would check the mail and catch up on paperwork."

"I remember those days," Helen said. "I always thought you'd be bored to death. What was there to do while he worked?"

"Didn't Dad ever tell you that he had one of the carpenters build a playhouse in the old safe room, below his office?" Amy asked, surprised. Helen shook her head with raised eyebrows.

"They furnished it with a small table and chairs that they built in the carpenter shop," Amy continued. "I loved that place."

"I didn't know there was anything in the basement but the cafeteria and boiler room," Helen replied.

"You couldn't access it from anywhere but the administrator's office. There was a small stairway you could get to from the closet. Originally, that's where they kept the payroll."

"Is it still there?"

"I don't know; I'm not even sure where to look for it. Dad's old office became a pharmacy storeroom when they remodeled the administrative wing. It would be interesting to know what happened to the tiny furniture, though."

"Is the storeroom still there?"

"No, that area is part of the new hall to the newborn nursery." Amy said thoughtfully, her eyes flickering with curiosity.

"*That's strange*," she mumbled. "*Where are the stairs?*" Amy was silent for a moment as something Wes said about Ramer suddenly made sense.

"What did you say, dear?" Helen Castleton asked as she finished the dishes and tossed the dishtowel onto the counter.

"Nothing," Amy replied.

Standing in the remodeled hall outside the nursery, Amy tried to reconstruct in her mind the original administrator's office and the placement of the stairs leading to the old safe room.

Assuming that the pharmacy wall is the same, Dad's desk must have been about here, Amy thought, standing in the middle of the hall. *The room was about twelve feet wide . . . that would place the closet and the stairway about where the display shelf is. The shelf isn't new; it looks like it's a remnant from the storeroom days, and it must have been used to seal the entrance.*

Moving closer she examined it. *Certainly the pharmacists must have known about the safe room. On the other hand, not many people were allowed in there; Ramer was always so possessive of the area.*

Her thoughts were interrupted by the muffled sound of hammering from the direction of the Pink Shop. From the space under the door, she noticed a light. Retrieving her keys, she unlocked the door to investigate.

Except for the toolbox on the counter, the room looked the same as when she closed the Pink Shop earlier that evening. Crossing the room, she looked at the tools, then noticed the hole in the floor, six inches or so behind the cash register. The cash drawer was empty. Quietly, she walked behind the counter and looked through the hole into the room below—*my old playhouse!*

Careful not to be seen, she looked closer. Someone was down there, assembling a cardboard box. The room was the same as she remembered but was cluttered with tables and bottles connected with tubing that resembled a chemistry set. *Who is down there and what is he doing?*

There was a noise behind her and she turned, startled. In the doorway to the Pink Shop stood Hank Ulman in filthy coveralls. His hair was covered with chalky dust and he was holding a crowbar. He smiled, exposing a mouthful of graying teeth.

"Well, it's little Amy Castleton," he chortled. "And she's come to play house."

37

The Boardroom

The fear tightened in Lexi's stomach as she studied the faces of the other members of the Board. Directly across the table, David Brannan peered anxiously through a pair of broken glasses perched precariously on his nose. Ryan Ramer had been kind enough to replace them—after punching David squarely in the face. To the left was Edward Wycoff, hands securely tied behind his back. Wycoff's eyes showed terror, stark and naked. That didn't make sense to Lexi. *Wycoff is Ramer's uncle . . . Isn't he in on this?*

Lexi took the opportunity to carefully study the pharmacist. With his coarse cranial features and darting black eyes, Ramer reminded her of a trapped animal. *So Ramer was responsible for Hap's death. I should have suspected him earlier,* Lexi thought to herself. *What does he plan to do with us?*

Lexi's stares irritated Ramer. He swore under his breath and checked his watch. "*Eighteen minutes . . .*" he whispered to himself, "*then the fireworks start. Hank should have been back by now; hope he knows what he's doing.*" Hank had made one last trip to the boiler room. "*In another ten minutes I'm out of here, whether he's back or not.*"

Cocking his gun, Ramer laid it on the highly polished boardroom table. He retrieved a small bundle from his coat pocket and unfolded it, placing its contents next to his revolver—one syringe and three small vials. *Too bad Wycoff showed up. Meetings must have finished early.*

Breathing heavily, he removed a handkerchief from his shirt pocket and wiped the sweat from his face. *Strange twist of fate, really. Uncle Ed . . . the final victim of his own hatred.* Picking up one of the vials, Ramer held it to the light. *Whole thing wouldn't have happened if Cluff hadn't stuck his nose where it shouldn't have been.* He snapped the head off the vial, nostrils flaring as the pungent odor wafted in the air. *Cluff is gone . . . in a few minutes they'll all be gone.*

Hands trembling with anger, Ramer rotated the vial between his thumb and forefinger to dissolve any remaining crystals and then picked up the syringe. *Coroner'll never pick this up,* he thought, *if there's anything left to autopsy.*

Sergeant O'Malley's frown dug deep furrows into his sunburned forehead. "Darndest thing I've ever seen," he said. He stared into the video monitor, scratching the scruff of his beard. "It don't look like no joke to me."

For the past four minutes, Sgt. O'Malley, Bradley Scott, chief engineer of Paradigm Solutions, and Wes Douglas watched Ryan Ramer take over a meeting in the boardroom of Brannan Community Hospital. Bradley had spent the previous day installing a video security system at the hospital and arranged a demonstration Saturday morning with O'Malley in the basement of the City Hall.

Wes was there at the request of David Brannan as Paradigm's consultant—his last assignment before leaving Park City. O'Malley picked up the dispatch radio in his office. "Unit Seven."

The scratchy response was immediate. It was Officer Charlie Thurgood. "Unit Seven here."

"Charlie, I think we have a hostage situation at the hospital. I'm in the middle of a demonstration of a video security system here and, on the screen, we see this guy burst into the boardroom with a gun. Sgt. Mason is off today, but Fuller's directing traffic on Main. Pick him up and then head over to investigate. I'll call the sheriff for backup. I'll see ya there."

"I'm rollin," Charlie said.

O'Malley spoke into the dispatch radio again. "A large fellow in a blue maintenance uniform may be implicated. He was in the room with the hostages but just left on an errand. See if you can intercept him before he returns."

Five minutes later, the phone in the boardroom rang, just as Ramer started to fill the first syringe. Since Lexi Cunningham was the only hostage who didn't have her hands tied, Ramer motioned with his gun for her to pick it up. She complied.

"Boardroom." Face expressionless, Lexi listened for what seemed like an eternity and then held out the phone.

"It's for you," she said.

Ramer's jaw dropped. "For me? Who is it?" he whispered.

Lexi said nothing and Ramer took the phone.

"Hullo," Ramer said, his eyes wide with curiosity.

"Ryan, this is Sergeant O'Malley." O'Malley chose his words carefully. Suspecting that Ryan Ramer was emotionally unstable, he purposefully kept his voice calm. "There are officers at each exit from the hospital, including the one leading from the boardroom to the hall. Throw your gun out and release the hostages. When the room is empty, come out slowly with your hands high above your head. We will give you further instructions at that time."

Ramer squinted at the floor with disbelief. *How did they know? Was it Hank? That doesn't make sense. He's in as deep as I am. It must be Amy Castleton. Maybe she escaped and the police were waiting for Hank when he went to the boiler room.*

"Stay on the line," Ramer said. He needed time to think. *If the police nabbed Hank before he armed the boiler, then the clock isn't ticking. There's time to negotiate. If not, I've gotta get out of here.* He lifted the receiver to his ear.

"Lemme talk to Hank."

"Hank's busy."

"Then unbusy him," Ramer said fiercely, "or I start shooting people." He discharged the gun through the door. Immediately, they put Hank Ulman on the phone.

"It's me."

"Did they get you before or after the … errand?" Ramer asked.

Knowing that their conversation was being monitored, Hank was brief. "After."

Ramer swore under his breath. "How did they know we were here?"

"Dunno."

"Have you told them anything?"

"Won't talk to no one but a lawyer."

"Good." Ramer paused. "Do you think they know about the … surprise?"

"I can't tell, but I want outta here!"

"That's enough," O'Malley said, taking the phone back. "The building is surrounded, Ryan. Throw your weapon out and release the hostages."

I'm not goin' to prison, Ramer whispered to himself. *Growing up in a boys' home was more than enough institutional life for me.*

"I have three nurses in here and four of the babies from the nursery," he bluffed.

"No you don't," O'Malley said briskly. "You have four hostages, all members of the Board."

Ramer searched the room for a camera, but couldn't see anything. "Okay," he said. "I'll trade three of the hostages for a car. The fourth is going with me."

"Is there a bomb?" O'Malley asked.

"No."

"We know there's a bomb, Ramer. You told the hostages there would be an explosion. Where is it? Does it have a timer?"

Ramer's eyes searched the room. *How do they know? Is the place bugged?*

"I'll tell you about the bomb when I have the car," he said. "I have a cell phone."

O'Malley persisted. "When is the bomb set to go off?"

"It isn't. It's armed or disarmed by radio," Ramer lied. "There's an electronic safety device," he continued. "I have to be at least three miles from the hospital to arm it. Give me three miles and, if no one is following me, I'll disarm the bomb."

The phone was silent while O'Malley conferred by radio with a SWAT team that was coming in from Salt Lake by helicopter. The estimated time of arrival was three minutes.

"You want a car, and you plan on taking a hostage with you?" O'Malley affirmed when he returned to the phone.

"Right."

"We'll get the car. Stay on the line."

Several minutes earlier, O'Malley and Wes met Officer Thurgood in the cafeteria, where Thurgood first detained Hank Ulman. On the way over, Wes informed Thurgood he received a phone call from Helen Castleton earlier that morning. Amy had not returned home. Wes suspected that Ramer had something to do with her disappearance and worried about foul play.

There was a speakerphone in the dietitian's office; O'Malley used it so Hank could listen when he called Ramer. "You heard the conversation," O'Malley said to Hank. "Ramer says there's a bomb, but no timer. Nothin's ticking; no reason to worry, right?" Hank said nothing. O'Malley noticed that Hank was perspiring profusely.

Hank looked at the clock and then at the thin wall that separated the cafeteria from the boiler. "I'm hot; let's go outside," he pled desperately.

"It's sixty-eight degrees in here," O'Malley said, pointing to the thermostat on the wall. He turned to Officer Thurgood. "I'm not hot. How about you Charlie?"

"Actually I'm kinda cold," Officer Thurgood said with a nervous shiver.

"I've got a medical condition. It's too hot in here for me. Take me out," Hank begged.

"The hospital's a good place to be if you aren't feeling well," O'Malley said. "Would you like me to call a nurse?"

"Tell us what's going on," Thurgood demanded, tiring of the small talk.

Hank's voice was tight. "I'm not talkin' to anyone without a lawyer. I have a right to be taken downtown."

O'Malley raised his eyebrows. "The only lawyer in town is Paul Jameson. He's the Little League coach. It's Saturday morning, and he doesn't like to be disturbed during practice. We'll wait here and call him at noon." O'Malley put his feet on the table and looked at his watch. "We got plenty of time."

Wes heard the loud *whomph whomph* of the helicopters as the SWAT team landed in the parking lot. Hank looked at the clock again, the fright clearly written on his face. "Okay, okay . . ." he said. "There's no time for the attorney. The boiler on the other side of that wall is going to blow in another four minutes. It shouldn't hurt the nursing units, but it will take the whole administrative wing! You can't stop it. The room's booby-trapped from the inside. Now get me outta here!" he screamed.

O'Malley was immediately on his feet talking to the SWAT team by radio. "Get the hostages out—all of them—*NOW!*" he shouted.

Wes, pumped full of adrenaline, grabbed Hank by the throat and threw him against the wall. "Helen Castleton called this morning; Amy went to the hospital and never came home. Where is she?" he demanded.

"In a room," gasped Hank, "below the floor of Pink Shop. We dug a hole and—"

"Take him!" Wes shouted as he shoved Hank at Thurgood. "I'll be back," he started to say, but his voice was obliterated by the sound of an explosion in the boardroom.

38

SWAT Team

Sergeant Chapman was recruited out of high school to pitch for the Pirates and had a fantastic arm. Within seven seconds of the call from O'Malley, he threw the concussion bomb right where he wanted it— through the heavy glass of the boardroom window and onto the center of the large maple conference table. *You're out!* he thought as he dove for cover.

The detonation blinded and deafened everyone in the boardroom. Immediately, four members of the SWAT team burst through the heavy maple doors, disarming Ramer and pinning him to the floor.

Downstairs, Wes jumped to his feet and bolted up the staircase to the Pink Shop. Kicking the door in, he found the hole Hank described, covered by a 3' x 3' square of plywood. Wasting no time, he jumped into it, handing Amy up to a SWAT team member that followed him from the hall. "Hit the fire alarm!" he shouted as he emerged from the hole, hoping the building would be evacuated before the explosion.

With three minutes to go, the SWAT team searched both floors of the administrative wing for Saturday employees, while O'Malley checked to see that the ICU Nursery was empty. In the distance, Wes heard *"Code Red, Code Red, Code Red"* over the intercom as the hospital's disaster plan was activated.

Amy and the Board members were being taken a safe distance from the hospital. Ramer and Hank were under the watch of the deputies.

With less than a minute to go, Wes and three remaining officers broke through the French doors of the administrator's office, crossed the lawn, and dove into an empty irrigation canal. The explosion from the boiler room was heard all the way to Heber City.

223

39

The Dedication

Two years later—

The locals couldn't remember a more beautiful autumn. An early chill turned the soft green of the aspen to shades of crimson, gold, and orange. As thirty-two-year-old Parker Richards stepped from his car onto the sidewalk of the new Brannan Community Hospital, it occurred to him that the festive colors were a harbinger of a new era for Park City. Only recently completed, the new hospital would be dedicated in less than two hours.

Parker was well prepared for the position for which he was hired. After completing a degree in accounting and an MBA in healthcare administration, he served as an administrative resident at the Mountainview Hospital in Las Vegas. His advisor was an able administrator and an effective teacher. Parker Richards' arrival in Park City was timed to coincide with the dedication of the new hospital.

The building is certainly modern, he thought. *As different from the old facility as the twentieth century is from the twenty-first. Fewer hospital beds, more outpatient services, a helicopter pad, and telemetry that linked the ICU to the University of Utah Medical Center.* Richards had only seen pictures of the old facility. An explosion and fire destroyed its administrative wing in 2004. No one died and, fortunately, the injuries were minor.

Crossing the lawn, he entered the modern lobby and took an elevator to administration on the third floor, where Birdie Bankhead, who had just been promoted to administrative assistant, met him. "Welcome," she said. "We're happy you could make the dedication. It's appropriate—a new hospital and our first assistant administrator."

She handed Parker a program for the dedication. "Wes is still meeting with the Board. I'm sure he'll be out in a few minutes. While you're waiting, you can look at this. Beautiful drawing, isn't it?" she said, pointing to the architect's drawing on the cover.

"Indeed," Parker affirmed.

"I'm on my way downstairs to check on seating for the dedication," Birdie continued. "If you need anything, Mary Anne will be happy to help you. You might congratulate her — she's just been promoted to administrative secretary."

A pretty blonde in her late twenties looked up from her new desk and blushed.

"Congratulations to both of you," Parker said, smiling.

Birdie picked up a bouquet of flowers delivered for the speaker's podium and hustled off to the elevator. Parker took a seat and studied the program. An introduction and welcome was to be offered by Wes Douglas, administrator. A musical number by the Park City High School marching band followed the ribbon cutting ceremony and the program would conclude with remarks by David Brannan, representing the Brannan family. The hospital had been made possible by a generous contribution from the Brannan Foundation, funded by the family's prospering software company.

As Parker finished reading the program, David's brother, Dr. Matt Brannan, entered the room accompanied by a lovely young woman carrying a three-month-old baby. Parker had seen Matt in the picture of the Brannan family that hung in the new boardroom. He was told that Dr. Brannan was finishing a residency at Johns Hopkins Hospital in Maryland and would be joining the staff in another year. Parker hadn't met the woman, however.

Mary Anne stood and greeted them at the door, hugging both of them.

"Parker, I don't think you have met Amy," she said, gently taking the baby. "She is the daughter of our former administrator, Hap Castleton." Parker reached out and shook Amy's hand.

"And this is Hap Douglas."

Parker looked puzzled. "Douglas?"

Mary Anne continued, holding the baby up. "Oh yes, Amy is Wes' wife."

"Amy and I were childhood friends," Dr. Brannan explained. "With family and staff tied up with preparations for the dedication, she was nice enough to pick us up at the airport. My wife, Emma, and I flew in for the dedication. Emma is coming over with her mother."

The administrator's door opened and David Brannan and Wes Douglas emerged. Wes and Amy embraced as Mary Anne continued to hold the baby.

"How's the residency?" Wes asked, shaking hands with Matt.

"Be done in a year," he said brightly.

Birdie returned with a cameraman from the *Deseret News*. "We need a picture for the paper," she said. As Wes, David Brannan and Parker Richards lined up by the architect's model, Mary Anne made small talk.

"I understand you've taken up flying," Mary Anne said, addressing Matt.

"I have!" Matt replied happily. "It gives me a break from studying. As a matter of fact, I'm picking up a new plane tomorrow in Salt Lake City. Before flying back to Baltimore, I hope to take Wes in it on a fishing trip."

"Hold still," the cameraman said as he snapped the picture and took two more.

"Where to?" Parker Richards asked when the cameraman had left.

"McCall, Idaho."

Matt took the baby from Mary Anne and held him high above his head. "It was a favorite spot of this little fellow's grandpa. Who knows," Matt continued, making a funny face at little Hap, "maybe I can turn your workaholic dad into a first-rate fisherman."

Wes smiled graciously. "It would be nice to take a break," he said, "and someday I would like to learn to fish." He shook his head as he put his arm around Amy. "But as for flying to McCall tomorrow, I think I'll just stay here and keep my feet on the ground."

With that, the group was off to the dedication.

Epilogue

It was 7:30 a.m. as the small Cessna Skyhawk 172P pulled onto the taxiway leading to Runway 16-left. The pilot, Dr. Matt Brannan, turned COM One to 118.3 to check in with the tower.

"Citation jet five miles inbound. Hold for arriving aircraft," the tower instructed. Matt applied the brakes and stopped the aircraft short of the runway. To the north, the jet, now at 7,000 feet, turned on its landing lights.

Matt throttled the aircraft to 1700 RPM to check the magnetos. The RPM drop didn't exceed 125 RPM—everything was in order. The Citation jet was three miles out, its landing gear down and engines on idle. Once more, Matt reviewed his checklist: *brakes, flaps, carburetor heat.*

Matt was happy that, after considerable arm-twisting, Wes had consented to join him on the fishing trip. It would give them the opportunity to mend some bridges. If Matt was going to return to the hospital after his residency, he would want a better relationship with the administrator.

Wes, through the medical staff, started the action that forced Matt to apply for a residency. Now, two years into the process, Matt saw that it was the best thing he ever did. One day at Baltimore Community Hospital, Matt ran into Emma Chandler, the skinny high school HOSA volunteer from the business office. Only she was no longer in braces or high school and her mature figure was anything but scrawny.

Matt never paid much attention to Emma at Brannan Community Hospital, but she had blossomed into the prettiest girl he had ever seen. They dated for a year and were married.

The Citation jet landed and turned left onto the taxiway.

"Cessna five-seven Zulu cleared for takeoff. Fly heading 320, climb to one three niner, contact departure on 124.3," came the tower's response.

"Ready?"

Wes smiled nervously and gave Matt a thumbs-up sign.

"Cessna five-seven Zulu, rolling." Matt released the brakes, pushed forward on the throttle, and started his take-off roll. As the plane left the runway, Matt and Wes thought of Hap Castleton. Three years ago, he took this same flight and the tragedy that followed set into motion a series of events that changed both of their lives.

History would not repeat itself. Matt and Wes would complete the trip for Hap and the experience would be the beginning of a better relationship between two professionals who would contribute significantly to the quality of healthcare in their communities.

Wes Douglas would eventually tire of the hassles of managed care, refocusing the direction of his hospital from primary to specialty care. Capitalizing on the genetic engineering breakthroughs of the first decade of the 21st century, the Brannan Genetic Endocrinology Medical Center would become regionally known for the implantation of cultured pancreatic beta cells in the treatment of insulin dependent diabetes. In later years, Wes would serve as the president of the American Specialty Care Center Association and would contribute to the quality of healthcare and reduction of costs through the development of similar high-volume specialty centers throughout the country.

Shaken by his close call with death, Edward Wycoff had retired from the Board. Reevaluating his value system, he would spend his remaining years trying, with some success, to build a relationship with his wife and children.

Del Cluff would recover from his injuries and return to work at the hospital. However, unable to get along with the other hospital employees, he would eventually return to school to get a Ph.D. Upon graduation, he would teach accounting at a large university.

Dr. Matt Brannan would return from his residency. As the focus of the hospital changed, he and Emma would leave Park City for a general practice in Montrose, California. Unlike Wes Douglas, he would never gain regional attention; but he would be remembered in the hearts of his patients for the quality of his care and the sincerity of his compassion.